Indiscretions of Archie

P. G. Wodehouse

Indiscretions of Archie

Copyright © 2020 Bibliotech Press
All rights reserved

The present edition is a reproduction of previous publication of this classic work. Minor typographical errors may have been corrected without note, however, for an authentic reading experience the spelling, punctuation, and capitalization have been retained from the original text.

ISBN: 978-1-64799-290-3

CONTENTS

CHAPTER I	DISTRESSING SCENE	1
CHAPTER II	A SHOCK FOR MR BREWSTER	4
CHAPTER III	MR BREWSTER DELIVERS SENTENCE	8
CHAPTER IV	WORK WANTED	13
CHAPTER V	STRANGE EXPERIENCES OF AN ARTIST'S MODEL	16
CHAPTER VI	THE BOMB	22
CHAPTER VII	MR ROSCOE SHERRIFF HAS AN IDEA ..	31
CHAPTER VIII	A DISTURBED NIGHT FOR DEAR OLD SQUIFFY	39
CHAPTER IX	A LETTER FROM PARKER	47
CHAPTER X	DOING FATHER A BIT OF GOOD	55
CHAPTER XI	SALVATORE CHOOSES THE WRONG MOMENT	64
CHAPTER XII	BRIGHT EYES—AND A FLY	69
CHAPTER XIII	RALLYING ROUND PERCY	77
CHAPTER XIV	THE SAD CASE OF LOONEY BIDDLE	87
CHAPTER XV	SUMMER STORMS	95
CHAPTER XVI	ARCHIE ACCEPTS A SITUATION	105
CHAPTER XVII	BROTHER BILL'S ROMANCE	111
CHAPTER XVIII	THE SAUSAGE CHAPPIE	115
CHAPTER XIX	REGGIE COMES TO LIFE	122
CHAPTER XX	THE-SAUSAGE-CHAPPIE-CLICKS	135
CHAPTER XXI	THE GROWING BOY	142
CHAPTER XXII	WASHY STEPS INTO THE HALL OF FAME	152
CHAPTER XXIII	MOTHER'S KNEE	160
CHAPTER XXIV	THE MELTING OF MR CONNOLLY	168
CHAPTER XXV	THE WIGMORE VENUS	176
CHAPTER XXVI	A TALE OF A GRANDFATHER	184

CHAPTER I

DISTRESSING SCENE

"I say, laddie!" said Archie.

"Sir?" replied the desk-clerk alertly. All the employes of the Hotel Cosmopolis were alert. It was one of the things on which Mr. Daniel Brewster, the proprietor, insisted. And as he was always wandering about the lobby of the hotel keeping a personal eye on affairs, it was never safe to relax.

"I want to see the manager."

"Is there anything I could do, sir?"

Archie looked at him doubtfully.

"Well, as a matter of fact, my dear old desk-clerk," he said, "I want to kick up a fearful row, and it hardly seems fair to lug you into it. Why you, I mean to say? The blighter whose head I want on a charger is the bally manager."

At this point a massive, grey-haired man, who had been standing close by, gazing on the lobby with an air of restrained severity, as if daring it to start anything, joined in the conversation.

"I am the manager," he said.

His eye was cold and hostile. Others, it seemed to say, might like Archie Moffam, but not he. Daniel Brewster was bristling for combat. What he had overheard had shocked him to the core of his being. The Hotel Cosmopolis was his own private, personal property, and the thing dearest to him in the world, after his daughter Lucille. He prided himself on the fact that his hotel was not like other New York hotels, which were run by impersonal companies and shareholders and boards of directors, and consequently lacked the paternal touch which made the Cosmopolis what it was. At other hotels things went wrong, and clients complained. At the Cosmopolis things never went wrong, because he was on the spot to see that they didn't, and as a result clients never complained. Yet here was this long, thin, string-bean of an Englishman actually registering annoyance and dissatisfaction before his very eyes.

"What is your complaint?" he enquired frigidly.

Archie attached himself to the top button of Mr. Brewster's coat, and was immediately dislodged by an irritable jerk of the other's substantial body.

"Listen, old thing! I came over to this country to nose about in search of a job, because there doesn't seem what you might call a

1

general demand for my services in England. Directly I was demobbed, the family started talking about the Land of Opportunity and shot me on to a liner. The idea was that I might get hold of something in America—"

He got hold of Mr. Brewster's coat-button, and was again shaken off.

"Between ourselves, I've never done anything much in England, and I fancy the family were getting a bit fed. At any rate, they sent me over here—"

Mr. Brewster disentangled himself for the third time.

"I would prefer to postpone the story of your life," he said coldly, "and be informed what is your specific complaint against the Hotel Cosmopolis."

"Of course, yes. The jolly old hotel. I'm coming to that. Well, it was like this. A chappie on the boat told me that this was the best place to stop at in New York—"

"He was quite right," said Mr. Brewster.

"Was he, by Jove! Well, all I can say, then, is that the other New York hotels must be pretty mouldy, if this is the best of the lot! I took a room here last night," said Archie quivering with self-pity, "and there was a beastly tap outside somewhere which went drip-drip-drip all night and kept me awake."

Mr. Brewster's annoyance deepened. He felt that a chink had been found in his armour. Not even the most paternal hotel-proprietor can keep an eye on every tap in his establishment.

"Drip-drip-drip!" repeated Archie firmly. "And I put my boots outside the door when I went to bed, and this morning they hadn't been touched. I give you my solemn word! Not touched."

"Naturally," said Mr. Brewster. "My employes are honest"

"But I wanted them cleaned, dash it!"

"There is a shoe-shining parlour in the basement. At the Cosmopolis shoes left outside bedroom doors are not cleaned."

"Then I think the Cosmopolis is a bally rotten hotel!"

Mr. Brewster's compact frame quivered. The unforgivable insult had been offered. Question the legitimacy of Mr. Brewster's parentage, knock Mr. Brewster down and walk on his face with spiked shoes, and you did not irremediably close all avenues to a peaceful settlement. But make a remark like that about his hotel, and war was definitely declared.

"In that case," he said, stiffening, "I must ask you to give up your room."

"I'm going to give it up! I wouldn't stay in the bally place another minute."

2

Mr. Brewster walked away, and Archie charged round to the cashier's desk to get his bill. It had been his intention in any case, though for dramatic purposes he concealed it from his adversary, to leave the hotel that morning. One of the letters of introduction which he had brought over from England had resulted in an invitation from a Mrs. van Tuyl to her house-party at Miami, and he had decided to go there at once.

"Well," mused Archie, on his way to the station, "one thing's certain. I'll never set foot in THAT bally place again!"

But nothing in this world is certain.

CHAPTER II

A SHOCK FOR MR. BREWSTER

Mr. Daniel Brewster sat in his luxurious suite at the Cosmopolis, smoking one of his admirable cigars and chatting with his old friend, Professor Binstead. A stranger who had only encountered Mr. Brewster in the lobby of the hotel would have been surprised at the appearance of his sitting-room, for it had none of the rugged simplicity which was the keynote of its owner's personal appearance. Daniel Brewster was a man with a hobby. He was what Parker, his valet, termed a connoozer. His educated taste in Art was one of the things which went to make the Cosmopolis different from and superior to other New York hotels. He had personally selected the tapestries in the dining-room and the various paintings throughout the building. And in his private capacity he was an enthusiastic collector of things which Professor Binstead, whose tastes lay in the same direction, would have stolen without a twinge of conscience if he could have got the chance.

The professor, a small man of middle age who wore tortoiseshell-rimmed spectacles, flitted covetously about the room, inspecting its treasures with a glistening eye. In a corner, Parker, a grave, lean individual, bent over the chafing-dish, in which he was preparing for his employer and his guest their simple lunch.

"Brewster," said Professor Binstead, pausing at the mantelpiece.

Mr. Brewster looked up amiably. He was in placid mood to-day. Two weeks and more had passed since the meeting with Archie recorded in the previous chapter, and he had been able to dismiss that disturbing affair from his mind. Since then, everything had gone splendidly with Daniel Brewster, for he had just accomplished his ambition of the moment by completing the negotiations for the purchase of a site further down-town, on which he proposed to erect a new hotel. He liked building hotels. He had the Cosmopolis, his first-born, a summer hotel in the mountains, purchased in the previous year, and he was toying with the idea of running over to England and putting up another in London, That, however, would have to wait. Meanwhile, he would concentrate on this new one down-town. It had kept him busy and worried, arranging for securing the site; but his troubles were over now.

"Yes?" he said.

Professor Binstead had picked up a small china figure of

delicate workmanship. It represented a warrior of pre-khaki days advancing with a spear upon some adversary who, judging from the contented expression on the warrior's face, was smaller than himself.

"Where did you get this?"

"That? Mawson, my agent, found it in a little shop on the east side."

"Where's the other? There ought to be another. These things go in pairs. They're valueless alone."

Mr. Brewster's brow clouded.

"I know that," he said shortly. "Mawson's looking for the other one everywhere. If you happen across it, I give you carte blanche to buy it for me."

"It must be somewhere."

"Yes. If you find it, don't worry about the expense. I'll settle up, no matter what it is."

"I'll bear it in mind," said Professor Binstead. "It may cost you a lot of money. I suppose you know that."

"I told you I don't care what it costs."

"It's nice to be a millionaire," sighed Professor Binstead.

"Luncheon is served, sir," said Parker.

He had stationed himself in a statutesque pose behind Mr. Brewster's chair, when there was a knock at the door. He went to the door, and returned with a telegram.

"Telegram for you, sir."

Mr. Brewster nodded carelessly. The contents of the chafing-dish had justified the advance advertising of their odour, and he was too busy to be interrupted.

"Put it down. And you needn't wait, Parker."

"Very good, sir."

The valet withdrew, and Mr. Brewster resumed his lunch.

"Aren't you going to open it?" asked Professor Binstead, to whom a telegram was a telegram.

"It can wait. I get them all day long. I expect it's from Lucille, saying what train she's making."

"She returns to-day?"

"Yes, Been at Miami." Mr. Brewster, having dwelt at adequate length on the contents of the chafing-dish, adjusted his glasses and took up the envelope. "I shall be glad—Great Godfrey!"

He sat staring at the telegram, his mouth open. His friend eyed him solicitously.

"No bad news, I hope?"

Mr. Brewster gurgled in a strangled way.

"Bad news? Bad—? Here, read it for yourself."

5

Professor Binstead, one of the three most inquisitive men in New York, took the slip of paper with gratitude.

"Returning New York to-day with darling Archie,'" he read. "'Lots of love from us both. Lucille.'" He gaped at his host. "Who is Archie?" he enquired.

"Who is Archie?" echoed Mr. Brewster helplessly. "Who is—? That's just what I would like to know."

"'Darling Archie,'" murmured the professor, musing over the telegram. "'Returning to-day with darling Archie.' Strange!"

Mr. Brewster continued to stare before him. When you send your only daughter on a visit to Miami minus any entanglements and she mentions in a telegram that she has acquired a darling Archie, you are naturally startled. He rose from the table with a bound. It had occurred to him that by neglecting a careful study of his mail during the past week, as was his bad habit when busy, he had lost an opportunity of keeping abreast with current happenings. He recollected now that a letter had arrived from Lucille some time ago, and that he had put it away unopened till he should have leisure to read it. Lucille was a dear girl, he had felt, but her letters when on a vacation seldom contained anything that couldn't wait a few days for a reading. He sprang for his desk, rummaged among his papers, and found what he was seeking.

It was a long letter, and there was silence in the room for some moments while he mastered its contents. Then he turned to the professor, breathing heavily.

"Good heavens!"

"Yes?" said Professor Binstead eagerly. "Yes?"

"Good Lord!"

"Well?"

"Good gracious!"

"What is it?" demanded the professor in an agony.

Mr. Brewster sat down again with a thud.

"She's married!"

"Married!"

"Married! To an Englishman!"

"Bless my soul!"

"She says," proceeded Mr. Brewster, referring to the letter again, "that they were both so much in love that they simply had to slip off and get married, and she hopes I won't be cross. Cross!" gasped Mr. Brewster, gazing wildly at his friend.

"Very disturbing!"

"Disturbing! You bet it's disturbing! I don't know anything about the fellow. Never heard of him in my life. She says he wanted a quiet wedding because he thought a fellow looked such a chump

6

getting married! And I must love him, because he's all set to love me very much!"

"Extraordinary!"

Mr. Brewster put the letter down.

"An Englishman!"

"I have met some very agreeable Englishmen," said Professor Binstead.

"I don't like Englishmen," growled Mr. Brewster. "Parker's an Englishman."

"Your valet?"

"Yes. I believe he wears my shirts on the sly,'" said Mr. Brewster broodingly, "If I catch him—! What would you do about this, Binstead?"

"Do?" The professor considered the point judiciary. "Well, really, Brewster, I do not see that there is anything you can do. You must simply wait and meet the man. Perhaps he will turn out an admirable son-in-law."

"H'm!" Mr. Brewster declined to take an optimistic view. "But an Englishman, Binstead!" he said with pathos. "Why," he went on, memory suddenly stirring, "there was an Englishman at this hotel only a week or two ago who went about knocking it in a way that would have amazed you! Said it was a rotten place! MY hotel!"

Professor Binstead clicked his tongue sympathetically. He understood his friend's warmth.

CHAPTER III

MR. BREWSTER DELIVERS SENTENCE

At about the same moment that Professor Binstead was clicking his tongue in Mr. Brewster's sitting-room, Archie Moffam sat contemplating his bride in a drawing-room on the express from Miami. He was thinking that this was too good to be true. His brain had been in something of a whirl these last few days, but this was one thought that never failed to emerge clearly from the welter.

Mrs. Archie Moffam, nee Lucille Brewster, was small and slender. She had a little animated face, set in a cloud of dark hair. She was so altogether perfect that Archie had frequently found himself compelled to take the marriage-certificate out of his inside pocket and study it furtively, to make himself realise that this miracle of good fortune had actually happened to him.

"Honestly, old bean—I mean, dear old thing,—I mean, darling," said Archie, "I can't believe it!"

"What?"

"What I mean is, I can't understand why you should have married a blighter like me."

Lucille's eyes opened. She squeezed his hand.

"Why, you're the most wonderful thing in the world, precious!—Surely you know that?"

"Absolutely escaped my notice. Are you sure?"

"Of course I'm sure! You wonder-child! Nobody could see you without loving you!"

Archie heaved an ecstatic sigh. Then a thought crossed his mind. It was a thought which frequently came to mar his bliss.

"I say, I wonder if your father will think that!"

"Of course he will!"

"We rather sprung this, as it were, on the old lad," said Archie dubiously. "What sort of a man IS your father?"

"Father's a darling, too."

"Rummy thing he should own that hotel," said Archie. "I had a frightful row with a blighter of a manager there just before I left for Miami. Your father ought to sack that chap. He was a blot on the landscape!"

It had been settled by Lucille during the journey that Archie should be broken gently to his father-in-law. That is to say, instead of bounding blithely into Mr. Brewster's presence hand in hand, the happy pair should separate for half an hour or so, Archie hanging around in the offing while Lucille saw her father and told him the whole story, or those chapters of it which she had omitted from her letter for want of space. Then, having impressed Mr. Brewster sufficiently with his luck in having acquired Archie for a son-in-law, she would lead him to where his bit of good fortune awaited him.

The programme worked out admirably in its earlier stages. When the two emerged from Mr. Brewster's room to meet Archie, Mr. Brewster's general idea was that fortune had smiled upon him in an almost unbelievable fashion and had presented him with a son-in-law who combined in almost equal parts the more admirable characteristics of Apollo, Sir Galahad, and Marcus Aurelius. True, he had gathered in the course of the conversation that dear Archie had no occupation and no private means; but Mr. Brewster felt that a great-souled man like Archie didn't need them. You can't have everything, and Archie, according to Lucille's account, was practically a hundred per cent man in soul, looks, manners, amiability, and breeding. These are the things that count. Mr. Brewster proceeded to the lobby in a glow of optimism and geniality.

Consequently, when he perceived Archie, he got a bit of a shock.

"Hullo—ullo—ullo!" said Archie, advancing happily.

"Archie, darling, this is father," said Lucille.

"Good Lord!" said Archie.

There was one of those silences. Mr. Brewster looked at Archie. Archie gazed at Mr. Brewster. Lucille, perceiving without understanding why that the big introduction scene had stubbed its toe on some unlooked-for obstacle, waited anxiously for enlightenment. Meanwhile, Archie continued to inspect Mr. Brewster, and Mr. Brewster continued to drink in Archie.

After an awkward pause of about three and a quarter minutes, Mr. Brewster swallowed once or twice, and finally spoke.

"Lu!"

"Yes, father?"

"Is this true?"

Lucille's grey eyes clouded over with perplexity and apprehension.

"True?"

"Have you really inflicted this—THIS on me for a son-in-law?" Mr. Brewster swallowed a few more times, Archie the while watching with a frozen fascination the rapid shimmying of his new relative's Adam's-apple. "Go away! I want to have a few words alone with this—This—WASSYOURDAMNAME?" he demanded, in an overwrought manner, addressing Archie for the first time.

9

"I told you, father. It's Moom."

"Moom?"

"It's spelt M-o-f-f-a-m, but pronounced Moom."

"To rhyme," said Archie, helpfully, "with Bluffinghame."

"Lu," said Mr. Brewster, "run away! I want to speak to-to-to"

"You called me THIS before," said Archie.

"You aren't angry, father, dear?" said Lucilla.

"Oh no! Oh no! I'm tickled to death!"

When his daughter had withdrawn, Mr. Brewster drew a long breath.

"Now then!" he said.

"Bit embarrassing, all this, what!" said Archie, chattily. "I mean to say, having met before in less happy circs. and what not. Rum coincidence and so forth! How would it be to bury the jolly old hatchet—start a new life—forgive and forget—learn to love each other—and all that sort of rot? I'm game if you are. How do we go? Is it a bet?"

Mr. Brewster remained entirely unsoftened by this manly appeal to his better feelings.

"What the devil do you mean by marrying my daughter?"

Archie reflected.

"Well, it sort of happened, don't you know! You know how these things ARE! Young yourself once, and all that. I was most frightfully in love, and Lu seemed to think it wouldn't be a bad scheme, and one thing led to another, and—well, there you are, don't you know!"

"And I suppose you think you've done pretty well for yourself?"

"Oh, absolutely! As far as I'm concerned, everything's topping! I've never felt so braced in my life!"

"Yes!" said Mr. Brewster, with bitterness, "I suppose, from your view-point, everything IS 'topping.' You haven't a cent to your name, and you've managed to fool a rich man's daughter into marrying you. I suppose you looked me up in Bradstreet before committing yourself?"

This aspect of the matter had not struck Archie until this moment.

"I say!" he observed, with dismay. "I never looked at it like that before! I can see that, from your point of view, this must look like a bit of a wash-out!"

"How do you propose to support Lucille, anyway?"

Archie ran a finger round the inside of his collar. He felt embarrassed, His father-in-law was opening up all kinds of new lines of thought.

"Well, there, old bean," he admitted, frankly, "you rather have me!" He turned the matter over for a moment. "I had a sort of idea of, as it were, working, if you know what I mean."

"Working at what?"

"Now, there again you stump me somewhat! The general scheme was that I should kind of look round, you know, and nose about and buzz to and fro till something turned up. That was, broadly speaking, the notion!"

"And how did you suppose my daughter was to live while you were doing all this?"

"Well, I think," said Archie, "I THINK we rather expected YOU to rally round a bit for the nonce!"

"I see! You expected to live on me?"

"Well, you put it a bit crudely, but—as far as I had mapped anything out—that WAS what you might call the general scheme of procedure. You don't think much of it, what? Yes? No?"

Mr. Brewster exploded.

"No! I do not think much of it! Good God! You go out of my hotel—MY hotel—calling it all the names you could think of—roasting it to beat the band—"

"Trifle hasty!" murmured Archie, apologetically. "Spoke without thinking. Dashed tap had gone DRIP-DRIP-DRIP all night—kept me awake—hadn't had breakfast—bygones be bygones—!"

"Don't interrupt! I say, you go out of my hotel, knocking it as no one has ever knocked it since it was built, and you sneak straight off and marry my daughter without my knowledge."

"Did think of wiring for blessing. Slipped the old bean, somehow. You know how one forgets things!"

"And now you come back and calmly expect me to fling my arms round you and kiss you, and support you for the rest of your life!"

"Only while I'm nosing about and buzzing to and fro."

"Well, I suppose I've got to support you. There seems no way out of it. I'll tell you exactly what I propose to do. You think my hotel is a pretty poor hotel, eh? Well, you'll have plenty of opportunity of judging, because you're coming to live here. I'll let you have a suite and I'll let you have your meals, but outside of that—nothing doing! Nothing doing! Do you understand what I mean?"

"Absolutely! You mean, 'Napoo!'"

"You can sign bills for a reasonable amount in my restaurant, and the hotel will look after your laundry. But not a cent do you get out me. And, if you want your shoes shined, you can pay for it

11

yourself in the basement. If you leave them outside your door, I'll instruct the floor-waiter to throw them down the air-shaft. Do you understand? Good! Now, is there anything more you want to ask?"

Archie smiled a propitiatory smile.

"Well, as a matter of fact, I was going to ask if you would stagger along and have a bite with us in the grill-room?"

"I will not!"

"I'll sign the bill," said Archie, ingratiatingly. "You don't think much of it? Oh, right-o!"

CHAPTER IV

WORK WANTED

It seemed to Archie, as he surveyed his position at the end of the first month of his married life, that all was for the best in the best of all possible worlds. In their attitude towards America, visiting Englishmen almost invariably incline to extremes, either detesting all that therein is or else becoming enthusiasts on the subject of the country, its climate, and its institutions. Archie belonged to the second class. He liked America and got on splendidly with Americans from the start. He was a friendly soul, a mixer; and in New York, that city of mixers, he found himself at home. The atmosphere of good-fellowship and the open-hearted hospitality of everybody he met appealed to him. There were moments when it seemed to him as though New York had simply been waiting for him to arrive before giving the word to let the revels commence.

Nothing, of course, in this world is perfect; and, rosy as were the glasses through which Archie looked on his new surroundings, he had to admit that there was one flaw, one fly in the ointment, one individual caterpillar in the salad. Mr. Daniel Brewster, his father-in-law, remained consistently unfriendly. Indeed, his manner towards his new relative became daily more and more a manner which would have caused gossip on the plantation if Simon Legree had exhibited it in his relations with Uncle Tom. And this in spite of the fact that Archie, as early as the third morning of his stay, had gone to him and in the most frank and manly way, had withdrawn his criticism of the Hotel Cosmopolis, giving it as his considered opinion that the Hotel Cosmopolis on closer inspection appeared to be a good egg, one of the best and brightest, and a bit of all right.

"A credit to you, old thing," said Archie cordially.

"Don't call me old thing!" growled Mr. Brewster.

"Right-o, old companion!" said Archie amiably.

Archie, a true philosopher, bore this hostility with fortitude, but it worried Lucille.

"I do wish father understood you better," was her wistful comment when Archie had related the conversation.

"Well, you know," said Archie, "I'm open for being understood any time he cares to take a stab at it."

"You must try and make him fond of you."

13

"But how? I smile winsomely at him and what not, but he doesn't respond."

"Well, we shall have to think of something. I want him to realise what an angel you are. You ARE an angel, you know."

"No, really?"

"Of course you are."

"It's a rummy thing," said Archie, pursuing a train of thought which was constantly with him, "the more I see of you, the more I wonder how you can have a father like—I mean to say, what I mean to say is, I wish I had known your mother; she must have been frightfully attractive."

"What would really please him, I know," said Lucille, "would be if you got some work to do. He loves people who work."

"Yes?" said Archie doubtfully. "Well, you know, I heard him interviewing that chappie behind the desk this morning, who works like the dickens from early morn to dewy eve, on the subject of a mistake in his figures; and, if he loved him, he dissembled it all right. Of course, I admit that so far I haven't been one of the toilers, but the dashed difficult thing is to know how to start. I'm nosing round, but the openings for a bright young man seem so scarce."

"Well, keep on trying. I feel sure that, if you could only find something to do, it doesn't matter what, father would be quite different."

It was possibly the dazzling prospect of making Mr. Brewster quite different that stimulated Archie. He was strongly of the opinion that any change in his father-in-law must inevitably be for the better. A chance meeting with James B. Wheeler, the artist, at the Pen-and-Ink Club seemed to open the way.

To a visitor to New York who has the ability to make himself liked it almost appears as though the leading industry in that city was the issuing of two-weeks' invitation-cards to clubs. Archie since his arrival had been showered with these pleasant evidences of his popularity; and he was now an honorary member of so many clubs of various kinds that he had not time to go to them all. There were the fashionable clubs along Fifth Avenue to which his friend Reggie van Tuyl, son of his Florida hostess, had introduced him. There were the businessmen's clubs of which he was made free by more solid citizens. And, best of all, there were the Lambs', the Players', the Friars', the Coffee-House, the Pen-and-Ink,—and the other resorts of the artist, the author, the actor, and the Bohemian. It was in these that Archie spent most of his time, and it was here that he made the acquaintance of J. B. Wheeler, the popular illustrator.

To Mr. Wheeler, over a friendly lunch, Archie had been

14

confiding some of his ambitions to qualify as the hero of one of the Get-on-or-get-out-young-man-step-lively-books.

"You want a job?" said Mr. Wheeler.

"I want a job," said Archie.

Mr. Wheeler consumed eight fried potatoes in quick succession. He was an able trencherman.

"I always looked on you as one of our leading lilies of the field," he said. "Why this anxiety to toil and spin?"

"Well, my wife, you know, seems to think it might put me one-up with the jolly old dad if I did something."

"And you're not particular what you do, so long as it has the outer aspect of work?"

"Anything in the world, laddie, anything in the world."

"Then come and pose for a picture I'm doing," said J. B. Wheeler. "It's for a magazine cover. You're just the model I want, and I'll pay you at the usual rates. Is it a go?"

"Pose?"

"You've only got to stand still and look like a chunk of wood. You can do that, surely?"

"I can do that," said Archie.

"Then come along down to my studio to-morrow."

"Right-o!" said Archie.

CHAPTER V

STRANGE EXPERIENCES OF AN ARTIST'S MODEL

"I say, old thing!"

Archie spoke plaintively. Already he was looking back ruefully to the time when he had supposed that an artist's model had a soft job. In the first five minutes muscles which he had not been aware that he possessed had started to ache like neglected teeth. His respect for the toughness and durability of artists' models was now solid. How they acquired the stamina to go through this sort of thing all day and then bound óff to Bohemian revels at night was more than he could understand.

"Don't wobble, confound you!" snorted Mr. Wheeler.

"Yes, but, my dear old artist," said Archie, "what you don't seem to grasp—what you appear not to realise—is that I'm getting a crick in the back."

"You weakling! You miserable, invertebrate worm. Move an inch and I'll murder you, and come and dance on your grave every Wednesday and Saturday. I'm just getting it."

"It's in the spine that it seems to catch me principally."

"Be a man, you faint-hearted string-bean!" urged J. B. Wheeler. "You ought to be ashamed of yourself. Why, a girl who was posing for me last week stood for a solid hour on one leg, holding a tennis racket over her head and smiling brightly withal."

"The female of the species is more india-rubbery than the male," argued Archie.

"Well, I'll be through in a few minutes. Don't weaken. Think how proud you'll be when you see yourself on all the bookstalls."

Archie sighed, and braced himself to the task once more. He wished he had never taken on this binge. In addition to his physical discomfort, he was feeling a most awful chump. The cover on which Mr. Wheeler was engaged was for the August number of the magazine, and it had been necessary for Archie to drape his reluctant form in a two-piece bathing suit of a vivid lemon colour; for he was supposed to be representing one of those jolly dogs belonging to the best families who dive off floats at exclusive seashore resorts. J. B. Wheeler, a stickler for accuracy, had wanted him to remove his socks and shoes; but there Archie had stood firm. He was willing to make an ass of himself, but not a silly ass.

"All right," said J. B. Wheeler, laying down his brush. "That

16

will do for to-day. Though, speaking without prejudice and with no wish to be offensive, if I had had a model who wasn't a weak-kneed, jelly-backboned son of Belial, I could have got the darned thing finished without having to have another sitting."

"I wonder why you chappies call this sort of thing 'sitting,'" said Archie, pensively, as he conducted tentative experiments in osteopathy on his aching back. "I say, old thing, I could do with a restorative, if you have one handy. But, of course, you haven't, I suppose," he added, resignedly. Abstemious as a rule, there were moments when Archie found the Eighteenth Amendment somewhat trying.

J. B. Wheeler shook his head.

"You're a little previous," he said. "But come round in another day or so, and I may be able to do something for you." He moved with a certain conspirator-like caution to a corner of the room, and, lifting to one side a pile of canvases, revealed a stout barrel, which, he regarded with a fatherly and benignant eye. "I don't mind telling you that, in the fullness of time, I believe this is going to spread a good deal of sweetness and light."

"Oh, ah," said Archie, interested. "Home-brew, what?"

"Made with these hands. I added a few more raisins yesterday, to speed things up a bit. There is much virtue in your raisin. And, talking of speeding things up, for goodness' sake try to be a bit more punctual to-morrow. We lost an hour of good daylight to-day."

"I like that! I was here on the absolute minute. I had to hang about on the landing waiting for you."

"Well, well, that doesn't matter," said J. B. Wheeler, impatiently, for the artist soul is always annoyed by petty details. "The point is that we were an hour late in getting to work. Mind you're here to-morrow at eleven sharp."

It was, therefore, with a feeling of guilt and trepidation that Archie mounted the stairs on the following morning; for in spite of his good resolutions he was half an hour behind time. He was relieved to find that his friend had also lagged by the wayside. The door of the studio was ajar, and he went in, to discover the place occupied by a lady of mature years, who was scrubbing the floor with a mop. He went into the bedroom and donned his bathing suit. When he emerged, ten minutes later, the charwoman had gone, but J. B. Wheeler was still absent. Rather glad of the respite, he sat down to kill time by reading the morning paper, whose sporting page alone he had managed to master at the breakfast table.

There was not a great deal in the paper to interest him. The usual bond-robbery had taken place on the previous day, and the police were reported hot on the trail of the Master-Mind who was

17

alleged to be at the back of these financial operations. A messenger named Henry Babcock had been arrested and was expected to become confidential. To one who, like Archie, had never owned a bond, the story made little appeal. He turned with more interest to a cheery half-column on the activities of a gentleman in Minnesota who, with what seemed to Archie, as he thought of Mr. Daniel Brewster, a good deal of resource and public spirit, had recently beaned his father-in-law with the family meat-axe. It was only after he had read this through twice in a spirit of gentle approval that it occurred to him that J. B. Wheeler was uncommonly late at the tryst. He looked at his watch, and found that he had been in the studio three-quarters of an hour.

Archie became restless. Long-suffering old bean though he was, he considered this a bit thick. He got up and went out on to the landing, to see if there were any signs of the blighter. There were none. He began to understand now what had happened. For some reason or other the bally artist was not coming to the studio at all that day. Probably he had called up the hotel and left a message to this effect, and Archie had just missed it. Another man might have waited to make certain that his message had reached its destination, but not woollen-headed Wheeler, the most casual individual in New York.

Thoroughly aggrieved, Archie turned back to the studio to dress and go away.

His progress was stayed by a solid, forbidding slab of oak. Somehow or other, since he had left the room, the door had managed to get itself shut.

"Oh, dash it!" said Archie.

The mildness of the expletive was proof that the full horror of the situation had not immediately come home to him. His mind in the first few moments was occupied with the problem of how the door had got that way. He could not remember shutting it. Probably he had done it unconsciously. As a child, he had been taught by sedulous elders that the little gentleman always closed doors behind him, and presumably his subconscious self was still under the influence. And then, suddenly, he realised that this infernal, officious ass of a subconscious self had deposited him right in the gumbo. Behind that closed door, unattainable as youthful ambition, lay his gent's heather-mixture with the green twill, and here he was, out in the world, alone, in a lemon-coloured bathing suit.

In all crises of human affairs there are two broad courses open to a man. He can stay where he is or he can go elsewhere. Archie, leaning on the banisters, examined these alternatives narrowly. If he stayed where he was he would have to spend the night on this dashed landing. If he legged it, in this kit, he would be gathered up by the constabulary before he had gone a hundred yards. He was no pessimist, but he was reluctantly forced to the conclusion that he was up against it.

It was while he was musing with a certain tenseness on these things that the sound of footsteps came to him from below. But almost in the first instant the hope that this might be J. B. Wheeler, the curse of the human race, died away. Whoever was coming up the stairs was running, and J. B. Wheeler never ran upstairs. He was not one of your lean, haggard, spiritual-looking geniuses. He made a large income with his brush and pencil, and spent most of it in creature comforts. This couldn't be J. B. Wheeler.

It was not. It was a tall, thin man whom he had never seen before. He appeared to be in a considerable hurry. He let himself into the studio on the floor below, and vanished without even waiting to shut the door.

He had come and disappeared in almost record time, but, brief though his passing had been, it had been long enough to bring consolation to Archie. A sudden bright light had been vouchsafed to Archie, and he now saw an admirably ripe and fruity scheme for ending his troubles. What could be simpler than to toddle down one flight of stairs and in an easy and debonair manner ask the chappie's permission to use his telephone? And what could be simpler, once he was at the 'phone, than to get in touch with somebody at the Cosmopolis who would send down a few trousers and what not in a kit bag. It was a priceless solution, thought Archie, as he made his way downstairs. Not even embarrassing, he meant to say. This chappie, living in a place like this, wouldn't bat an eyelid at the spectacle of a fellow trickling about the place in a bathing suit. They would have a good laugh about the whole thing.

"I say, I hate to bother you—dare say you're busy and all that sort of thing—but would you mind if I popped in for half a second and used your 'phone?"

That was the speech, the extremely gentlemanly and well-phrased speech which Archie had prepared to deliver the moment the man appeared. The reason he did not deliver it was that the man did not appear. He knocked, but nothing stirred.

"I say!"

Archie now perceived that the door was ajar, and that on an envelope attached with a tack to one of the panels was the name "Elmer M. Moon" He pushed the door a little farther open and tried again.

"Oh, Mr. Moon! Mr. Moon!" He waited a moment. "Oh, Mr. Moon! Mr. Moon! Are you there, Mr. Moon?"

19

He blushed hotly. To his sensitive ear the words had sounded exactly like the opening line of the refrain of a vaudeville song-hit. He decided to waste no further speech on a man with such an unfortunate surname until he could see him face to face and get a chance of lowering his voice a bit. Absolutely absurd to stand outside a chappie's door singing song-hits in a lemon-coloured bathing suit. He pushed the door open and walked in; and his subconscious self, always the gentleman, closed it gently behind him.

"Up!" said a low, sinister, harsh, unfriendly, and unpleasant voice.

"Eh?" said Archie, revolving sharply on his axis.

He found himself confronting the hurried gentleman who had run upstairs. This sprinter had produced an automatic pistol, and was pointing it in a truculent manner at his head. Archie stared at his host, and his host stared at him.

"Put your hands up," he said.

"Oh, right-o! Absolutely!" said Archie. "But I mean to say—"

The other was drinking him in with considerable astonishment. Archie's costume seemed to have made a powerful impression upon him.

"Who the devil are you?" he enquired.

"Me? Oh, my name's—"

"Never mind your name. What are you doing here?"

"Well, as a matter of fact, I popped in to ask if I might use your 'phone. You see—"

A certain relief seemed to temper the austerity of the other's gaze. As a visitor, Archie, though surprising, seemed to be better than he had expected.

"I don't know what to do with you," he said, meditatively.

"If you'd just let me toddle to the 'phone—"

"Likely!" said the man. He appeared to reach a decision. "Here, go into that room."

He indicated with a jerk of his head the open door of what was apparently a bedroom at the farther end of the studio.

"I take it," said Archie, chattily, "that all this may seem to you not a little rummy."

"Get on!"

"I was only saying—"

"Well, I haven't time to listen. Get a move on!"

The bedroom was in a state of untidiness which eclipsed anything which Archie had ever witnessed. The other appeared to be moving house. Bed, furniture, and floor were covered with articles of clothing. A silk shirt wreathed itself about Archie's ankles as he

20

stood gaping, and, as he moved farther into the room, his path was paved with ties and collars.

"Sit down!" said Elmer M. Moon, abruptly.

"Right-o! Thanks," said Archie, "I suppose you wouldn't like me to explain, and what not, what?"

"No!" said Mr. Moon. "I haven't got your spare time. Put your hands behind that chair."

Archie did so, and found them immediately secured by what felt like a silk tie. His assiduous host then proceeded to fasten his ankles in a like manner. This done, he seemed to feel that he had done all that was required of him, and he returned to the packing of a large suitcase which stood by the window.

"I say!" said Archie.

Mr. Moon, with the air of a man who has remembered something which he had overlooked, shoved a sock in his guest's mouth and resumed his packing. He was what might be called an impressionist packer. His aim appeared to be speed rather than neatness. He bundled his belongings in, closed the bag with some difficulty, and, stepping to the window, opened it. Then he climbed out on to the fire-escape, dragged the suit-case after him, and was gone.

Archie, left alone, addressed himself to the task of freeing his prisoned limbs. The job proved much easier than he had expected. Mr. Moon, that hustler, had wrought for the moment, not for all time. A practical man, he had been content to keep his visitor shackled merely for such a period as would permit him to make his escape unhindered. In less than ten minutes Archie, after a good deal of snake-like writhing, was pleased to discover that the thingummy attached to his wrists had loosened sufficiently to enable him to use his hands. He untied himself and got up.

He now began to tell himself that out of evil cometh good. His encounter with the elusive Mr. Moon had not been an agreeable one, but it had had this solid advantage, that it had left him right in the middle of a great many clothes. And Mr. Moon, whatever his moral defects, had the one excellent quality of taking about the same size as himself. Archie, casting a covetous eye upon a tweed suit which lay on the bed, was on the point of climbing into the trousers when on the outer door of the studio there sounded a forceful knocking.

"Open up here!"

CHAPTER VI

THE BOMB

Archie bounded silently out into the other room and stood listening tensely. He was not a naturally querulous man, but he did feel at this point that Fate was picking on him with a somewhat undue severity.

"In th' name av th' Law!"

There are times when the best of us lose our heads. At this juncture Archie should undoubtedly have gone to the door, opened it, explained his presence in a few well-chosen words, and generally have passed the whole thing off with ready tact. But the thought of confronting a posse of police in his present costume caused him to look earnestly about him for a hiding-place.

Up against the farther wall was a settee with a high, arching back, which might have been put there for that special purpose. He inserted himself behind this, just as a splintering crash announced that the Law, having gone through the formality of knocking with its knuckles, was now getting busy with an axe. A moment later the door had given way, and the room was full of trampling feet. Archie wedged himself against the wall with the quiet concentration of a clam nestling in its shell, and hoped for the best.

It seemed to him that his immediate future depended for better or for worse entirely on the native intelligence of the Force. If they were the bright, alert men he hoped they were, they would see all that junk in the bedroom and, deducing from it that their quarry had stood not upon the order of his going but had hopped it, would not waste time in searching a presumably empty apartment. If, on the other hand, they were the obtuse, flat-footed persons who occasionally find their way into the ranks of even the most enlightened constabularies, they would undoubtedly shift the settee and drag him into a publicity from which his modest soul shrank. He was enchanted, therefore, a few moments later, to hear a gruff voice state that th' mutt had beaten it down th' fire-escape. His opinion of the detective abilities of the New York police force rose with a bound.

There followed a brief council of war, which, as it took place in the bedroom, was inaudible to Archie except as a distant growling noise. He could distinguish no words, but, as it was succeeded by a general trampling of large boots in the direction of the door and then by silence, he gathered that the pack, having drawn the studio and found it empty, had decided to return to other and more profitable duties. He gave them a reasonable interval for removing themselves, and then poked his head cautiously over the settee.

All was peace. The place was empty. No sound disturbed the stillness.

Archie emerged. For the first time in this morning of disturbing occurrences he began to feel that God was in his heaven and all right with the world. At last things were beginning to brighten up a bit, and life might be said to have taken on some of the aspects of a good egg. He stretched himself, for it is cramping work lying under settees, and, proceeding to the bedroom, picked up the tweed trousers again.

Clothes had a fascination for Archie. Another man, in similar circumstances, might have hurried over his toilet; but Archie, faced by a difficult choice of ties, rather strung the thing out. He selected a specimen which did great credit to the taste of Mr. Moon, evidently one of our snappiest dressers, found that it did not harmonise with the deeper meaning of the tweed suit, removed it, chose another, and was adjusting the bow and admiring the effect, when his attention was diverted by a slight sound which was half a cough and half a sniff; and, turning, found himself gazing into the clear blue eyes of a large man in uniform, who had stepped into the room from the fire-escape. He was swinging a substantial club in a negligent sort of way, and he looked at Archie with a total absence of bonhomie.

"Ah!" he observed.

"Oh, THERE you are!" said Archie, subsiding weakly against the chest of drawers. He gulped. "Of course, I can see you're thinking all this pretty tolerably weird and all that," he proceeded, in a propitiatory voice.

The policeman attempted no analysis of his emotions, He opened a mouth which a moment before had looked incapable of being opened except with the assistance of powerful machinery, and shouted a single word.

"Cassidy!"

A distant voice gave tongue in answer. It was like alligators roaring to their mates across lonely swamps.

There was a rumble of footsteps in the region of the stairs, and presently there entered an even larger guardian of the Law than the first exhibit. He, too, swung a massive club, and, like his colleague, he gazed frostily at Archie.

"God save Ireland!" he remarked.

23

The words appeared to be more in the nature of an expletive than a practical comment on the situation. Having uttered them, he draped himself in the doorway like a colossus, and chewed gum.

"Where ja get him?" he enquired, after a pause.

"Found him in here attimpting to disguise himself."

"I told Cap. he was hiding somewheres, but he would have it that he'd beat it down th' escape," said the gum-chewer, with the sombre triumph of the underling whose sound advice has been overruled by those above him. He shifted his wholesome (or, as some say, unwholesome) morsel to the other side of his mouth, and for the first time addressed Archie directly. "Ye're pinched!" he observed.

Archie started violently. The bleak directness of the speech roused him with a jerk from the dream-like state into which he had fallen. He had not anticipated this. He had assumed that there would be a period of tedious explanations to be gone through before he was at liberty to depart to the cosy little lunch for which his interior had been sighing wistfully this long time past; but that he should be arrested had been outside his calculations. Of course, he could put everything right eventually; he could call witnesses to his character and the purity of his intentions; but in the meantime the whole dashed business would be in all the papers, embellished with all those unpleasant flippancies to which your newspaper reporter is so prone to stoop when he sees half a chance. He would feel a frightful chump. Chappies would rot him about it to the most fearful extent. Old Brewster's name would come into it, and he could not disguise it from himself that his father-in-law, who liked his name in the papers as little as possible, would be sorer than a sunburned neck.

"No, I say, you know! I mean, I mean to say!"

"Pinched!" repeated the rather larger policeman.

"And annything ye say," added his slightly smaller colleague, "will be used agenst ya 't the trial."

"And if ya try t'escape," said the first speaker, twiddling his club, "ya'll getja block knocked off."

And, having sketched out this admirably clear and neatly-constructed scenario, the two relapsed into silence. Officer Cassidy restored his gum to circulation. Officer Donahue frowned sternly at his boots.

"But, I say," said Archie, "it's all a mistake, you know. Absolutely a frightful error, my dear old constables. I'm not the lad you're after at all. The chappie you want is a different sort of fellow altogether. Another blighter entirely."

24

New York policemen never laugh when on duty. There is probably something in the regulations against it. But Officer Donahue permitted the left corner of his mouth to twitch slightly, and a momentary muscular spasm disturbed the calm of Officer Cassidy's granite features, as a passing breeze ruffles the surface of some bottomless lake.

"That's what they all say!" observed Officer Donahue.

"It's no use tryin' that line of talk," said Officer Cassidy. "Babcock's squealed."

"Sure. Squealed 's morning," said Officer Donahue.

Archie's memory stirred vaguely.

"Babcock?" he said. "Do you know, that name seems familiar to me, somehow. I'm almost sure I've read it in the paper or something."

"Ah, cut it out!" said Officer Cassidy, disgustedly. The two constables exchanged a glance of austere disapproval. This hypocrisy pained them. "Read it in th' paper or something!"

"By Jove! I remember now. He's the chappie who was arrested in that bond business. For goodness' sake, my dear, merry old constables," said Archie, astounded, "you surely aren't labouring under the impression that I'm the Master-Mind they were talking about in the paper? Why, what an absolutely priceless notion! I mean to say, I ask you, what! Frankly, laddies, do I look like a Master-Mind?"

Officer Cassidy heaved a deep sigh, which rumbled up from his interior like the first muttering of a cyclone.

"If I'd known," he said, regretfully, "that this guy was going to turn out a ruddy Englishman, I'd have taken a slap at him with m' stick and chanced it!"

Officer Donahue considered the point well taken.

"Ah!" he said, understandingly. He regarded Archie with an unfriendly eye. "I know th' sort well! Trampling on th' face av th' poor!"

"Ya c'n trample on the poor man's face," said Officer Cassidy, severely; "but don't be surprised if one day he bites you in the leg!"

"But, my dear old sir," protested Archie, "I've never trampled—"

"One of these days," said Officer Donahue, moodily, "the Shannon will flow in blood to the sea!"

"Absolutely! But—"

Officer Cassidy uttered a glad cry.

"Why couldn't we hit him a lick," he suggested, brightly, "an' tell th' Cap. he resisted us in th' exercise of our jooty?"

25

An instant gleam of approval and enthusiasm came into Officer Donahue's eyes. Officer Donahue was not a man who got these luminous inspirations himself, but that did not prevent him appreciating them in others and bestowing commendation in the right quarter. There was nothing petty or grudging about Officer Donahue.

"Ye're the lad with the head, Tim!" he exclaimed admiringly.

"It just sorta came to me," said Mr. Cassidy, modestly.

"It's a great idea, Timmy!"

"Just happened to think of it," said Mr. Cassidy, with a coy gesture of self-effacement.

Archie had listened to the dialogue with growing uneasiness. Not for the first time since he had made their acquaintance, he became vividly aware of the exceptional physical gifts of these two men. The New York police force demands from those who would join its ranks an extremely high standard of stature and sinew, but it was obvious that jolly old Donahue and Cassidy must have passed in first shot without any difficulty whatever.

"I say, you know," he observed, apprehensively.

And then a sharp and commanding voice spoke from the outer room.

"Donahue! Cassidy! What the devil does this mean?"

Archie had a momentary impression that an angel had fluttered down to his rescue. If this was the case, the angel had assumed an effective disguise—that of a police captain. The new arrival was a far smaller man than his subordinates—so much smaller that it did Archie good to look at him. For a long time he had been wishing that it were possible to rest his eyes with the spectacle of something of a slightly less out-size nature than his two companions.

"Why have you left your posts?"

The effect of the interruption on the Messrs. Cassidy and Donahue was pleasingly instantaneous. They seemed to shrink to almost normal proportions, and their manner took on an attractive deference.

Officer Donahue saluted.

"If ye plaze, sorr—"

Officer Cassidy also saluted, simultaneously.

"'Twas like this, sorr—"

The captain froze Officer Cassidy with a glance and, leaving him congealed, turned to Officer Donahue.

"Oi wuz standing on th' fire-escape, sorr," said Officer

26

Donahue, in a tone of obsequious respect which not only delighted, but astounded Archie, who hadn't known he could talk like that, "accordin' to instructions, when I heard a suspicious noise. I crope in, sorr, and found this duck—found the accused, sorr—in front of the mirror, examinin' himself. I then called to Officer Cassidy for assistance. We pinched—arrested um, sorr."

The captain looked at Archie. It seemed to Archie that he looked at him coldly and with contempt.

"Who is he?"

"The Master-Mind, sorr."

"The what?"

"The accused, sorr. The man that's wanted."

"You may want him. I don't," said the captain. Archie, though relieved, thought he might have put it more nicely. "This isn't Moon. It's not a bit like him."

"Absolutely not!" agreed Archie, cordially. "It's all a mistake, old companion, as I was trying to—"

"Cut it out!"

"Oh, right-o!"

"You've seen the photographs at the station. Do you mean to tell me you see any resemblance?"

"If ye plaze, sorr," said Officer Cassidy, coming to life.

"Well?"

"We thought he'd bin disguising himself, the way he wouldn't be recognised."

"You're a fool!" said the captain.

"Yes, sorr," said Officer Cassidy, meekly.

"So are you, Donahue."

"Yes, sorr."

Archie's respect for this chappie was going up all the time. He seemed to be able to take years off the lives of these massive blighters with a word. It was like the stories you read about lion-tamers. Archie did not despair of seeing Officer Donahue and his old college chum Cassidy eventually jumping through hoops.

"Who are you?" demanded the captain, turning to Archie.

"Well, my name is—"

"What are you doing here?"

"Well, it's rather a longish story, you know. Don't want to bore you, and all that."

"I'm here to listen. You can't bore ME."

"Dashed nice of you to put it like that," said Archie, gratefully. "I mean to say, makes it easier and so forth. What I mean is, you know how rotten you feel telling the deuce of a long yarn and wondering if the party of the second part is wishing you would turn off the tap and go home. I mean—"

"If," said the captain, "you're reciting something, stop. If you're trying to tell me what you're doing here, make it shorter and easier."

Archie saw his point. Of course, time was money—the modern spirit of hustle—all that sort of thing.

"Well, it was this bathing suit, you know," he said.

"What bathing suit?"

"Mine, don't you know, A lemon-coloured contrivance. Rather bright and so forth, but in its proper place not altogether a bad egg. Well, the whole thing started, you know, with my standing on a bally pedestal sort of arrangement in a diving attitude—for the cover, you know. I don't know if you have ever done anything of that kind yourself, but it gives you a most fearful crick in the spine. However, that's rather beside the point, I suppose—don't know why I mentioned it. Well, this morning he was dashed late, so I went out—"

"What the devil are you talking about?"

Archie looked at him, surprised.

"Aren't I making it clear?"

"No."

"Well, you understand about the bathing suit, don't you? The jolly old bathing suit, you've grasped that, what?"

"No."

"Oh, I say," said Archie. "That's rather a nuisance. I mean to say, the bathing suit's what you might call the good old pivot of the whole dashed affair, you see. Well, you understand about the cover, what? You're pretty clear on the subject of the cover?"

"What cover?"

"Why, for the magazine."

"What magazine?"

"Now there you rather have me. One of these bright little periodicals, you know, that you see popping to and fro on the bookstalls."

"I don't know what you're talking about," said the captain. He looked at Archie with an expression of distrust and hostility. "And I'll tell you straight out I don't like the looks of you. I believe you're a pal of his."

"No longer," said Archie, firmly. "I mean to say, a chappie who makes you stand on a bally pedestal sort of arrangement and get a

28

crick in the spine, and then doesn't turn up and leaves you biffing all over the countryside in a bathing suit—"

The reintroduction of the bathing suit motive seemed to have the worst effect on the captain. He flushed darkly.

"Are you trying to josh me? I've a mind to soak you!"

"If ye plaze, sorr," cried Officer Donahue and Officer Cassidy in chorus. In the course of their professional career they did not often hear their superior make many suggestions with which they saw eye to eye, but he had certainly, in their opinion, spoken a mouthful now.

"No, honestly, my dear old thing, nothing was farther from my thoughts—"

He would have spoken further, but at this moment the world came to an end. At least, that was how it sounded. Somewhere in the immediate neighbourhood something went off with a vast explosion, shattering the glass in the window, peeling the plaster from the ceiling, and sending him staggering into the inhospitable arms of Officer Donahue.

The three guardians of the Law stared at one another.

"If ye plaze, sorr," said. Officer Cassidy, saluting.

"Well?"

"May I spake, sorr?"

"Well?"

"Something's exploded, sorr!"

The information, kindly meant though it was, seemed to annoy the captain.

"What the devil did you think I thought had happened?" he demanded, with not a little irritation, "It was a bomb!"

Archie could have corrected this diagnosis, for already a faint but appealing aroma of an alcoholic nature was creeping into the room through a hole in the ceiling, and there had risen before his eyes the picture of J. B. Wheeler affectionately regarding that barrel of his on the previous morning in the studio upstairs. J. B. Wheeler had wanted quick results, and he had got them. Archie had long since ceased to regard J. B. Wheeler as anything but a tumour on the social system, but he was bound to admit that he had certainly done him a good turn now. Already these honest men, diverted by the superior attraction of this latest happening, appeared to have forgotten his existence.

"Sorr!" said Officer Donahue.

"Well?"

"It came from upstairs, sorr."

29

"Of course it came from upstairs. Cassidy!"

"Sorr?"

"Get down into the street, call up the reserves, and stand at the front entrance to keep the crowd back. We'll have the whole city here in five minutes."

"Right, sorr."

"Don't let anyone in."

"No, sorr."

"Well, see that you don't. Come along, Donahue, now. Look slippy."

"On the spot, sorr!" said Officer Donahue.

A moment later Archie had the studio to himself. Two minutes later he was picking his way cautiously down the fire-escape after the manner of the recent Mr. Moon. Archie had not seen much of Mr. Moon, but he had seen enough to know that in certain crises his methods were sound and should be followed. Elmer Moon was not a good man; his ethics were poor and his moral code shaky; but in the matter of legging it away from a situation of peril and discomfort he had no superior.

CHAPTER VII

MR. ROSCOE SHERRIFF HAS AN IDEA

Archie inserted a fresh cigarette in his long holder and began to smoke a little moodily. It was about a week after his disturbing adventures in J. B. Wheeler's studio, and life had ceased for the moment to be a thing of careless enjoyment. Mr. Wheeler, mourning over his lost home-brew and refusing, like Niobe, to be comforted, has suspended the sittings for the magazine cover, thus robbing Archie of his life-work. Mr. Brewster had not been in genial mood of late. And, in addition to all this, Lucille was away on a visit to a school-friend. And when Lucille went away, she took with her the sunshine. Archie was not surprised at her being popular and in demand among her friends, but that did not help him to become reconciled to her absence.

He gazed rather wistfully across the table at his friend, Roscoe Sherriff, the Press-agent, another of his Pen-and-Ink Club acquaintances. They had just finished lunch, and during the meal Sherriff, who, like most men of action, was fond of hearing the sound of his own voice and liked exercising it on the subject of himself, had been telling Archie a few anecdotes about his professional past. From these the latter had conceived a picture of Roscoe Sherriff's life as a prismatic thing of energy and adventure and well-paid withal—just the sort of life, in fact, which he would have enjoyed leading himself. He wished that he, too, like the Press-agent, could go about the place "slipping things over" and "putting things across." Daniel Brewster, he felt, would have beamed upon a son-in-law like Roscoe Sherriff.

"The more I see of America," sighed Archie, "the more it amazes me. All you birds seem to have been doing things from the cradle upwards. I wish I could do things!"

"Well, why don't you?"

Archie flicked the ash from his cigarette into the finger-bowl.

"Oh, I don't know, you know," he said, "Somehow, none of our family ever have. I don't know why it is, but whenever a Moffam starts out to do things he infallibly makes a bloomer. There was a Moffam in the Middle Ages who had a sudden spasm of energy and set out to make a pilgrimage to Jerusalem, dressed as a wandering friar. Rum ideas they had in those days."

"Did he get there?"

"Absolutely not! Just as he was leaving the front door his favourite hound mistook him for a tramp—or a varlet, or a scurvy knave, or whatever they used to call them at that time—and bit him in the fleshy part of the leg."

"Well, at least he started."

"Enough to make a chappie start, what?"

Roscoe Sherriff sipped his coffee thoughtfully. He was an apostle of Energy, and it seemed to him that he could make a convert of Archie and incidentally do himself a bit of good. For several days he had been, looking for someone like Archie to help him in a small matter which he had in mind.

"If you're really keen on doing things," he said, "there's something you can do for me right away."

Archie beamed. Action was what his soul demanded.

"Anything, dear boy, anything! State your case!"

"Would you have any objection to putting up a snake for me?"

"Putting up a snake?"

"Just for a day or two."

"But how do you mean, old soul? Put him up where?"

"Wherever you live. Where do you live? The Cosmopolis, isn't it? Of course! You married old Brewster's daughter. I remember reading about it."

"But, I say, laddie, I don't want to spoil your day and disappoint you and so forth, but my jolly old father-in-law would never let me keep a snake. Why, it's as much as I can do to make him let me stop on in the place."

"He wouldn't know."

"There's not much that goes on in the hotel that he doesn't know," said Archie, doubtfully.

"He mustn't know. The whole point of the thing is that it must be a dead secret."

Archie flicked some more ash into the finger-bowl.

"I don't seem absolutely to have grasped the affair in all its aspects, if you know what I mean," he said. "I mean to say—in the first place—why would it brighten your young existence if I entertained this snake of yours?"

"It's not mine. It belongs to Mme. Brudowska. You've heard of her, of course?"

"Oh yes. She's some sort of performing snake female in vaudeville or something, isn't she, or something of that species or order?"

"You're near it, but not quite right. She is the leading exponent of high-brow tragedy on any stage in the civilized world."

"Absolutely! I remember now. My wife lugged me to see her perform one night. It all comes back to me. She had me wedged in an orchestra-stall before I knew what I was up against, and then it was too late. I remember reading in some journal or other that she had a pet snake, given her by some Russian prince or other, what?"

"That," said Sherriff, "was the impression I intended to convey when I sent the story to the papers. I'm her Press-agent. As a matter of fact, I bought Peter-its name's Peter-myself down on the East Side. I always believe in animals for Press-agent stunts. I've nearly always had good results. But with Her Nibs I'm handicapped. Shackled, so to speak. You might almost say my genius is stifled. Or strangled, if you prefer it."

"Anything you say," agreed Archie, courteously, "But how? Why is your what-d'you-call-it what's-its-named?"

"She keeps me on a leash. She won't let me do anything with a kick in it. If I've suggested one rip-snorting stunt, I've suggested twenty, and every time she turns them down on the ground that that sort of thing is beneath the dignity of an artist in her position. It doesn't give a fellow a chance. So now I've made up my mind to do her good by stealth. I'm going to steal her snake."

"Steal it? Pinch it, as it were?"

"Yes. Big story for the papers, you see. She's grown very much attached to Peter. He's her mascot. I believe she's practically kidded herself into believing that Russian prince story. If I can sneak it away and keep it away for a day or two, she'll do the rest. She'll make such a fuss that the papers will be full of it."

"I see."

"Wow, any ordinary woman would work in with me. But not Her Nibs. She would call it cheap and degrading and a lot of other things. It's got to be a genuine steal, and, if I'm caught at it, I lose my job. So that's where you come in."

"But where am I to keep the jolly old reptile?"

"Oh, anywhere. Punch a few holes in a hat-box, and make it up a shakedown inside. It'll be company for you."

"Something in that. My wife's away just now and it's a bit lonely in the evenings."

"You'll never be lonely with Peter around. He's a great scout. Always merry and bright."

"He doesn't bite, I suppose, or sting or what-not?"

"He may what-not occasionally. It depends on the weather. But, outside of that, he's as harmless as a canary."

"Dashed dangerous things, canaries," said Archie, thoughtfully. "They peck at you."

33

"Don't weaken!" pleaded the Press-agent

"Oh, all right. I'll take him. By the way, touching the matter of browsing and sluicing. What do I feed him on?"

"Oh, anything. Bread-and-milk or fruit or soft-boiled egg or dog-biscuit or ants'-eggs. You know—anything you have yourself. Well, I'm much obliged for your hospitality. I'll do the same for you another time. Now I must be getting along to see to the practical end of the thing. By the way, Her Nibs lives at the Cosmopolis, too. Very convenient. Well, so long. See you later."

Archie, left alone, began for the first time to have serious doubts. He had allowed himself to be swayed by Mr. Sherriff's magnetic personality, but now that the other had removed himself he began to wonder if he had been entirely wise to lend his sympathy and co-operation to the scheme. He had never had intimate dealings with a snake before, but he had kept silkworms as a child, and there had been the deuce of a lot of fuss and unpleasantness over them. Getting into the salad and what-not. Something seemed to tell him that he was asking for trouble with a loud voice, but he had given his word and he supposed he would have to go through with it.

He lit another cigarette and wandered out into Fifth Avenue. His usually smooth brow was ruffled with care. Despite the eulogies which Sherriff had uttered concerning Peter, he found his doubts increasing. Peter might, as the Press-agent had stated, be a great scout, but was his little Garden of Eden on the fifth floor of the Cosmopolis Hotel likely to be improved by the advent of even the most amiable and winsome of serpents? However—

"Moffam! My dear fellow!"

The voice, speaking suddenly in his ear from behind, roused Archie from his reflections. Indeed, it roused him so effectually that he jumped a clear inch off the ground and bit his tongue. Revolving on his axis, he found himself confronting a middle-aged man with a face like a horse. The man was dressed in something of an old-world style. His clothes had an English cut. He had a drooping grey moustache. He also wore a grey bowler hat flattened at the crown— but who are we to judge him?

"Archie Moffam! I have been trying to find you all the morning."

Archie had placed him now. He had not seen General Mannister for several years—not, indeed, since the days when he used to meet him at the home of young Lord Seacliff, his nephew. Archie had been at Eton and Oxford with Seacliff, and had often visited him in the Long Vacation.

34

"Halloa, General! What ho, what ho! What on earth are you doing over here?"

"Let's get out of this crush, my boy." General Mannister steered Archie into a side-street, "That's better." He cleared his throat once or twice, as if embarrassed. "I've brought Seacliff over," he said, finally.

"Dear old Squiffy here? Oh, I say! Great work!"

General Mannister did not seem to share his enthusiasm. He looked like a horse with a secret sorrow. He coughed three times, like a horse who, in addition to a secret sorrow, had contracted asthma.

"You will find Seacliff changed," he said. "Let me see, how long is it since you and he met?"

Archie reflected.

"I was demobbed just about a year ago. I saw him in Paris about a year before that. The old egg got a bit of shrapnel in his foot or something, didn't he? Anyhow, I remember he was sent home."

"His foot is perfectly well again now. But, unfortunately, the enforced inaction led to disastrous results. You recollect, no doubt, that Seacliff always had a—a tendency;—a—a weakness—it was a family failing—"

"Mopping it up, do you mean? Shifting it? Looking on the jolly old stuff when it was red and what not, what?"

"Exactly."

Archie nodded.

"Dear old Squiffy was always rather-a lad for the wassail-bowl. When I met him in Paris, I remember, he was quite tolerably blotto."

"Precisely. And the failing has, I regret to say, grown on him since he returned from the war. My poor sister was extremely worried. In fact, to cut a long story short, I induced him to accompany me to America. I am attached to the British Legation in Washington now, you know."

"Oh, really?"

"I wished Seacliff to come with me to Washington, but he insists on remaining in New York. He stated specifically that the thought of living in Washington gave him the—what was the expression he used?"

"The pip?"

"The pip. Precisely."

"But what was the idea of bringing him to America?"

"This admirable Prohibition enactment has rendered America—to my mind—the ideal place for a young man of his

35

views." The General looked at his watch. "It is most fortunate that I happened to run into you, my dear fellow. My train for Washington leaves in another hour, and I have packing to do. I want to leave poor Seacliff in your charge while I am gone."

"Oh, I say! What!"

"You can look after him. I am credibly informed that even now there are places in New York where a determined young man may obtain the—er—stuff, and I should be infinitely obliged—and my poor sister would be infinitely grateful—if you would keep an eye on him." He hailed a taxi-cab. "I am sending Seacliff round to the Cosmopolis to-night. I am sure you, will do everything you can. Good-bye, my boy, good-bye."

Archie continued his walk. This, he felt, was beginning to be a bit thick. He smiled a bitter, mirthless smile as he recalled the fact that less than half an hour had elapsed since he had expressed a regret that he did not belong to the ranks of those who do things. Fate since then had certainly supplied him with jobs with a lavish hand. By bed-time he would be an active accomplice to a theft, valet and companion to a snake he had never met, and—as far as could gather the scope of his duties—a combination of nursemaid and private detective to dear old Squiffy.

It was past four o'clock when he returned to the Cosmopolis. Roscoe Sherriff was pacing the lobby of the hotel nervously, carrying a small hand-bag.

"Here you are at last! Good heavens, man, I've been waiting two hours."

"Sorry, old bean. I was musing a bit and lost track of the time."

The Press-agent looked cautiously round. There was nobody within earshot.

"Here he is!" he said.

"Who?"

"Peter."

"Where?" said Archie, staring blankly.

"In this bag. Did you expect to find him strolling arm-in-arm with me round the lobby? Here you are! Take him!"

He was gone. And Archie, holding the bag, made his way to the lift. The bag squirmed gently in his grip.

The only other occupant of the lift was a striking-looking woman of foreign appearance, dressed in a way that made Archie feel that she must be somebody or she couldn't look like that. Her face, too, seemed vaguely familiar. She entered the lift at the second floor where the tea-room is, and she had the contented expression of one who had tea'd to her satisfaction. She got off at the same floor as Archie, and walked swiftly, in a lithe, pantherist way, round the bend in the corridor. Archie followed more slowly. When he reached the door of his room, the passage was empty. He inserted the key in his door, turned it, pushed the door open, and pocketed the key. He was about to enter when the bag again squirmed gently in his grip.

From the days of Pandora, through the epoch of Bluebeard's wife, down to the present time, one of the chief failings of humanity has been the disposition to open things that were better closed. It would have been simple for Archie to have taken another step and put a door between himself and the world, but there came to him the irresistible desire to peep into the bag now—not three seconds later, but now. All the way up in the lift he had been battling with the temptation, and now he succumbed.

The bag was one of those simple bags with a thingummy which you press. Archie pressed it. And, as it opened, out popped the head of Peter. His eyes met Archie's. Over his head there seemed to be an invisible mark of interrogation. His gaze was curious, but kindly. He appeared to be saying to himself, "Have I found a friend?"

Serpents, or Snakes, says the Encyclopaedia, are reptiles of the saurian class Ophidia, characterised by an elongated, cylindrical, limbless, scaly form, and distinguished from lizards by the fact that the halves (RAMI) of the lower jaw are not solidly united at the chin, but movably connected by an elastic ligament. The vertebra are very numerous, gastrocentrous, and procoelous. And, of course, when they put it like that, you can see at once that a man might spend hours with combined entertainment and profit just looking at a snake.

Archie would no doubt have done this; but long before he had time really to inspect the halves (RAMI) of his new friend's lower jaw and to admire its elastic fittings, and long before the gastrocentrous and procoelous character of the other's vertebrae had made any real impression on him, a piercing scream almost at his elbow—startled him out of his scientific reverie. A door opposite had opened, and the woman of the elevator was standing staring at him with an expression of horror and fury that went through, him like a knife. It was the expression which, more than anything else, had made Mme. Brudowska what she was professionally. Combined with a deep voice and a sinuous walk, it enabled her to draw down a matter of a thousand dollars per week.

Indeed, though the fact gave him little pleasure, Archie, as a matter of fact, was at this moment getting about—including war-tax—two dollars and seventy-five cents worth of the great emotional star for nothing. For, having treated him gratis to the look of horror and fury, she now moved towards him with the sinuous walk and spoke in the tone which she seldom permitted herself to use before the curtain of act two, unless there was a whale of a situation that called for it in act one.

"Thief!"

It was the way she said it.

Archie staggered backwards as though he had been hit between the eyes, fell through the open door of his room, kicked it to with a flying foot, and collapsed on the bed. Peter, the snake, who had fallen on the floor with a squashy sound, looked surprised and pained for a moment; then, being a philosopher at heart, cheered up and began hunting for flies under the bureau.

CHAPTER VIII

A DISTURBED NIGHT FOR DEAR OLD SQUIFFY

Peril sharpens the intellect. Archie's mind as a rule worked in rather a languid and restful sort of way, but now it got going with a rush and a whir. He glared round the room. He had never seen a room so devoid of satisfactory cover. And then there came to him a scheme, a ruse. It offered a chance of escape. It was, indeed, a bit of all right.

Peter, the snake, loafing contentedly about the carpet, found himself seized by what the Encyclopaedia calls the "distensible gullet" and looked up reproachfully. The next moment he was in his bag again; and Archie, bounding silently into the bathroom, was tearing the cord off his dressing-gown.

There came a banging at the door. A voice spoke sternly. A masculine voice this time.

"Say! Open this door!"

Archie rapidly attached the dressing-gown cord to the handle of the bag, leaped to the window, opened it, tied the cord to a projecting piece of iron on the sill, lowered Peter and the bag into the depths, and closed the window again. The whole affair took but a few seconds. Generals have received the thanks of their nations for displaying less resource on the field of battle.

He opened the-door. Outside stood the bereaved woman, and beside her a bullet-headed gentleman with a bowler hat on the back of his head, in whom Archie recognised the hotel detective.

The hotel detective also recognised Archie, and the stern cast of his features relaxed. He even smiled a rusty but propitiatory smile. He imagined—erroneously—that Archie, being the son-in-law of the owner of the hotel, had a pull with that gentleman; and he resolved to proceed warily lest he jeopardise his job.

"Why, Mr. Moffam!" he said, apologetically. "I didn't know it was you I was disturbing."

"Always glad to have a chat," said Archie, cordially. "What seems to be the trouble?"

"My snake!" cried the queen of tragedy. "Where is my snake?"

Archie, looked at the detective. The detective looked at Archie.

"This lady," said the detective, with a dry little cough, "thinks her snake is in your room, Mr. Moffam."

"Snake?"

"Snake's what the lady said."

39

"My snake! My Peter!" Mme. Brudowska's voice shook with emotion. "He is here—here in this room."

Archie shook his head.

"No snakes here! Absolutely not! I remember noticing when I came in."

"The snake is here—here in this room. This man had it in a bag! I saw him! He is a thief!"

"Easy, ma'am!" protested the detective. "Go easy! This gentleman is the boss's son-in-law."

"I care not who he is! He has my snake! Here—' here in this room!"

"Mr. Moffam wouldn't go round stealing snakes."

"Rather not," said Archie. "Never stole a snake in my life. None of the Moffams have ever gone about stealing snakes. Regular family tradition! Though I once had an uncle who kept gold-fish."

"Here he is! Here! My Peter!"

Archie looked at the detective. The detective looked at Archie. "We must humour her!" their glances said.

"Of course," said Archie, "if you'd like to search the room, what? What I mean to say is, this is Liberty Hall. Everybody welcome! Bring the kiddies!"

"I will search the room!" said Mme. Brudowska.

The detective glanced apologetically at Archie.

"Don't blame me for this, Mr. Moffam," he urged.

"Rather not! Only too glad you've dropped in!"

He took up an easy attitude against the window, and watched the empress of the emotional drama explore. Presently she desisted, baffled. For an instant she paused, as though about to speak, then swept from the room. A moment later a door banged across the passage.

"How do they get that way?" queried the detective, "Well, g'bye, Mr. Moffam. Sorry to have butted in."

The door closed. Archie waited a few moments, then went to the window and hauled in the slack. Presently the bag appeared over the edge of the window-sill.

"Good God!" said Archie.

In the rush and swirl of recent events he must have omitted to see that the clasp that fastened the bag was properly closed; for the bag, as it jumped on to the window-sill, gaped at him like a yawning face. And inside it there was nothing.

Archie leaned as far out of the window as he could manage without committing suicide. Far below him, the traffic took its usual course and the pedestrians moved to and fro upon the pavements. There was no crowding, no excitement. Yet only a few moments before a long green snake with three hundred ribs, a distensible gullet, and gastrocentrous vertebras must have descended on that street like the gentle rain from Heaven upon the place beneath. And nobody seemed even interested. Not for the first time since he had arrived in America, Archie marvelled at the cynical detachment of the New Yorker, who permits himself to be surprised at nothing.

He shut the window and moved away with a heavy Heart. He had not had the pleasure of an extended acquaintanceship with Peter, but he had seen enough of him to realise his sterling qualities. Somewhere beneath Peter's three hundred ribs there had lain a heart of gold, and Archie mourned for his loss.

Archie had a dinner and theatre engagement that night, and it was late when he returned to the hotel. He found his father-in-law prowling restlessly about the lobby. There seemed to be something on Mr. Brewster's mind. He came up to Archie with a brooding frown on his square face.

"Who's this man Seacliff?" he demanded, without preamble. "I hear he's a friend of yours."

"Oh, you've met him, what?" said Archie. "Had a nice little chat together, yes? Talked of this and that, no!"

"We have not said a word to each other."

"Really? Oh, well, dear old Squiffy is one of those strong, silent fellers you know. You mustn't mind if he's a bit dumb. He never says much, but it's whispered round the clubs that he thinks a lot. It was rumoured in the spring of nineteen-thirteen that Squiffy was on the point of making a bright remark, but it never came to anything."

Mr. Brewster struggled with his feelings.

"Who is he? You seem to know him."

"Oh yes. Great pal of mine, Squiffy. We went through Eton, Oxford, and the Bankruptcy Court together. And here's a rummy coincidence. When they examined ME, I had no assets. And, when they examined Squiffy, HE had no assets! Rather extraordinary, what?"

Mr. Brewster seemed to be in no mood for discussing coincidences.

"I might have known he was a friend of yours!" he said, bitterly. "Well, if you want to see him, you'll have to do it outside my hotel."

"Why, I thought he was stopping here."

"He is—to-night. To-morrow he can look for some other hotel to break up."

"Great Scot! Has dear old Squiffy been breaking the place up?"

41

Mr. Brewster snorted.

"I am informed that this precious friend of yours entered my grill-room at eight o'clock. He must have been completely intoxicated, though the head waiter tells me he noticed nothing at the time."

Archie nodded approvingly.

"Dear old Squiffy was always like that. It's a gift. However woozled he might be, it was impossible to detect it with the naked eye. I've seen the dear old chap many a time whiffled to the eyebrows, and looking as sober as a bishop. Soberer! When did it begin to dawn on the lads in the grill-room that the old egg had been pushing the boat out?"

"The head waiter," said Mr. Brewster, with cold fury, "tells me that he got a hint of the man's condition when he suddenly got up from his table and went the round of the room, pulling off all the table-cloths, and breaking everything that was on them. He then threw a number of rolls at the diners, and left. He seems to have gone straight to bed."

"Dashed sensible of him, what? Sound, practical chap, Squiffy. But where on earth did he get the—er—materials?"

"From his room. I made enquiries. He has six large cases in his room."

"Squiffy always was a chap of infinite resource! Well, I'm dashed sorry this should have happened, don't you know."

"If it hadn't been for you, the man would never have come here." Mr. Brewster brooded coldly. "I don't know why it is, but ever since you came to this hotel I've had nothing but trouble."

"Dashed sorry!" said Archie, sympathetically.

"Grrh!" said Mr. Brewster.

Archie made his way meditatively to the lift. The injustice of his father-in-law's attitude pained him. It was absolutely rotten and all that to be blamed for everything that went wrong in the Hotel Cosmopolis.

While this conversation was in progress, Lord Seacliff was enjoying a refreshing sleep in his room on the fourth floor. Two hours passed. The noise of the traffic in the street below faded away. Only the rattle of an occasional belated cab broke the silence. In the hotel all was still. Mr. Brewster had gone to bed. Archie, in his room, smoked meditatively. Peace may have been said to reign.

At half-past two Lord Seacliff awoke. His hours of slumber were always irregular. He sat up in bed and switched the light on. He was a shock-headed young man with a red face and a hot brown eye. He yawned and stretched himself. His head was aching a little. The room seemed to him a trifle close. He got out of bed and threw open the window. Then, returning to bed, he picked up a book and began to read. He was conscious of feeling a little jumpy, and reading generally sent him to sleep.

Much has been written on the subject of bed-books. The general consensus of opinion is that a gentle, slow-moving story makes the best opiate. If this be so, dear old Squiffy's choice of literature had been rather injudicious. His book was The Adventures of Sherlock Holmes, and the particular story, which he selected for perusal was the one entitled, "The Speckled Band." He was not a great reader, but, when he read, he liked something with a bit of zip to it.

Squiffy became absorbed. He had read the story before, but a long time back, and its complications were fresh to him. The tale, it may be remembered, deals with the activities of an ingenious gentleman who kept a snake, and used to loose it into people's bedrooms as a preliminary to collecting on their insurance. It gave Squiffy pleasant thrills, for he had always had a particular horror of snakes. As a child, he had shrunk from visiting the serpent house at the Zoo; and, later, when he had come to man's estate and had put off childish things, and settled down in real earnest to his self-appointed mission of drinking up all the alcoholic fluid in England, the distaste for Ophidia had lingered. To a dislike for real snakes had been added a maturer shrinking from those which existed only in his imagination. He could still recall his emotions on the occasion, scarcely three months before, when he had seen a long, green serpent which a majority of his contemporaries had assured him wasn't there.

Squiffy read on:—

"Suddenly another sound became audible—a very gentle, soothing sound, like that of a small jet of steam escaping continuously from a kettle."

Lord Seacliff looked up from his book with a start Imagination was beginning to play him tricks. He could have sworn that he had actually heard that identical sound. It had seemed to come from the window. He listened again. No! All was still. He returned to his book and went on reading.

"It was a singular sight that met our eyes. Beside the table, on a wooden chair, sat Doctor Grimesby Rylott, clad in a long dressing-gown. His chin was cocked upward and his eyes were fixed in a dreadful, rigid stare at the corner of the ceiling. Round his brow he had a peculiar yellow band, with brownish speckles, which seemed to be bound tightly round his head."

"I took a step forward. In an instant his strange head-gear began to move, and there reared itself from among his hair the squat, diamond-shaped head and puffed neck of a loathsome serpent..."

"Ugh!" said Squiffy.

He closed the book and put it down. His head was aching worse than ever. He wished now that he had read something else. No fellow could read himself to sleep with this sort of thing. People ought not to write this sort of thing.

His heart gave a bound. There it was again, that hissing sound. And this time he was sure it came from the window.

He looked at the window, and remained staring, frozen. Over the sill, with a graceful, leisurely movement, a green snake was crawling. As it crawled, it raised its head and peered from side to side, like a shortsighted man looking for his spectacles. It hesitated a moment on the edge of the sill, then wriggled to the floor and began to cross the room. Squiffy stared on.

It would have pained Peter deeply, for he was a snake of great sensibility, if he had known how much his entrance had disturbed the occupant of the room. He himself had no feeling but gratitude for the man who had opened the window and so enabled him to get in out of the rather nippy night air. Ever since the bag had swung open and shot him out onto the sill of the window below Archie's, he had been waiting patiently for something of the kind to happen. He was a snake who took things as they came, and was prepared to rough it a bit if necessary; but for the last hour or two he had been hoping that somebody would do something practical in the way of getting him in out of the cold. When at home, he had an eiderdown quilt to sleep on, and the stone of the window-sill was a little trying to a snake of regular habits. He crawled thankfully across the floor under Squiffy's bed. There was a pair of trousers there, for his host had undressed when not in a frame of mind to fold his clothes neatly and place them upon a chair. Peter looked the trousers over. They were not an eiderdown quilt, but they would serve. He curled up in them and went to sleep. He had had an exciting day, and was glad to turn in.

After about ten minutes, the tension of Squiffy's attitude relaxed. His heart, which had seemed to suspend its operations, began beating again. Reason reasserted itself. He peeped cautiously under the bed. He could see nothing.

Squiffy was convinced. He told himself that he had never really believed in Peter as a living thing. It stood to reason that there couldn't really be a snake in his room. The window looked out on emptiness. His room was several stories above the ground. There was a stern, set expression on Squiffy's face as he climbed out of bed. It was the expression of a man who is turning over a new leaf, starting a new life. He looked about the room for some implement which would carry out the deed he had to do, and finally pulled out one of the curtain-rods. Using this as a lever, he broke open the topmost of the six cases which stood in the corner. The soft wood cracked and split. Squiffy drew out a straw-covered bottle. For a moment he stood looking at it, as a man might gaze at a friend on the point of death. Then, with a sudden determination, he went into the bathroom. There was a crash of glass and a gurgling sound.

Half an hour later the telephone in Archie's room rang. "I say, Archie, old top," said the voice of Squiffy.

"Halloa, old bean! Is that you?"

"I say, could you pop down here for a second? I'm rather upset."

"Absolutely! Which room?"

"Four-forty-one."

"I'll be with you eftsoons or right speedily."

"Thanks, old man."

"What appears to be the difficulty?"

"Well, as a matter of fact, I thought I saw a snake!"

"A snake!"

"I'll tell you all about it when you come down."

Archie found Lord Seacliff seated on his bed. An arresting aroma of mixed drinks pervaded the atmosphere.

"I say! What?" said Archie, inhaling.

"That's all right. I've been pouring my stock away. Just finished the last bottle."

"But why?"

"I told you. I thought I saw a snake!"

"Green?"

Squiffy shivered slightly.

"Frightfully green!"

Archie hesitated. He perceived that there are moments when silence is the best policy. He had been worrying himself over the unfortunate case of his friend, and now that Fate seemed to have provided a solution, it would be rash to interfere merely to ease the old bean's mind. If Squiffy was going to reform because he thought he had seen an imaginary snake, better not to let him know that the snake was a real one.

"Dashed serious!" he said.

"Bally dashed serious!" agreed Squiffy. "I'm going to cut it out!"

"Great scheme!"

"You don't think," asked Squiffy, with a touch of hopefulness, "that it could have been a real snake?"

"Never heard of the management supplying them."

"I thought it went under the bed."

"Well, take a look."

Squiffy shuddered.

"Not me! I say, old top, you know, I simply can't sleep in this room now. I was wondering if you could give me a doss somewhere in yours."

"Rather! I'm in five-forty-one. Just above. Trot along up. Here's the key. I'll tidy up a bit here, and join you in a minute."

Squiffy put on a dressing-gown and disappeared. Archie looked under the bed. From the trousers the head of Peter popped up with its usual expression of amiable enquiry. Archie nodded pleasantly, and sat down on the bed. The problem of his little friend's immediate future wanted thinking over.

He lit a cigarette and remained for a while in thought. Then he rose. An admirable solution had presented itself. He picked Peter up and placed him in the pocket of his dressing-gown. Then, leaving the room, he mounted the stairs till he reached the seventh floor. Outside a room half-way down the corridor he paused.

From within, through the open transom, came the rhythmical snoring of a good man taking his rest after the labours of the day. Mr. Brewster was always a heavy sleeper.

"There's always a way," thought Archie, philosophically, "if a chappie only thinks of it."

His father-in-law's snoring took on a deeper note. Archie extracted Peter from his pocket and dropped him gently through the transom.

CHAPTER IX

A LETTER FROM PARKER

As the days went by and he settled down at the Hotel Cosmopolis, Archie, looking about him and revising earlier judgments, was inclined to think that of all his immediate circle he most admired Parker, the lean, grave valet of Mr. Daniel Brewster. Here was a man who, living in the closest contact with one of the most difficult persons in New York, contrived all the while to maintain an unbowed head, and, as far as one could gather from appearances, a tolerably cheerful disposition. A great man, judge him by what standard you pleased. Anxious as he was to earn an honest living, Archie would not have changed places with Parker for the salary of a movie-star.

It was Parker who first directed Archie's attention to the hidden merits of Pongo. Archie had drifted into his father-in-law's suite one morning, as he sometimes did in the effort to establish more amicable relations, and had found it occupied only by the valet, who was dusting the furniture and bric-a-brac with a feather broom rather in the style of a man-servant at the rise of the curtain of an old-fashioned farce. After a courteous exchange of greetings, Archie sat down and lit a cigarette. Parker went on dusting.

"The guv'nor," said Parker, breaking the silence, "has some nice little objay dar, sir."

"Little what?"

"Objay dar, sir."

Light dawned upon Archie.

"Of course, yes. French for junk. I see what you mean now. Dare say you're right, old friend. Don't know much about these things myself."

Parker gave an appreciative flick at a vase on the mantelpiece.

"Very valuable, some of the guv'nor's things." He had picked up the small china figure of the warrior with the spear, and was grooming it with the ostentatious care of one brushing flies off a sleeping Venus. He regarded this figure with a look of affectionate esteem which seemed to Archie absolutely uncalled-for. Archie's taste in Art was not precious. To his untutored eye the thing was only one degree less foul than his father-in-law's Japanese prints, which he had always observed with silent loathing. "This one, now," continued Parker. "Worth a lot of money. Oh, a lot of money."

47

"What, Pongo?" said Archie incredulously.

"Sir?"

"I always call that rummy-looking what-not Pongo. Don't know what else you could call him, what!"

The valet seemed to disapprove of this levity. He shook his head and replaced the figure on the mantelpiece.

"Worth a lot of money," he repeated. "Not by itself, no."

"Oh, not by itself?"

"No, sir. Things like this come in pairs. Somewhere or other there's the companion-piece to this here, and if the guv'nor could get hold of it, he'd have something worth having. Something that connoozers would give a lot of money for. But one's no good without the other. You have to have both, if you understand my meaning, sir."

"I see. Like filling a straight flush, what?"

"Precisely, sir."

Archie gazed at Pongo again, with the dim hope of discovering virtues not immediately apparent to the casual observer. But without success. Pongo left him cold—even chilly. He would not have taken Pongo as a gift, to oblige a dying friend.

"How much would the pair be worth?" he asked. "Ten dollars?"

Parker smiled a gravely superior smile. "A leetle more than that, sir. Several thousand dollars, more like it."

"Do you mean to say," said Archie, with honest amazement, "that there are chumps going about loose—absolutely loose—who would pay that for a weird little object like Pongo?"

"Undoubtedly, sir. These antique china figures are in great demand among collectors."

Archie looked at Pongo once more, and shook his head.

"Well, well, well! It takes all sorts to make a world, what!"

What might be called the revival of Pongo, the restoration of Pongo to the ranks of the things that matter, took place several weeks later, when Archie was making holiday at the house which his father-in-law had taken for the summer at Brookport. The curtain of the second act may be said to rise on Archie strolling back from the golf-links in the cool of an August evening. From time to time he sang slightly, and wondered idly if Lucille would put the finishing touch upon the all-rightness of everything by coming to meet him and sharing his homeward walk.

She came in view at this moment, a trim little figure in a white skirt and a pale blue sweater. She waved to Archie; and Archie, as always at the sight of her, was conscious of that jumpy, fluttering sensation about the heart, which, translated into words, would have formed the question, "What on earth could have made a girl like that fall in love with a chump like me?" It was a question which he was continually asking himself, and one which was perpetually in the mind also of Mr. Brewster, his father-in-law. The matter of Archie's unworthiness to be the husband of Lucille was practically the only one on which the two men saw eye to eye.

"Hallo—allo—allo!" said Archie. "Here we are, what! I was just hoping you would drift over the horizon."

Lucille kissed him.

"You're a darling," she said. "And you look like a Greek god in that suit."

"Glad you like it." Archie squinted with some complacency down his chest. "I always say it doesn't matter what you pay for a suit, so long as it's right. I hope your jolly old father will feel that way when he settles up for it."

"Where is father? Why didn't he come back with you?"

"Well, as a matter of fact, he didn't seem any too keen on my company. I left him in the locker-room chewing a cigar. Gave me the impression of having something on his mind."

"Oh, Archie! You didn't beat him AGAIN?"

Archie looked uncomfortable. He gazed out to sea with something of embarrassment.

"Well, as a matter of fact, old thing, to be absolutely frank, I, as it were, did!"

"Not badly?"

"Well, yes! I rather fancy I put it across him with some vim and not a little emphasis. To be perfectly accurate, I licked him by ten and eight."

"But you promised me you would let him beat you to-day. You know how pleased it would have made him."

"I know. But, light of my soul, have you any idea how dashed difficult it is to get beaten by your festive parent at golf?"

"Oh, well!" Lucille sighed. "It can't be helped, I suppose." She felt in the pocket of her sweater. "Oh, there's a letter for you. I've just been to fetch the mail. I don't know who it can be from. The handwriting looks like a vampire's. Kind of scrawly."

Archie inspected the envelope. It provided no solution.

"That's rummy! Who could be writing to me?"

"Open it and see."

"Dashed bright scheme! I will, Herbert Parker. Who the deuce is Herbert Parker?"

"Parker? Father's valet's name was Parker. The one he dismissed when he found he was wearing his shirts."

"Do you mean to say any reasonable chappie would willingly wear the sort of shirts your father—? I mean to say, there must have been some mistake."

"Do read the letter. I expect he wants to use your influence with father to have him taken back."

"MY influence? With your FATHER? Well, I'm dashed. Sanguine sort of Johnny, if he does. Well, here's what he says. Of course, I remember jolly old Parker now—great pal of mine."

> Dear Sir,—It is some time since the undersigned had the honour of conversing with you, but I am respectfully trusting that you may recall me to mind when I mention that until recently I served Mr. Brewster, your father-in-law, in the capacity of valet. Owing to an unfortunate misunderstanding, I was dismissed from that position and am now temporarily out of a job. "How art thou fallen from Heaven, O Lucifer, son of the morning!" (Isaiah xiv. 12.)

"You know," said Archie, admiringly, "this bird is hot stuff! I mean to say he writes dashed well."

> It is not, however, with my own affairs that I desire to trouble you, dear sir. I have little doubt that all will be well with me and that I shall not fall like a sparrow to the ground. "I have been young and now am old; yet have I not seen the righteous forsaken, nor his seed begging bread" (Psalms xxxvii. 25). My object in writing to you is as follows. You may recall that I had the pleasure of meeting you one morning in Mr. Brewster's suite, when we had an interesting talk on the subject of Mr. B.'s objets d'art. You may recall being particularly interested in a small china figure. To assist your memory, the figure to which I allude is the one which you whimsically referred to as Pongo. I informed you, if you remember, that, could the accompanying figure be secured, the pair would be extremely valuable.

> I am glad to say, dear sir, that this has now transpired, and is on view at Beale's Art Galleries on West Forty-Fifth Street, where it will be sold to-morrow at auction, the sale commencing at two-thirty sharp. If Mr. Brewster cares to attend, he will, I fancy, have little trouble in securing it at a reasonable price. I confess that I had thought of refraining from apprising my late employer of this matter, but more Christian feelings have

prevailed. *"If thine enemy hunger, feed him; if he thirst, give him drink; for in so doing thou shalt heap coals of fire on his head" (Romans xii. 20). Nor, I must confess, am I altogether uninfluenced by the thought that my action in this matter may conceivably lead to Mr. B. consenting to forget the past and to reinstate me in my former position. However, I am confident that I can leave this to his good feeling.*

I remain, respectfully yours,
Herbert Parker.

Lucille clapped her hands.

"How splendid! Father will be pleased!"

"Yes. Friend Parker has certainly found a way to make the old dad fond of him. Wish I could!"

"But you can, silly! He'll be delighted when you show him that letter."

"Yes, with Parker. Old Herb. Parker's is the neck he'll fall on—not mine."

Lucille reflected.

"I wish—" she began. She stopped. Her eyes lit up. "Oh, Archie, darling, I've got an idea!"

"Decant it."

"Why don't you slip up to New York to-morrow and buy the thing, and give it to father as a surprise?"

Archie patted her hand kindly. He hated to spoil her girlish day-dreams.

"Yes," he said. "But reflect, queen of my heart! I have at the moment of going to press just two dollars fifty in specie, which I took off your father this after-noon. We were playing twenty-five cents a Hole. He coughed it up without enthusiasm—in fact, with a nasty hacking sound—but I've got it. But that's all I have got."

"That's all right. You can pawn that ring and that bracelet of mine."

"Oh, I say, what! Pop the family jewels?"

"Only for a day or two. Of course, once you've got the thing, father will pay us back. He would give you all the money we asked him for, if he knew what it was for. But I want to surprise him. And if you were to go to him and ask him for a thousand dollars without telling him what it was for, he might refuse."

"He might!" said Archie. "He might!"

"It all works out splendidly. To-morrow's the Invitation Handicap, and father's been looking forward to it for weeks. He'd

51

hate to have to go up to town himself and not play in it. But you can slip up and slip back without his knowing anything about it."

Archie pondered.

"It sounds a ripe scheme. Yes, it has all the ear-marks of a somewhat fruity wheeze! By Jove, it IS a fruity wheeze! It's an egg!"

"An egg?"

"Good egg, you know. Halloa, here's a postscript. I didn't see it."

> *P.S.—I should be glad if you would convey my most cordial respects to Mrs. Moffam. Will you also inform her that I chanced to meet Mr. William this morning on Broadway, just off the boat. He desired me to send his regards and to say that he would be joining you at Brookport in the course of a day or so. Mr. B. will be pleased to have him back. "A wise son maketh a glad father" (Proverbs x. 1).*

"Who's Mr. William?" asked Archie.

"My brother Bill, of course. I've told you all about him."

"Oh yes, of course. Your brother Bill. Rummy to think I've got a brother-in-law I've never seen."

"You see, we married so suddenly. When we married, Bill was in Yale."

"Good God! What for?"

"Not jail, silly. Yale. The university."

"Oh, ah, yes."

"Then he went over to Europe for a trip to broaden his mind. You must look him up to-morrow when you get back to New York. He's sure to be at his club."

"I'll make a point of it. Well, vote of thanks to good old Parker! This really does begin to look like the point in my career where I start to have your forbidding old parent eating out of my hand."

"Yes, it's an egg, isn't it!"

"Queen of my soul," said Archie enthusiastically, "it's an omelette!"

The business negotiations in connection with the bracelet and the ring occupied Archie on his arrival in New York to an extent which made it impossible for him to call on Brother Bill before lunch. He decided to postpone the affecting meeting of brothers-in-law to a more convenient season, and made his way to his favourite table at the Cosmopolis grill-room for a bite of lunch preliminary to the fatigues of the sale. He found Salvatore hovering about as usual, and instructed him to come to the rescue with a minute steak.

Salvatore was the dark, sinister-looking waiter who attended, among other tables, to the one at the far end of the grill-room at which Archie usually sat. For several weeks Archie's conversations with the other had dealt exclusively with the bill of fare and its contents; but gradually he had found himself becoming more personal. Even before the war and its democratising influences, Archie had always lacked that reserve which characterises many Britons; and since the war he had looked on nearly everyone he met as a brother. Long since, through the medium of a series of friendly chats, he had heard all about Salvatore's home in Italy, the little newspaper and tobacco shop which his mother owned down on Seventh Avenue, and a hundred other personal details. Archie had an insatiable curiosity about his fellow-man.

"Well done," said Archie.

"Sare?"

"The steak. Not too rare, you know."

"Very good, sare."

Archie looked at the waiter closely. His tone had been subdued and sad. Of course, you don't expect a waiter to beam all over his face and give three rousing cheers simply because you have asked him to bring you a minute steak, but still there was something about Salvatore's manner that disturbed Archie. The man appeared to have the pip. Whether he was merely homesick and brooding on the lost delights of his sunny native land, or whether his trouble was more definite, could only be ascertained by enquiry. So Archie enquired.

"What's the matter, laddie?" he said sympathetically. "Something on your mind?"

"Sare?"

"I say, there seems to be something on your mind. What's the trouble?"

The waiter shrugged his shoulders, as if indicating an unwillingness to inflict his grievances on one of the tipping classes.

"Come on!" persisted Archie encouragingly. "All pals here. Barge along, old thing, and let's have it."

Salvatore, thus admonished, proceeded in a hurried undertone—with one eye on the headwaiter—to lay bare his soul. What he said was not very coherent, but Archie could make out enough of it to gather that it was a sad story of excessive hours and insufficient pay. He mused awhile. The waiter's hard case touched him.

53

"I'll tell you what," he said at last. "When jolly old Brewster conies back to town—he's away just now—I'll take you along to him and we'll beard the old boy in his den. I'll introduce you, and you get that extract from Italian opera-off your chest which you've just been singing to me, and you'll find it'll be all right. He isn't what you might call one of my greatest admirers, but everybody says he's a square sort of cove and he'll see you aren't snootered. And now, laddie, touching the matter of that steak."

The waiter disappeared, greatly cheered, and Archie, turning, perceived that his friend Reggie van Tuyl was entering the room. He waved to him to join his table. He liked Reggie, and it also occurred to him that a man of the world like the heir of the van Tuyls, who had been popping about New York for years, might be able to give him some much-needed information on the procedure at an auction sale, a matter on which he himself was profoundly ignorant.

CHAPTER X

DOING FATHER A BIT OF GOOD

Reggie Van Tuyl approached the table languidly, and sank down into a chair. He was a long youth with a rather subdued and deflated look, as though the burden of the van Tuyl millions was more than his frail strength could support. Most things tired him.

"I say, Reggie, old top," said Archie, "you're just the lad I wanted to see. I require the assistance of a blighter of ripe intellect. Tell me, laddie, do you know anything about sales?"

Reggie eyed him sleepily.

"Sales?"

"Auction sales."

Reggie considered.

"Well, they're sales, you know." He checked a yawn. "Auction sales, you understand."

"Yes," said Archie encouragingly. "Something—the name or something—seemed to tell me that."

"Fellows put things up for sale you know, and other fellows— other fellows go in and—and buy 'em, if you follow me."

"Yes, but what's the procedure? I mean, what do I do? That's what I'm after. I've got to buy something at Beale's this afternoon. How do I set about it?"

"Well," said Reggie, drowsily, "there are several ways of bidding, you know. You can shout, or you can nod, or you can twiddle your fingers—" The effort of concentration was too much for him. He leaned back limply in his chair. "I'll tell you what. I've nothing to do this afternoon. I'll come with you and show you."

When he entered the Art Galleries a few minutes later, Archie was glad of the moral support of even such a wobbly reed as Reggie van Tuyl. There is something about an auction room which weighs heavily upon the novice. The hushed interior was bathed in a dim, religious light; and the congregation, seated on small wooden chairs, gazed in reverent silence at the pulpit, where a gentleman of commanding presence and sparkling pince-nez was delivering a species of chant. Behind a gold curtain at the end of the room mysterious forms flitted to and fro. Archie, who had been expecting something on the lines of the New York Stock Exchange, which he had once been privileged to visit when it was in a more than usually feverish mood, found the atmosphere oppressively ecclesiastical. He

55

sat down and looked about him. The presiding priest went on with his chant.

"Sixteen-sixteen-sixteen-sixteen-sixteen—worth three hundred—sixteen-sixteen-sixteen-sixteen-sixteen—ought to bring five hundred—sixteen-sixteen-seventeen-seventeen-eighteen-eighteen nineteen-nineteen-nineteen."

He stopped and eyed the worshippers with a glittering and reproachful eye. They had, it seemed, disappointed him. His lips curled, and he waved a hand towards a grimly uncomfortable-looking chair with insecure legs and a good deal of gold paint about it. "Gentlemen! Ladies and gentlemen! You are not here to waste my time; I am not here to waste yours. Am I seriously offered nineteen dollars for this eighteenth-century chair, acknowledged to be the finest piece sold in New York for months and months? Am I—twenty? I thank you. Twenty-twenty-twenty-twenty. YOUR opportunity! Priceless. Very few extant. Twenty-five-five-five-five-thirty-thirty. Just what you are looking for. The only one in the City of New York. Thirty-five-five-five-five. Forty-forty-forty-forty-forty. Look at those legs! Back it into the light, Willie. Let the light fall on those legs!"

Willie, a sort of acolyte, manoeuvred the chair as directed. Reggie van Tuyl, who had been yawning in a hopeless sort of way, showed his first flicker of interest.

"Willie," he observed, eyeing that youth more with pity than reproach, "has a face like Jo-Jo the dog-faced boy, don't you think so?"

Archie nodded briefly. Precisely the same criticism had occurred to him.

"Forty-five-five-five-five-five," chanted the high-priest. "Once forty-five. Twice forty-five. Third and last call, forty-five. Sold at forty-five. Gentleman in the fifth row."

Archie looked up and down the row with a keen eye. He was anxious to see who had been chump enough to give forty-five dollars for such a frightful object. He became aware of the dog-faced Willie leaning towards him.

"Name, please?" said the canine one.

"Eh, what?" said Archie. "Oh, my name's Moffam, don't you know." The eyes of the multitude made him feel a little nervous "Er—glad to meet you and all that sort of rot."

"Ten dollars deposit, please," said Willie.

"I don't absolutely follow you, old bean. What is the big thought at the back of all this?"

"Ten dollars deposit on the chair."

"What chair?"

56

"You bid forty-five dollars for the chair."

"Me?"

"You nodded," said Willie, accusingly. "If," he went on, reasoning closely, "you didn't want to bid, why did you nod?"

Archie was embarrassed. He could, of course, have pointed out that he had merely nodded in adhesion to the statement that the other had a face like Jo-Jo the dog-faced boy; but something seemed to tell him that a purist might consider the excuse deficient in tact. He hesitated a moment, then handed over a ten-dollar bill, the price of Willie's feelings. Willie withdrew like a tiger slinking from the body of its victim.

"I say, old thing," said Archie to Reggie, "this is a bit thick, you know. No purse will stand this drain."

Reggie considered the matter. His face seemed drawn under the mental strain.

"Don't nod again," he advised. "If you aren't careful, you get into the habit of it. When you want to bid, just twiddle your fingers. Yes, that's the thing. Twiddle!"

He sighed drowsily. The atmosphere of the auction room was close; you weren't allowed to smoke; and altogether he was beginning to regret that he had come. The service continued. Objects of varying unattractiveness came and went, eulogised by the officiating priest, but coldly received by the congregation. Relations between the former and the latter were growing more and more distant. The congregation seemed to suspect the priest of having an ulterior motive in his eulogies, and the priest seemed to suspect the congregation of a frivolous desire to waste his time. He had begun to speculate openly as to why they were there at all. Once, when a particularly repellent statuette of a nude female with an unwholesome green skin had been offered at two dollars and had found no bidders—the congregation appearing silently grateful for his statement that it was the only specimen of its kind on the continent—he had specifically accused them of having come into the auction room merely with the purpose of sitting down and taking the weight off their feet.

"If your thing—your whatever-it-is, doesn't come up soon, Archie," said Reggie, fighting off with an effort the mists of sleep, "I rather think I shall be toddling along. What was it you came to get?"

"It's rather difficult to describe. It's a rummy-looking sort of what-not, made of china or something. I call it Pongo. At least, this one isn't Pongo, don't you know—it's his little brother, but presumably equally foul in every respect. It's all rather complicated, I know, but—hallo!" He pointed excitedly. "By Jove! We're off! There it is! Look! Willie's unleashing it now!"

57

Willie, who had disappeared through the gold curtain, had now returned, and was placing on a pedestal a small china figure of delicate workmanship. It was the figure of a warrior in a suit of armour advancing with raised spear upon an adversary. A thrill permeated Archie's frame. Parker had not been mistaken. This was undoubtedly the companion-figure to the redoubtable Pongo. The two were identical. Even from where he sat Archie could detect on the features of the figure on the pedestal the same expression of insufferable complacency which had alienated his sympathies from the original Pongo.

The high-priest, undaunted by previous rebuffs, regarded the figure with a gloating enthusiasm wholly unshared by the congregation, who were plainly looking upon Pongo's little brother as just another of those things.

"This," he said, with a shake in his voice, "is something very special. China figure, said to date back to the Ming Dynasty. Unique. Nothing like it on either side of the Atlantic. If I were selling this at Christie's in London, where people," he said, nastily, "have an educated appreciation of the beautiful, the rare, and the exquisite, I should start the bidding at a thousand dollars. This afternoon's experience has taught me that that might possibly be too high." His pince-nez sparkled militantly, as he gazed upon the stolid throng. "Will anyone offer me a dollar for this unique figure?"

"Leap at it, old top," said Reggie van Tuyl. "Twiddle, dear boy, twiddle! A dollar's reasonable."

Archie twiddled.

"One dollar I am offered," said the high-priest, bitterly. "One gentleman here is not afraid to take a chance. One gentleman here knows a good thing when he sees one." He abandoned the gently sarcastic manner for one of crisp and direct reproach. "Come, come, gentlemen, we are not here to waste time. Will anyone offer me one hundred dollars for this superb piece of—" He broke off, and seemed for a moment almost unnerved. He stared at someone in one of the seats in front of Archie. "Thank you," he said, with a sort of gulp. "One hundred dollars I am offered! One hundred—one hundred—one hundred—"

Archie was startled. This sudden, tremendous jump, this wholly unforeseen boom in Pongos, if one might so describe it, was more than a little disturbing. He could not see who his rival was, but it was evident that at least one among those present did not intend to allow Pongo's brother to slip by without a fight. He looked helplessly at Reggie for counsel, but Reggie had now definitely given up the struggle. Exhausted nature had done its utmost, and now he was leaning back with closed eyes, breathing softly through his nose. Thrown on his own resources, Archie could think of no better course than to twiddle his fingers again. He did so, and the high-priest's chant took on a note of positive exuberance.

"Two hundred I am offered. Much better! Turn the pedestal round, Willie, and let them look at it. Slowly! Slowly! You aren't spinning a roulette-wheel. Two hundred. Two-two-two-two-two." He became suddenly lyrical. "Two-two-two—There was a young lady named Lou, who was catching a train at two-two. Said the porter, 'Don't worry or hurry or scurry. It's a minute or two to two-two!' Two-two-two-two-two!"

Archie's concern increased. He seemed to be twiddling at this voluble man across seas of misunderstanding. Nothing is harder to interpret to a nicety than a twiddle, and Archie's idea of the language of twiddles and the high-priest's idea did not coincide by a mile. The high-priest appeared to consider that, when Archie twiddled, it was his intention to bid in hundreds, whereas in fact Archie had meant to signify that he raised the previous bid by just one dollar. Archie felt that, if given time, he could make this clear to the high-priest, but the latter gave him no time. He had got his audience, so to speak, on the run, and he proposed to hustle them before they could rally.

"Two hundred—two hundred—two—three—thank you, sir—three-three-three-four-four-five-five-six-six-seven-seven-seven—"

Archie sat limply in his wooden chair. He was conscious of a feeling which he had only experienced twice in his life—once when he had taken his first lesson in driving a motor and had trodden on the accelerator instead of the brake; the second time more recently, when he had made his first down-trip on an express lift. He had now precisely the same sensation of being run away with by an uncontrollable machine, and of having left most of his internal organs at some little distance from the rest of his body. Emerging from this welter of emotion, stood out the one clear fact that, be the opposition bidding what it might, he must nevertheless secure the prize. Lucille had sent him to New York expressly to do so. She had sacrificed her jewellery for the cause. She relied on him. The enterprise had become for Archie something almost sacred. He felt dimly like a knight of old hot on the track of the Holy Grail.

He twiddled again. The ring and the bracelet had fetched nearly twelve hundred dollars. Up to that figure his hat was in the ring.

"Eight hundred I am offered. Eight hundred. Eight-eight-eight-eight—"

A voice spoke from somewhere at the back of the room. A quiet, cold, nasty, determined voice.

"Nine!"

Archie rose from his seat and spun round. This mean attack from the rear stung his fighting spirit. As he rose, a young man sitting immediately in front of him rose too and stared likewise. He was a square-built resolute-looking young man, who reminded Archie vaguely of somebody he had seen before. But Archie was too busy trying to locate the man at the back to pay much attention to him. He detected him at last, owing to the fact that the eyes of everybody in that part of the room were fixed upon him. He was a small man of middle age, with tortoise-shell-rimmed spectacles. He might have been a professor or something of the kind. Whatever he was, he was obviously a man to be reckoned with. He had a rich sort of look, and his demeanour was the demeanour of a man who is prepared to fight it out on these lines if it takes all the summer.

"Nine hundred I am offered. Nine-nine-nine-nine—"

Archie glared defiantly at the spectacled man.

"A thousand!" he cried.

The irruption of high finance into the placid course of the afternoon's proceedings had stirred the congregation out of its lethargy. There were excited murmurs. Necks were craned, feet shuffled. As for the high-priest, his cheerfulness was now more than restored, and his faith in his fellow-man had soared from the depths to a very lofty altitude. He beamed with approval. Despite the warmth of his praise he would have been quite satisfied to see Pongo's little brother go at twenty dollars, and the reflection that the bidding had already reached one thousand and that his commission was twenty per cent, had engendered a mood of sunny happiness.

"One thousand is bid!" he carolled. "Now, gentlemen, I don't want to hurry you over this. You are all connoisseurs here, and you don't want to see a priceless china figure of the Ming Dynasty get away from you at a sacrifice price. Perhaps you can't all see the figure where it is. Willie, take it round and show it to 'em. We'll take a little intermission while you look carefully at this wonderful figure. Get a move on, Willie! Pick up your feet!"

Archie, sitting dazedly, was aware that Reggie van Tuyl had finished his beauty sleep and was addressing the young man in the seat in front.

"Why, hallo," said Reggie. "I didn't know you were back. You remember me, don't you? Reggie van Tuyl. I know your sister very well. Archie, old man, I want you to meet my friend, Bill Brewster. Why, dash it!" He chuckled sleepily. "I was forgetting. Of course! He's your—"

"How are you?" said the young man. "Talking of my sister," he

60

said to Reggie, "I suppose you haven't met her husband by any chance? I suppose you know she married some awful chump?"

"Me," said Archie.

"How's that?"

"I married your sister. My name's Moffam."

The young man seemed a trifle taken aback.

"Sorry," he said.

"Not at all," said Archie.

"I was only going by what my father said in his letters," he explained, in extenuation.

Archie nodded.

"I'm afraid your jolly old father doesn't appreciate me. But I'm hoping for the best. If I can rope in that rummy-looking little china thing that Jo-Jo the dog-faced boy is showing the customers, he will be all over me. I mean to say, you know, he's got another like it, and, if he can get a full house, as it were, I'm given to understand he'll be bucked, cheered, and even braced."

The young man stared.

"Are YOU the fellow who's been bidding against me?"

"Eh, what? Were you bidding against ME?"

"I wanted to buy the thing for my father. I've a special reason for wanting to get in right with him just now. Are you buying it for him, too?"

"Absolutely. As a surprise. It was Lucille's idea. His valet, a chappie named Parker, tipped us off that the thing was to be sold."

"Parker? Great Scot! It was Parker who tipped ME off. I met him on Broadway, and he told me about it."

"Rummy he never mentioned it in his letter to me. Why, dash it, we could have got the thing for about two dollars if we had pooled our bids."

"Well, we'd better pool them now, and extinguish that pill at the back there. I can't go above eleven hundred. That's all I've got."

"I can't go above eleven hundred myself."

"There's just one thing. I wish you'd let me be the one to hand the thing over to Father. I've a special reason for wanting to make a hit with him."

"Absolutely!" said Archie, magnanimously. "It's all the same to me. I only wanted to get him generally braced, as it were, if you know what I mean."

"That's awfully good of you."

"Not a bit, laddie, no, no, and far from it. Only too glad."

Willie had returned from his rambles among the connoisseurs, and Pongo's brother was back on his pedestal. The high-priest cleared his throat and resumed his discourse.

61

"Now that you have all seen this superb figure we will—I was offered one thousand—one thousand-one-one-one-one—eleven hundred. Thank you, sir. Eleven hundred I am offered."

The high-priest was now exuberant. You could see him doing figures in his head.

"You do the bidding," said Brother Bill.

"Right-o!" said Archie.

He waved a defiant hand.

"Thirteen," said the man at the back.

"Fourteen, dash it!"

"Fifteen!"

"Sixteen!"

"Seventeen!"

"Eighteen!"

"Nineteen!"

"Two thousand!"

The high-priest did everything but sing. He radiated good will and bonhomie.

"Two thousand I am offered. Is there any advance on two thousand? Come, gentlemen, I don't want to give this superb figure away. Twenty-one hundred. Twenty-one-one-one-one. This is more the sort of thing I have been accustomed to. When I was at Sotheby's Rooms in London, this kind of bidding was a commonplace. Twenty-two-two-two-two-two. One hardly noticed it. Three-three-three. Twenty-three-three-three. Twenty-three hundred dollars I am offered."

He gazed expectantly at Archie, as a man gazes at some favourite dog whom he calls upon to perform a trick. But Archie had reached the end of his tether. The hand that had twiddled so often and so bravely lay inert beside his trouser-leg, twitching feebly. Archie was through.

"Twenty-three hundred," said the high-priest, ingratiatingly.

Archie made no movement. There was a tense pause. The high-priest gave a little sigh, like one waking from a beautiful dream.

"Twenty-three hundred," he said. "Once twenty-three. Twice twenty-three. Third, last, and final call, twenty-three. Sold at twenty-three hundred. I congratulate you, sir, on a genuine bargain!"

Reggie van Tuyl had dozed off again. Archie tapped his brother-in-law on the shoulder.

"May as well be popping, what?"

They threaded their way sadly together through the crowd,

and made for the street. They passed into Fifth Avenue without breaking the silence.

"Bally nuisance," said Archie, at last.

"Rotten!"

"Wonder who that chappie was?"

"Some collector, probably."

"Well, it can't be helped," said Archie.

Brother Bill attached himself to Archie's arm, and became communicative.

"I didn't want to mention it in front of van Tuyl," he said, "because he's such a talking-machine, and it would have been all over New York before dinner-time. But you're one of the family, and you can keep a secret."

"Absolutely! Silent tomb and what not."

"The reason I wanted that darned thing was because I've just got engaged to a girl over in England, and I thought that, if I could hand my father that china figure-thing with one hand and break the news with the other, it might help a bit. She's the most wonderful girl!"

"I'll bet she is," said Archie, cordially.

"The trouble is she's in the chorus of one of the revues over there, and Father is apt to kick. So I thought—oh, well, it's no good worrying now. Come along where it's quiet, and I'll tell you all about her."

"That'll be jolly," said Archie.

CHAPTER XI

SALVATORE CHOOSES THE WRONG MOMENT

Archie reclaimed the family jewellery from its temporary home next morning; and, having done so, sauntered back to the Cosmopolis. He was surprised, on entering the lobby, to meet his father-in-law. More surprising still, Mr. Brewster was manifestly in a mood of extraordinary geniality. Archie could hardly believe his eyes when the other waved cheerily to him—nor his ears a moment later when Mr. Brewster, addressing him as "my boy," asked him how he was and mentioned that the day was a warm one.

Obviously this jovial frame of mind must be taken advantage of; and Archie's first thought was of the downtrodden Salvatore, to the tale of whose wrongs he had listened so sympathetically on the previous day. Now was plainly the moment for the waiter to submit his grievance, before some ebb-tide caused the milk of human kindness to flow out of Daniel Brewster. With a swift "Cheerio!" in his father-in-law's direction, Archie bounded into the grill-room. Salvatore, the hour for luncheon being imminent but not yet having arrived, was standing against the far wall in an attitude of thought.

"Laddie!" cried Archie.

"Sare?"

"A most extraordinary thing has happened. Good old Brewster has suddenly popped up through a trap and is out in the lobby now. And what's still more weird, he's apparently bucked."

"Sare?"

"Braced, you know. In the pink. Pleased about something. If you go to him now with that yarn of yours, you can't fail. He'll kiss you on both cheeks and give you his bank-roll and collar-stud. Charge along and ask the head-waiter if you can have ten minutes off."

Salvatore vanished in search of the potentate named, and Archie returned to the lobby to bask in the unwonted sunshine.

"Well, well, well, what!" he said. "I thought you were at Brookport."

"I came up this morning to meet a friend of mine," replied Mr. Brewster genially. "Professor Binstead."

"Don't think I know him."

"Very interesting man," said Mr. Brewster, still with the same uncanny amiability. "He's a dabbler in a good many things—science,

64

phrenology, antiques. I asked him to bid for me at a sale yesterday. There was a little china figure—"

Archie's jaw fell.

"China figure?" he stammered feebly.

"Yes. The companion to one you may have noticed on my mantelpiece upstairs. I have been trying to get the pair of them for years. I should never have heard of this one if it had not been for that valet of mine, Parker. Very good of him to let me know of it, considering I had fired him. Ah, here is Binstead."—He moved to greet the small, middle-aged man with the tortoiseshell-rimmed spectacles who was bustling across the lobby.—"Well, Binstead, so you got it?"

"Yes."

"I suppose the price wasn't particularly stiff?"

"Twenty-three hundred."

"Twenty-three hundred!" Mr. Brewster seemed to reel in his tracks. "Twenty-three HUNDRED!"

"You gave me carte blanche."

"Yes, but twenty-three hundred!"

"I could have got it for a few dollars, but unfortunately I was a little late, and, when I arrived, some young fool had bid it up to a thousand, and he stuck to me till I finally shook him off at twenty-three hundred. Why, this is the very man! Is he a friend of yours?"

Archie coughed.

"More a relation than a friend, what? Son-in-law, don't you know!"

Mr. Brewster's amiability had vanished.

"What damned foolery have you been up to NOW?" he demanded. "Can't I move a step without stubbing my toe on you? Why the devil did you bid?"

"We thought it would be rather a fruity scheme. We talked it over and came to the conclusion that it was an egg. Wanted to get hold of the rummy little object, don't you know, and surprise you."

"Who's we?"

"Lucille and I."

"But how did you hear of it at all?"

"Parker, the valet-chappie, you know, wrote me a letter about it."

"Parker! Didn't he tell you that he had told me the figure was to be sold?"

"Absolutely not!" A sudden suspicion came to Archie. He was normally a guileless young man, but even to him the extreme fishiness of the part played by Herbert Parker had become apparent. "I say, you know, it looks to me as if friend Parker had

65

been having us all on a bit, what? I mean to say it was jolly old Herb, who tipped your son off—Bill, you know—to go and bid for the thing."

"Bill! Was Bill there?"

"Absolutely in person! We were bidding against each other like the dickens till we managed to get together and get acquainted. And then this bird—this gentleman—sailed in and started to slip it across us."

Professor Binstead chuckled—the care-free chuckle of a man who sees all those around him smitten in the pocket, while he himself remains untouched.

"A very ingenious rogue, this Parker of yours, Brewster. His method seems to have been simple but masterly. I have no doubt that either he or a confederate obtained the figure and placed it with the auctioneer, and then he ensured a good price for it by getting us all to bid against each other. Very ingenious!"

Mr. Brewster struggled with his feelings. Then he seemed to overcome them and to force himself to look on the bright side.

"Well, anyway," he said. "I've got the pair of figures, and that's what I wanted. Is that it in that parcel?"

"This is it. I wouldn't trust an express company to deliver it. Suppose we go up to your room and see how the two look side by side."

They crossed the lobby to the lift.-The cloud was still on Mr. Brewster's brow as they stepped out and made their way to his suite. Like most men who have risen from poverty to wealth by their own exertions, Mr. Brewster objected to parting with his money unnecessarily, and it was plain that that twenty-three hundred dollars still rankled.

Mr. Brewster unlocked the door and crossed the room. Then, suddenly, he halted, stared, and stared again. He sprang to the bell and pressed it, then stood gurgling wordlessly.

"Anything wrong, old bean?" queried Archie, solicitously.

"Wrong! Wrong! It's gone!"

"Gone?"

"The figure!"

The floor-waiter had manifested himself silently in answer to the bell, and was standing in the doorway.

"Simmons!" Mr. Brewster turned to him wildly. "Has anyone been in this suite since I went away?"

"No, sir."

"Nobody?"

"Nobody except your valet, sir—Parker. He said he had come

66

to fetch some things away. I supposed he had come from you, sir, with instructions."

"Get out!"

Professor Binstead had unwrapped his parcel, and had placed the Pongo on the table. There was a weighty silence. Archie picked up the little china figure and balanced it on the palm of his hand. It was a small thing, he reflected philosophically, but it had made quite a stir in the world.

Mr. Brewster fermented for a while without speaking.

"So," he said, at last, in a voice trembling with self-pity, "I have been to all this trouble—"

"And expense," put in Professor Binstead, gently.

"Merely to buy back something which had been stolen from me! And, owing to your damned officiousness," he cried, turning on Archie, "I have had to pay twenty-three hundred dollars for it! I don't know why they make such a fuss about Job. Job never had anything like you around!"

"Of course," argued Archie, "he had one or two boils."

"Boils! What are boils?"

"Dashed sorry," murmured Archie. "Acted for the best. Meant well. And all that sort of rot!"

Professor Binstead's mind seemed occupied to the exclusion of all other aspects of the affair, with the ingenuity of the absent Parker.

"A cunning scheme!" he said. "A very cunning scheme! This man Parker must have a brain of no low order. I should like to feel his bumps!"

"I should like to give him some!" said the stricken Mr. Brewster. He breathed a deep breath. "Oh, well," he said, "situated as I am, with a crook valet and an imbecile son-in-law, I suppose I ought to be thankful that I've still got my own property, even if I have had to pay twenty-three hundred dollars for the privilege of keeping it." He rounded on Archie, who was in a reverie. The thought of the unfortunate Bill had just crossed Archie's mind. It would be many moons, many weary moons, before Mr. Brewster would be in a suitable mood to listen sympathetically to the story of love's young dream. "Give me that figure!"

Archie continued to toy absently with Pongo. He was wondering now how best to break this sad occurrence to Lucille. It would be a disappointment for the poor girl.

"GIVE ME THAT FIGURE!"

Archie started violently. There was an instant in which Pongo seemed to hang suspended, like Mohammed's coffin, between heaven and earth, then the force of gravity asserted itself. Pongo fell

67

with a sharp crack and disintegrated. And as it did so there was a knock at the door, and in walked a dark, furtive person, who to the inflamed vision of Mr. Daniel Brewster looked like something connected with the executive staff of the Black Hand. With all time at his disposal, the unfortunate Salvatore had selected this moment for stating his case.

"Get out!" bellowed Mr. Brewster. "I didn't ring for a waiter."

Archie, his mind reeling beneath the catastrophe, recovered himself sufficiently to do the honours. It was at his instigation that Salvatore was there, and, greatly as he wished that he could have seen fit to choose a more auspicious moment for his business chat, he felt compelled to do his best to see him through.

"Oh, I say, half a second," he said. "You don't quite understand. As a matter of fact, this chappie is by way of being downtrodden and oppressed and what not, and I suggested that he should get hold of you and speak a few well-chosen words. Of course, if you'd rather—some other time—"

But Mr. Brewster was not permitted to postpone the interview. Before he could get his breath, Salvatore had begun to talk. He was a strong, ambidextrous talker, whom it was hard to interrupt; and it was not for some moments that Mr. Brewster succeeded in getting a word in. When he did, he spoke to the point. Though not a linguist, he had been able to follow the discourse closely enough to realise that the waiter was dissatisfied with conditions in his hotel; and Mr. Brewster, as has been indicated, had a short way with people who criticised the Cosmopolis.

"You're fired!" said Mr. Brewster.

"Oh, I say!" protested Archie.

Salvatore muttered what sounded like a passage from Dante.

"Fired!" repeated Mr. Brewster resolutely. "And I wish to heaven," he added, eyeing his son-in-law malignantly, "I could fire you!"

"Well," said Professor Binstead cheerfully, breaking the grim silence which followed this outburst, "if you will give me your cheque, Brewster, I think I will be going. Two thousand three hundred dollars. Make it open, if you will, and then I can run round the corner and cash it before lunch. That will be capital!"

CHAPTER XII

BRIGHT EYES—AND A FLY

The Hermitage (unrivalled scenery, superb cuisine, Daniel Brewster, proprietor) was a picturesque summer hotel in the green heart of the mountains, built by Archie's father-in-law shortly after he assumed control of the Cosmopolis. Mr. Brewster himself seldom went there, preferring to concentrate his attention on his New York establishment; and Archie and Lucille, breakfasting in the airy dining-room some ten days after the incidents recorded in the last chapter, had consequently to be content with two out of the three advertised attractions of the place. Through the window at their side quite a slab of the unrivalled scenery was visible; some of the superb cuisine was already on the table; and the fact that the eye searched in vain for Daniel Brewster, proprietor, filled Archie, at any rate, with no sense of aching loss. He bore it with equanimity and even with positive enthusiasm. In Archie's opinion, practically all a place needed to make it an earthly Paradise was for Mr. Daniel Brewster to be about forty-seven miles away from it.

It was at Lucille's suggestion that they had come to the Hermitage. Never a human sunbeam, Mr. Brewster had shown such a bleak front to the world, and particularly to his son-in-law, in the days following the Pongo incident, that Lucille had thought that he and Archie would for a time at least be better apart—a view with which her husband cordially agreed. He had enjoyed his stay at the Hermitage, and now he regarded the eternal hills with the comfortable affection of a healthy man who is breakfasting well.

"It's going to be another perfectly topping day," he observed, eyeing the shimmering landscape, from which the morning mists were swiftly shredding away like faint puffs of smoke. "Just the day you ought to have been here."

"Yes, it's too bad I've got to go. New York will be like an oven."

"Put it off."

"I can't, I'm afraid. I've a fitting."

Archie argued no further. He was a married man of old enough standing to know the importance of fittings.

"Besides," said Lucille, "I want to see father." Archie repressed an exclamation of astonishment. "I'll be back to-morrow evening. You will be perfectly happy."

"Queen of my soul, you know I can't be happy with you away. You know—"

69

"Yes?" murmured Lucille, appreciatively. She never tired of hearing Archie say this sort of thing.

Archie's voice had trailed off. He was looking across the room.

"By Jove!" he exclaimed. "What an awfully pretty woman!"

"Where?"

"Over there. Just coming in, I say, what wonderful eyes! I don't think I ever saw such eyes. Did you notice her eyes? Sort of flashing! Awfully pretty woman!"

Warm though the morning was, a suspicion of chill descended upon the breakfast-table. A certain coldness seemed to come into Lucille's face. She could not always share Archie's fresh young enthusiasms.

"Do you think so?"

"Wonderful figure, too!"

"Yes?"

"Well, what I mean to say, fair to medium," said Archie, recovering a certain amount of that intelligence which raises man above the level of the beasts of the field. "Not the sort of type I admire myself, of course."

"You know her, don't you?"

"Absolutely not and far from it," said Archie, hastily. "Never met her in my life."

"You've seen her on the stage. Her name's Vera Silverton. We saw her in—"

"Of course, yes. So we did. I say, I wonder what she's doing here? She ought to be in New York, rehearsing. I remember meeting what's-his-name—you know—chappie who writes plays and what not—George Benham—I remember meeting George Benham, and he told me she was rehearsing in a piece of his called—I forget the name, but I know it was called something or other. Well, why isn't she?"

"She probably lost her temper and broke her contract and came away. She's always doing that sort of thing. She's known for it. She must be a horrid woman."

"Yes."

"I don't want to talk about her. She used to be married to someone, and she divorced him. And then she was married to someone else, and he divorced her. And I'm certain her hair wasn't that colour two years ago, and I don't think a woman ought to make up like that, and her dress is all wrong for the country, and those pearls can't be genuine, and I hate the way she rolls her eyes about, and pink doesn't suit her a bit. I think she's an awful woman, and I wish you wouldn't keep on talking about her."

"Right-o!" said Archie, dutifully.

70

They finished breakfast, and Lucille went up to pack her bag. Archie strolled out on to the terrace outside the hotel, where he smoked, communed with nature, and thought of Lucille. He always thought of Lucille when he was alone, especially when he chanced to find himself in poetic surroundings like those provided by the unrivalled scenery encircling the Hotel Hermitage. The longer he was married to her the more did the sacred institution seem to him a good egg. Mr. Brewster might regard their marriage as one of the world's most unfortunate incidents, but to Archie it was, and always had been, a bit of all right. The more he thought of it the more did he marvel that a girl like Lucille should have been content to link her lot with that of a Class C specimen like himself. His meditations were, in fact, precisely what a happily-married man's meditations ought to be.

He was roused from them by a species of exclamation or cry almost at his elbow, and turned to find that the spectacular Miss Silverton was standing beside him. Her dubious hair gleamed in the sunlight, and one of the criticised eyes was screwed up. The other gazed at Archie with an expression of appeal.

"There's something in my eye," she said.

"No, really!"

"I wonder if you would mind? It would be so kind of you!"

Archie would have preferred to remove himself, but no man worthy of the name can decline to come to the rescue of womanhood in distress. To twist the lady's upper lid back and peer into it and jab at it with the corner of his handkerchief was the only course open to him. His conduct may be classed as not merely blameless but definitely praiseworthy. King Arthur's knights used to do this sort of thing all the time, and look what people think of them. Lucille, therefore, coming out of the hotel just as the operation was concluded, ought not to have felt the annoyance she did. But, of course, there is a certain superficial intimacy about the attitude of a man who is taking a fly out of a woman's eye which may excusably jar upon the sensibilities of his wife. It is an attitude which suggests a sort of rapprochement or camaraderie or, as Archie would have put it, what not.

"Thanks so much!" said Miss Silverton.

"Oh no, rather not," said Archie.

"Such a nuisance getting things in your eye."

"Absolutely!"

"I'm always doing it!"

"Rotten luck!"

"But I don't often find anyone as clever as you to help me."

71

Lucille felt called upon to break in on this feast of reason and flow of soul.

"Archie," she said, "if you go and get your clubs now, I shall just have time to walk round with you before my train goes."

"Oh, ah!" said Archie, perceiving her for the first time. "Oh, ah, yes, right-o, yes, yes, yes!"

On the way to the first tee it seemed to Archie that Lucille was distrait and abstracted in her manner; and it occurred to him, not for the first time in his life, what a poor support a clear conscience is in moments of crisis. Dash it all, he didn't see what else he could have done. Couldn't leave the poor female staggering about the place with squads of flies wedged in her eyeball. Nevertheless—

"Rotten thing getting a fly in your eye," he hazarded at length. "Dashed awkward, I mean."

"Or convenient."

"Eh?"

"Well, it's a very good way of dispensing with an introduction."

"Oh, I say! You don't mean you think—"

"She's a horrid woman!"

"Absolutely! Can't think what people see in her."

"Well, you seemed to enjoy fussing over her!"

"No, no! Nothing of the kind! She inspired me with absolute what-d'you-call-it—the sort of thing chappies do get inspired with, you know."

"You were beaming all over your face."

"I wasn't. I was just screwing up my face because the sun was in my eye."

"All sorts of things seem to be in people's eyes this morning!"

Archie was saddened. That this sort of misunderstanding should have occurred on such a topping day and at a moment when they were to be torn
asunder for about thirty-six hours made him feel—well, it gave him the pip. He had an idea that there were words which would have straightened
everything out, but he was not an eloquent young man and could not find them. He felt aggrieved. Lucille, he considered, ought to have known that he was immune as regarded females with flashing eyes and experimentally-coloured hair. Why, dash it, he could have extracted flies from the eyes of Cleopatra with one hand and Helen of Troy with the other, simultaneously, without giving them a second thought. It was in depressed mood that he played a listless nine holes; nor had life brightened for him when he came back to the hotel two hours later, after seeing Lucille off in the train to New York. Never till now had they had

anything remotely resembling a quarrel. Life, Archie felt, was a bit of
a wash-out. He was disturbed and jumpy, and the sight of Miss Silverton,
talking to somebody on a settee in the corner of the hotel lobby, sent
him shooting off at right angles and brought him up with a bump against
the desk behind which the room-clerk sat.

The room-clerk, always of a chatty disposition, was saying something to him, but Archie did not listen. He nodded mechanically. It was something about his room. He caught the word "satisfactory."

"Oh, rather, quite!" said Archie.

A fussy devil, the room-clerk! He knew perfectly well that Archie found his room satisfactory. These chappies gassed on like this so as to try to make you feel that the management took a personal interest in you. It was part of their job. Archie beamed absently and went in to lunch. Lucille's empty seat stared at him mournfully, increasing his sense of desolation.

He was half-way through his lunch, when the chair opposite ceased to be vacant. Archie, transferring his gaze from the scenery outside the window, perceived that his friend, George Benham, the playwright, had materialised from nowhere and was now in his midst.

"Hallo!" he said.

George Benham was a grave young man whose spectacles gave him the look of a mournful owl. He seemed to have something on his mind besides the artistically straggling mop of black hair which swept down over his brow. He sighed wearily, and ordered fish-pie.

"I thought I saw you come through the lobby just now," he said.

"Oh, was that you on the settee, talking to Miss Silverton?"

"She was talking to ME," said the playwright, moodily.

"What are you doing here?" asked Archie. He could have wished Mr. Benham elsewhere, for he intruded on his gloom, but, the chappie being amongst those present, it was only civil to talk to him. "I thought you were in New York, watching the rehearsals of your jolly old drama."

"The rehearsals are hung up. And it looks as though there wasn't going to be any drama. Good Lord!" cried George Benham, with honest warmth, "with opportunities opening out before one on every side—with life extending prizes to one with both hands—when you see coal-heavers making fifty dollars a week and the fellows who clean out the sewers going happy and singing about their work— why does a man deliberately choose a job like writing plays? Job was the only man that ever lived who was really qualified to write a play, and he would have found it pretty tough going if his leading woman had been anyone like Vera Silverton!"

Archie—and it was this fact, no doubt, which accounted for his possession of such a large and varied circle of friends—was always able to shelve his own troubles in order to listen to other people's hard-luck stories.

"Tell me all, laddie," he said. "Release the film! Has she walked out on you?"

"Left us flat! How did you hear about it? Oh, she told you, of course?"

Archie hastened to try to dispel the idea that he was on any such terms of intimacy with Miss Silverton.

"No, no! My wife said she thought it must be something of that nature or order when we saw her come in to breakfast. I mean to say," said Archie, reasoning closely, "woman can't come into breakfast here and be rehearsing in New York at the same time. Why did she administer the raspberry, old friend?"

Mr. Benham helped himself to fish-pie, and spoke dully through the steam.

"Well, what happened was this. Knowing her as intimately as you do—"

"I DON'T know her!"

"Well, anyway, it was like this. As you know, she has a dog—"

"I didn't know she had a dog," protested Archie. It seemed to him that the world was in conspiracy to link him with this woman.

"Well, she has a dog. A beastly great whacking brute of a bulldog. And she brings it to rehearsal." Mr. Benham's eyes filled with tears, as in his emotion he swallowed a mouthful of fish-pie some eighty-three degrees Fahrenheit hotter than it looked. In the intermission caused by this disaster his agile mind skipped a few chapters of the story, and, when he was able to speak again, he said, "So then there was a lot of trouble. Everything broke loose!"

"Why?" Archie was puzzled. "Did the management object to her bringing the dog to rehearsal?"

"A lot of good that would have done! She does what she likes in the theatre."

"Then why was there trouble?"

"You weren't listening," said Mr. Benham, reproachfully. "I told you. This dog came snuffling up to where I was sitting—it was quite dark in the body of the theatre, you know—and I got up to say something about something that was happening on the stage, and somehow I must have given it a push with my foot."

"I see," said Archie, beginning to get the run of the plot. "You kicked her dog."

"Pushed it. Accidentally. With my foot."

"I understand. And when you brought off this kick—"

"Push," said Mr. Benham, austerely.

"This kick or push. When you administered this kick or push"

"It was more a sort of light shove."

"Well, when you did whatever you did, the trouble started?"

Mr. Benham gave a slight shiver.

"She talked for a while, and then walked out, taking the dog with her. You see, this wasn't the first time it had happened."

"Good Lord! Do you spend your whole time doing that sort of thing?"

"It wasn't me the first time. It was the stage-manager. He didn't know whose dog it was, and it came waddling on to the stage, and he gave it a sort of pat, a kind of flick—"

"A slosh?"

"NOT a slosh," corrected Mr. Benham, firmly. "You might call it a tap—with the promptscript. Well, we had a lot of difficulty smoothing her over that time. Still, we managed to do it, but she said that if anything of the sort occurred again she would chuck up her part."

"She must be fond of the dog," said Archie, for the first time feeling a touch of goodwill and sympathy towards the lady.

"She's crazy about, it. That's what made it so awkward when I happened—quite inadvertently—to give it this sort of accidental shove. Well, we spent the rest of the day trying to get her on the 'phone at her apartment, and finally we heard that she had come here. So I took the next train, and tried to persuade her to come back. She wouldn't listen. And that's how matters stand."

"Pretty rotten!" said Archie, sympathetically.

"You can bet it's pretty rotten—for me. There's nobody else who can play the part. Like a chump, I wrote the thing specially for her. It means the play won't be produced at all, if she doesn't do it. So you're my last hope!"

Archie, who was lighting a cigarette, nearly swallowed it.

"I am?"

"I thought you might persuade her. Point out to her what a lot hangs on her coming back. Jolly her along, YOU know the sort of thing!"

"But, my dear old friend, I tell you I don't know her!"

Mr. Benham's eyes opened behind their zareba of glass.

"Well, she knows YOU. When you came through the lobby just now she said that you were the only real human being she had ever met."

"Well, as a matter of fact, I did take a fly out of her eye. But—"

"You did? Well, then, the whole thing's simple. All you have to do is to ask her how her eye is, and tell her she has the most beautiful eyes you ever saw, and coo a bit."

"But, my dear old son!" The frightful programme which his friend had mapped out stunned Archie. "I simply can't! Anything to oblige and all that sort of thing, but when it comes to cooing, distinctly Napoo!"

"Nonsense! It isn't hard to coo."

"You don't understand, laddie. You're not a married man. I mean to say, whatever you say for or against marriage—personally I'm all for it and consider it a ripe egg—the fact remains that it practically makes a chappie a spent force as a cooer. I don't want to dish you in any way, old bean, but I must firmly and resolutely decline to coo."

Mr. Benham rose and looked at his watch.

"I'll have to be moving," he said. "I've got to get back to New York and report. I'll tell them that I haven't been able to do anything myself, but that I've left the matter in good hands. I know you will do your best."

"But, laddie!"

"Think," said Mr. Benham, solemnly, "of all that depends on it! The other actors! The small-part people thrown out of a job! Myself—but no! Perhaps you had better touch very lightly or not at all on my connection with the thing. Well, you know how to handle it. I feel I can leave it to you. Pitch it strong! Good-bye, my dear old man, and a thousand thanks. I'll do the same for you another time." He moved towards the door, leaving Archie transfixed. Half-way there he turned and came back. "Oh, by the way," he said, "my lunch. Have it put on your bill, will you? I haven't time to stay and settle. Good-bye! Good-bye!"

CHAPTER XIII

RALLYING ROUND PERCY

It amazed Archie through the whole of a long afternoon to reflect how swiftly and unexpectedly the blue and brilliant sky of life can cloud over and with what abruptness a man who fancies that his feet are on solid ground can find himself immersed in Fate's gumbo. He recalled, with the bitterness with which one does recall such things, that that morning he had risen from his bed without a care in the world, his happiness unruffled even by the thought that Lucille would be leaving him for a short space. He had sung in his bath. Yes, he had chirruped like a bally linnet. And now—

Some men would have dismissed the unfortunate affairs of Mr. George Benham from their mind as having nothing to do with themselves, but Archie had never been made of this stern stuff. The fact that Mr. Benham, apart from being an agreeable companion with whom he had lunched occasionally in New York, had no claims upon him affected him little. He hated to see his fellowman in trouble. On the other hand, what could he do? To seek Miss Silverton out and plead with her—even if he did it without cooing— would undoubtedly establish an intimacy between them which, instinct told him, might tinge her manner after Lucille's return with just that suggestion of Auld Lang Syne which makes things so awkward.

His whole being shrank from extending to Miss Silverton that inch which the female artistic temperament is so apt to turn into an ell; and when, just as he was about to go in to dinner, he met her in the lobby and she smiled brightly at him and informed him that her eye was now completely recovered, he shied away like a startled mustang of the prairie, and, abandoning his intention of worrying the table d'hote in the same room with the amiable creature, tottered off to the smoking-room, where he did the best he could with sandwiches and coffee.

Having got through the time as best he could till eleven o'clock, he went up to bed.

The room to which he and Lucille had been assigned by the management was on the second floor, pleasantly sunny by day and at night filled with cool and heartening fragrance of the pines. Hitherto Archie had always enjoyed taking a final smoke on the balcony overlooking the woods, but, to-night such was his mental

77

stress that he prepared to go to bed directly he had closed the door. He turned to the cupboard to get his pyjamas.

His first thought, when even after a second scrutiny no pyjamas were visible, was that this was merely another of those things which happen on days when life goes wrong. He raked the cupboard for a third time with an annoyed eye. From every hook hung various garments of Lucille's, but no pyjamas. He was breathing a soft malediction preparatory to embarking on a point-to-point hunt for his missing property, when something in the cupboard caught his eye and held him for a moment puzzled.

He could have sworn that Lucille did not possess a mauve neglige. Why, she had told him a dozen times that mauve was a colour which she did not like. He frowned perplexedly; and as he did so, from near the window came a soft cough.

Archie spun round and subjected the room to as close a scrutiny as that which he had bestowed upon the cupboard. Nothing was visible. The window opening on to the balcony gaped wide. The balcony was manifestly empty.

"URRF!"

This time there was no possibility of error. The cough had come from the immediate neighbourhood of the window.

Archie was conscious of a pringly sensation about the roots of his closely-cropped back-hair, as he moved cautiously across the room. The affair was becoming uncanny; and, as he tip-toed towards the window, old ghost stories, read in lighter moments before cheerful fires with plenty of light in the room, flitted through his mind. He had the feeling—precisely as every chappie in those stories had had—that he was not alone.

Nor was he. In a basket behind an arm-chair, curled up, with his massive chin resting on the edge of the wicker-work, lay a fine bulldog.

"Urrf!" said the bulldog.

"Good God!" said Archie.

There was a lengthy pause in which the bulldog looked earnestly at Archie and Archie looked earnestly at the bulldog.

Normally, Archie was a dog-lover. His hurry was never so great as to prevent him stopping, when in the street, and introducing himself to any dog he met. In a strange house, his first act was to assemble the canine population, roll it on its back or backs, and punch it in the ribs. As a boy, his earliest ambition had been to become a veterinary surgeon; and, though the years had cheated him of his career, he knew all about dogs, their points, their manners, their customs, and their treatment in sickness and in health. In short, he loved dogs, and, had they met under happier

78

conditions, he would undoubtedly have been on excellent terms with this one within the space of a minute. But, as things were, he abstained from fraternising and continued to goggle dumbly.

And then his eye, wandering aside, collided with the following objects: a fluffy pink dressing-gown, hung over the back of a chair, an entirely strange suit-case, and, on the bureau, a photograph in a silver frame of a stout gentleman in evening-dress whom he had never seen before in his life.

Much has been written of the emotions of the wanderer who, returning to his childhood home, finds it altered out of all recognition; but poets have neglected the theme—far more poignant—of the man who goes up to his room in an hotel and finds it full of somebody else's dressing-gowns and bulldogs.

Bulldogs! Archie's heart jumped sideways and upwards with a wiggling movement, turning two somersaults, and stopped beating. The hideous truth, working its way slowly through the concrete, had at last penetrated to his brain. He was not only in somebody else's room, and a woman's at that. He was in the room belonging to Miss Vera Silverton.

He could not understand it. He would have been prepared to stake the last cent he could borrow from his father-in-law on the fact that he had made no error in the number over the door. Yet, nevertheless, such was the case, and, below par though his faculties were at the moment, he was sufficiently alert to perceive that it behoved him to withdraw.

He leaped to the door, and, as he did so, the handle began to turn.

The cloud which had settled on Archie's mind lifted abruptly. For an instant he was enabled to think about a hundred times more quickly than was his leisurely wont. Good fortune had brought him to within easy reach of the electric-light switch. He snapped it back, and was in darkness. Then, diving silently and swiftly to the floor, he wriggled under the bed. The thud of his head against what appeared to be some sort of joist or support, unless it had been placed there by the maker as a practical joke, on the chance of this kind of thing happening some day, coincided with the creak of the opening door. Then the light was switched on again, and the bulldog in the corner gave a welcoming woofle.

"And how is mamma's precious angel?"

Rightly concluding that the remark had not been addressed to himself and that no social obligation demanded that he reply, Archie pressed his cheek against the boards and said nothing. The question was not repeated, but from the other side of the room came the sound of a patted dog.

"Did he think his muzzer had fallen down dead and was never coming up?"

The beautiful picture which these words conjured up filled Archie with that yearning for the might-have-been which is always so painful. He was finding his position physically as well as mentally distressing. It was cramped under the bed, and the boards were harder than anything he had ever encountered. Also, it appeared to be the practice of the housemaids at the Hotel Hermitage to use the space below the beds as a depository for all the dust which they swept off the carpet, and much of this was insinuating itself into his nose and mouth. The two things which Archie would have liked most to do at that moment were first to kill Miss Silverton—if possible, painfully—and then to spend the remainder of his life sneezing.

After a prolonged period he heard a drawer open, and noted the fact as promising. As the old married man, he presumed that it signified the putting away of hair-pins. About now the dashed woman would be looking at herself in the glass with her hair down. Then she would brush it. Then she would twiddle it up into thingummies. Say, ten minutes for this. And after that she would go to bed and turn out the light, and he would be able, after giving her a bit of time to go to sleep, to creep out and leg it. Allowing at a conservative estimate three-quarters of—

"Come out!"

Archie stiffened. For an instant a feeble hope came to him that this remark, like the others, might be addressed to the dog.

"Come out from under that bed!" said a stern voice. "And mind how you come! I've got a pistol!"

"Well, I mean to say, you know," said Archie, in a propitiatory voice, emerging from his lair like a tortoise and smiling as winningly as a man can who has just bumped his head against the leg of a bed, "I suppose all this seems fairly rummy, but—"

"For the love of Mike!" said Miss Silverton.

The point seemed to Archie well taken and the comment on the situation neatly expressed.

"What are you doing in my room?"

"Well, if it comes to that, you know—shouldn't have mentioned it if you hadn't brought the subject up in the course of general chit-chat—what are you doing in mine?"

"Yours?"

"Well, apparently there's been a bloomer of some species somewhere, but this was the room I had last night," said Archie.

"But the desk-clerk said that he had asked you if it would be quite satisfactory to you giving it up to me, and you said yes. I come

80

here every summer, when I'm not working, and I always have this room."

"By Jove! I remember now. The chappie did say something to me about the room, but I was thinking of something else and it rather went over the top. So that's what he was talking about, was it?"

Miss Silverton was frowning. A moving-picture director, scanning her face, would have perceived that she was registering disappointment.

"Nothing breaks right for me in this darned world," she said, regretfully. "When I caught sight of your leg sticking out from under the bed, I did think that everything was all lined up for a real find and, at last, I could close my eyes and see the thing in the papers. On the front page, with photographs: 'Plucky Actress Captures Burglar.' Darn it!"

"Fearfully sorry, you know!"

"I just needed something like that. I've got a Press-agent, and I will say for him that he eats well and sleeps well and has just enough intelligence to cash his monthly cheque without forgetting what he went into the bank for, but outside of that you can take it from me he's not one of the world's workers! He's about as much solid use to a girl with aspirations as a pain in the lower ribs. It's three weeks since he got me into print at all, and then the brightest thing he could think up was that my favourite breakfast-fruit was an apple. Well, I ask you!"

"Rotten!" said Archie.

"I did think that for once my guardian angel had gone back to work and was doing something for me. 'Stage Star and Midnight Marauder,'" murmured Miss Silverton, wistfully. "'Footlight Favourite Foils Felon.'"

"Bit thick!" agreed Archie, sympathetically. "Well, you'll probably be wanting to get to bed and all that sort of rot, so I may as well be popping, what! Cheerio!"

A sudden gleam came into Miss Silverton's compelling eyes.

"Wait!"

"Eh?"

"Wait! I've got an idea!" The wistful sadness had gone from her manner. She was bright and alert. "Sit down!"

"Sit down?"

"Sure. Sit down and take the chill off the arm-chair. I've thought of something."

Archie sat down as directed. At his elbow the bulldog eyed him gravely from the basket.

"Do they know you in this hotel?"

"Know me? Well, I've been here about a week."

"I mean, do they know who you are? Do they know you're a good citizen?"

"Well, if it comes to that, I suppose they don't. But—"

"Fine!" said Miss Silverton, appreciatively. "Then it's all right. We can carry on!"

"Carry on!"

"Why, sure! All I want is to get the thing into the papers. It doesn't matter to me if it turns out later that there was a mistake and that you weren't a burglar trying for my jewels after all. It makes just as good a story either way. I can't think why that never struck me before. Here have I been kicking because you weren't a real burglar, when it doesn't amount to a hill of beans whether you are or not. All I've got to do is to rush out and yell and rouse the hotel, and they come in and pinch you, and I give the story to the papers, and everything's fine!"

Archie leaped from his chair.

"I say! What!"

"What's on your mind?" enquired Miss Silverton, considerately. "Don't you think it's a nifty scheme?"

"Nifty! My dear old soul! It's frightful!"

"Can't see what's wrong with it," grumbled Miss Silverton. "After I've had someone get New York on the long-distance 'phone and give the story to the papers you can explain, and they'll let you out. Surely to goodness you don't object, as a personal favour to me, to spending an hour or two in a cell? Why, probably they haven't got a prison at all out in these parts, and you'll simply be locked in a room. A child of ten could do it on his head," said Miss Silverton. "A child of six," she emended.

"But, dash it—I mean—what I mean to say—I'm married!"

"Yes?" said Miss Silverton, with the politeness of faint interest. "I've been married myself. I wouldn't say it's altogether a bad thing, mind you, for those that like it, but a little of it goes a long way. My first husband," she proceeded, reminiscently, "was a travelling man. I gave him a two-weeks' try-out, and then I told him to go on travelling. My second husband—now, HE wasn't a gentleman in any sense of the word. I remember once—"

"You don't grasp the point. The jolly old point! You fail to grasp it. If this bally thing comes out, my wife will be most frightfully sick!"

Miss Silverton regarded him with pained surprise.

"Do you mean to say you would let a little thing like that stand in the way of my getting on the front page of all the papers—WITH photographs? Where's your chivalry?"

82

"Never mind my dashed chivalry!"

"Besides, what does it matter if she does get a little sore? She'll soon get over it. You can put that right. Buy her a box of candy. Not that I'm strong for candy myself. What I always say is, it may taste good, but look what it does to your hips! I give you my honest word that, when I gave up eating candy, I lost eleven ounces the first week. My second husband—no, I'm a liar, it was my third— my third husband said—Say, what's the big idea? Where are you going?"

"Out!" said Archie, firmly. "Bally out!"

A dangerous light flickered in Miss Silverton's eyes.

"That'll be all of that!" she said, raising the pistol. "You stay right where you are, or I'll fire!"

"Right-o!"

"I mean it!"

"My dear old soul," said Archie, "in the recent unpleasantness in France I had chappies popping off things like that at me all day and every day for close on five years, and here I am, what! I mean to say, if I've got to choose between staying here and being pinched in your room by the local constabulary and having the dashed thing get into the papers and all sorts of trouble happening, and my wife getting the wind up and—I say, if I've got to choose—"

"Suck a lozenge and start again!" said Miss Silverton.

"Well, what I mean to say is, I'd much rather take a chance of getting a bullet in the old bean than that. So loose it off and the best o' luck!"

Miss Silverton lowered the pistol, sank into a chair, and burst into tears.

"I think you're the meanest man I ever met!" she sobbed. "You know perfectly well the bang would send me into a fit!"

"In that case," said Archie, relieved, "cheerio, good luck, pip-pip, toodle-oo, and good-bye-ee! I'll be shifting!"

"Yes, you will!" cried Miss Silverton, energetically, recovering with amazing swiftness from her collapse. "Yes, you will, I by no means suppose! You think, just because I'm no champion with a pistol, I'm helpless. You wait! Percy!"

"My name is not Percy."

"I never said it was. Percy! Percy, come to muzzer!"

There was a creaking rustle from behind the arm-chair. A heavy body flopped on the carpet. Out into the room, heaving himself along as though sleep had stiffened his joints, and breathing stertorously through his tilted nose, moved the fine bulldog. Seen in the open, he looked even more formidable than he had done in his basket.

"Guard him, Percy! Good dog, guard him! Oh, heavens! What's the matter with him?"

And with these words the emotional woman, uttering a wail of anguish, flung herself on the floor beside the animal.

Percy was, indeed, in manifestly bad shape. He seemed quite unable to drag his limbs across the room. There was a curious arch in his back, and, as his mistress touched him, he cried out plaintively,

"Percy! Oh, what IS the matter with him? His nose is burning!"

Now was the time, with both sections of the enemy's forces occupied, for Archie to have departed softly from the room. But never, since the day when at the age of eleven he had carried a large, damp, and muddy terrier with a sore foot three miles and deposited him on the best sofa in his mother's drawing-room, had he been able to ignore the spectacle of a dog in trouble.

"He does look bad, what!"

"He's dying! Oh, he's dying! Is it distemper? He's never had distemper."

Archie regarded the sufferer with the grave eye of the expert. He shook his head.

"It's not that," he said. "Dogs with distemper make a sort of snifting noise."

"But he IS making a snifting noise!"

"No, he's making a snuffling noise. Great difference between snuffling and snifting. Not the same thing at all. I mean to say, when they snift they snift, and when they snuffle they—as it were—snuffle. That's how you can tell. If you ask ME"—he passed his hand over the dog's back. Percy uttered another cry. "I know what's the matter with him."

"A brute of a man kicked him at rehearsal. Do you think he's injured internally?"

"It's rheumatism," said Archie. "Jolly old rheumatism. That's all that's the trouble."

"Are you sure?"

"Absolutely!"

"But what can I do?"

"Give him a good hot bath, and mind and dry him well. He'll have a good sleep then, and won't have any pain. Then, first thing to-morrow, you want to give him salicylate of soda."

"I'll never remember that."—"I'll write it down for you. You ought to give him from ten to twenty grains three times a day in an ounce of water. And rub him with any good embrocation."

"And he won't die?"

"Die! He'll live to be as old as you are!-I mean to say—"

"I could kiss you!" said Miss Silverton, emotionally.

Archie backed hastily.

"No, no, absolutely not! Nothing like that required, really!"

"You're a darling!"

"Yes. I mean no. No, no, really!"

"I don't know what to say. What can I say?"

"Good night," said Archie.

"I wish there was something I could do! If you hadn't been here, I should have gone off my head!"

A great idea flashed across Archie's brain.

"Do you really want to do something?"

"Anything!"

"Then I do wish, like a dear sweet soul, you would pop straight back to New York to-morrow and go on with those rehearsals."

Miss Silverton shook her head.

"I can't do that!"

"Oh, right-o! But it isn't much to ask, what!"

"Not much to ask! I'll never forgive that man for kicking Percy!"

"Now listen, dear old soul. You've got the story all wrong. As a matter of fact, jolly old Benham told me himself that he has the greatest esteem and respect for Percy, and wouldn't have kicked him for the world. And, you know it was more a sort of push than a kick. You might almost call it a light shove. The fact is, it was beastly dark in the theatre, and he was legging it sideways for some reason or other, no doubt with the best motives, and unfortunately he happened to stub his toe on the poor old bean."

"Then why didn't he say so?"

"As far as I could make out, you didn't give him a chance."

Miss Silverton wavered.

"I always hate going back after I've walked out on a show," she said. "It seems so weak!"

"Not a bit of it! They'll give three hearty cheers and think you a topper. Besides, you've got to go to New York in any case. To take Percy to a vet., you know, what!"

"Of course. How right you always are!" Miss Silverton hesitated again. "Would you really be glad if I went back to the show?"

"I'd go singing about the hotel! Great pal of mine, Benham. A thoroughly cheery old bean, and very cut up about the whole affair. Besides, think of all the coves thrown out of work—the thingummabobs and the poor what-d'you-call-'ems!"

"Very well."

"You'll do it?"

"Yes."

"I say, you really are one of the best! Absolutely like mother made! That's fine! Well, I think I'll be saying good night."

"Good night. And thank you so much!"

"Oh, no, rather not!"

Archie moved to the door.

"Oh, by the way."

"Yes?"

"If I were you, I think I should catch the very first train you can get to New York. You see—er—you ought to take Percy to the vet. as soon as ever you can."

"You really do think of everything," said Miss Silverton.

"Yes," said Archie, meditatively.

CHAPTER XIV

THE SAD CASE OF LOONEY BIDDLE

Archie was a simple soul, and, as is the case with most simple souls, gratitude came easily to him. He appreciated kind treatment. And when, on the following day, Lucille returned to the Hermitage, all smiles and affection, and made no further reference to Beauty's Eyes and the flies that got into them, he was conscious of a keen desire to show some solid recognition of this magnanimity. Few wives, he was aware, could have had the nobility and what not to refrain from occasionally turning the conversation in the direction of the above-mentioned topics. It had not needed this behaviour on her part to convince him that Lucille was a topper and a corker and one of the very best, for he had been cognisant of these facts since the first moment he had met her: but what he did feel was that she deserved to be rewarded in no uncertain manner. And it seemed a happy coincidence to him that her birthday should be coming along in the next week or so. Surely, felt Archie, he could whack up some sort of a not unjuicy gift for that occasion—something pretty ripe that would make a substantial hit with the dear girl. Surely something would come along to relieve his chronic impecuniosity for just sufficient length of time to enable him to spread himself on this great occasion.

And, as if in direct answer to prayer, an almost forgotten aunt in England suddenly, out of an absolutely blue sky, shot no less a sum than five hundred dollars across the ocean. The present was so lavish and unexpected that Archie had the awed feeling of one who participates in a miracle. He felt, like Herbert Parker, that the righteous was not forsaken. It was the sort of thing that restored a fellow's faith in human nature. For nearly a week he went about in a happy trance: and when, by thrift and enterprise—that is to say, by betting Reggie van Tuyl that the New York Giants would win the opening game of the series against the Pittsburg baseball team—he contrived to double his capital, what it amounted to was simply that life had nothing more to offer. He was actually in a position to go to a thousand dollars for Lucille's birthday present. He gathered in Mr. van Tuyl, of whose taste in these matters he had a high opinion, and dragged him off to a jeweller's on Broadway.

The jeweller, a stout, comfortable man, leaned on the counter and fingered lovingly the bracelet which he had lifted out of its nest of blue plush. Archie, leaning on the other side of the counter, inspected the bracelet searchingly, wishing that he knew more about these things; for he had rather a sort of idea that the merchant was scheming to do him in the eyeball. In a chair by his side, Reggie van Tuyl, half asleep as usual, yawned despondently. He had permitted Archie to lug him into this shop; and he wanted to buy something and go. Any form of sustained concentration fatigued Reggie.

"Now this," said the jeweller, "I could do at eight hundred and fifty dollars."

"Grab it!" murmured Mr. van Tuyl.

The jeweller eyed him approvingly, a man after his own heart; but Archie looked doubtful. It was all very well for Reggie to tell him to grab it in that careless way. Reggie was a dashed millionaire, and no doubt bought bracelets by the pound or the gross or what not; but he himself was in an entirely different position.

"Eight hundred and fifty dollars!" he said, hesitating.

"Worth it," mumbled Reggie van Tuyl.

"More than worth it," amended the jeweller. "I can assure you that it is better value than you could get anywhere on Fifth Avenue."

"Yes?" said Archie. He took the bracelet and twiddled it thoughtfully. "Well, my dear old jeweller, one can't say fairer than that, can one—or two, as the case may be!" He frowned. "Oh, well, all right! But it's rummy that women are so fearfully keen on these little thingummies, isn't it? I mean to say, can't see what they see in them. Stones, and all that. Still, there, it is, of course!"

"There," said the jeweller, "as you say, it is, sir."

"Yes, there it is!"

"Yes, there it is," said the jeweller, "fortunately for people in my line of business. Will you take it with you, sir?"

Archie reflected.

"No. No, not take it with me. The fact is, you know, my wife's coming back from the country to-night, and it's her birthday to-morrow, and the thing's for her, and, if it was popping about the place to-night, she might see it, and it would sort of spoil the surprise. I mean to say, she doesn't know I'm giving it her, and all that!"

"Besides," said Reggie, achieving a certain animation now that the tedious business interview was concluded, "going to the ball-game this afternoon—might get pocket picked—yes, better have it sent."

"Where shall I send it, sir?"

"Eh? Oh, shoot it along to Mrs. Archibald Moffam, at the Cosmopolis. Not to-day, you know. Buzz it in first thing to-morrow."

Having completed the satisfactory deal, the jeweller threw off the business manner and became chatty.

"So you are going to the ball-game? It should be an interesting contest."

Reggie van Tuyl, now—by his own standards—completely awake, took exception to this remark.

"Not a bit of it!" he said, decidedly. "No contest! Can't call it a contest! Walkover for the Pirates!"

Archie was stung to the quick. There is that about baseball which arouses enthusiasm and the partisan spirit in the unlikeliest bosoms. It is almost impossible for a man to live in America and not become gripped by the game; and Archie had long been one of its warmest adherents. He was a whole-hearted supporter of the Giants, and his only grievance against Reggie, in other respects an estimable young man, was that the latter, whose money had been inherited from steel-mills in that city, had an absurd regard for the Pirates of Pittsburg.

"What absolute bally rot!" he exclaimed. "Look what the Giants did to them yesterday!"

"Yesterday isn't to-day," said Reggie.

"No, it'll be a jolly sight worse," said Archie. "Looney Biddle'll be pitching for the Giants to-day."

"That's just what I mean. The Pirates have got him rattled. Look what happened last time."

Archie understood, and his generous nature chafed at the innuendo. Looney Biddle—so-called by an affectionately admiring public as the result of certain marked eccentricities—was beyond dispute the greatest left-handed pitcher New York had possessed in the last decade. But there was one blot on Mr. Biddle's otherwise stainless scutcheon. Five weeks before, on the occasion of the Giants' invasion of Pittsburg, he had gone mysteriously to pieces. Few native-born partisans, brought up to baseball from the cradle, had been plunged into a profounder gloom on that occasion than Archie; but his soul revolted at the thought that that sort of thing could ever happen again.

"I'm not saying," continued Reggie, "that Biddle isn't a very fair pitcher, but it's cruel to send him against the Pirates, and somebody ought to stop it. His best friends should interfere. Once a team gets a pitcher rattled, he's never any good against them again. He loses his nerve."

The jeweller nodded approval of this sentiment.

"They never come back," he said, sententiously.

The fighting blood of the Moffams was now thoroughly stirred. Archie eyed his friend sternly. Reggie was a good chap—in many respects an extremely sound egg—but he must not be allowed

89

to talk rot of this description about the greatest left-handed pitcher of the age.

"It seems to me, old companion," he said, "that a small bet is indicated at this juncture. How about it?"

"Don't want to take your money."

"You won't have to! In the cool twilight of the merry old summer evening I, friend of my youth and companion of my riper years, shall be trousering yours."

Reggie yawned. The day was very hot, and this argument was making him feel sleepy again.

"Well, just as you like, of course. Double or quits on yesterday's bet, if that suits you."

For a moment Archie hesitated. Firm as his faith was in Mr. Biddle's stout left arm, he had not intended to do the thing on quite this scale. That thousand dollars of his was earmarked for Lucille's birthday present, and he doubted whether he ought to risk it. Then the thought that the honour of New York was in his hands decided him. Besides, the risk was negligible. Betting on Looney Biddle was like betting on the probable rise of the sun in the east. The thing began to seem to Archie a rather unusually sound and conservative investment. He remembered that the jeweller, until he drew him firmly but kindly to earth and urged him to curb his exuberance and talk business on a reasonable plane, had started brandishing bracelets that cost about two thousand. There would be time to pop in at the shop this evening after the game and change the one he had selected for one of those. Nothing was too good for Lucille on her birthday.

"Right-o!" he said. "Make it so, old friend!"

Archie walked back to the Cosmopolis. No misgivings came to mar his perfect contentment. He felt no qualms about separating Reggie from another thousand dollars. Except for a little small change in the possession of the Messrs. Rockefeller and Vincent Astor, Reggie had all the money in the world and could afford to lose. He hummed a gay air as he entered the lobby and crossed to the cigar-stand to buy a few cigarettes to see him through the afternoon.

The girl behind the cigar counter welcomed him with a bright smile. Archie was popular with all the employes of the Cosmopolis.

"'S a great day, Mr. Moffam!"

"One of the brightest and best," Agreed Archie. "Could you dig me out two, or possibly three, cigarettes of the usual description? I shall want something to smoke at the ball-game."

"You going to the ball-game?"

"Rather! Wouldn't miss it for a fortune."

"No?"

"Absolutely no! Not with jolly old Biddle pitching."

The cigar-stand girl laughed amusedly.

"Is he pitching this afternoon? Say, that feller's a nut? D'you know him?"

"Know him? Well, I've seen him pitch and so forth."

"I've got a girl friend who's engaged to him!"

Archie looked at her with positive respect. It would have been more dramatic, of course, if she had been engaged to the great man herself, but still the mere fact that she had a girl friend in that astounding position gave her a sort of halo.

"No, really!" he said. "I say, by Jove, really! Fancy that!"

"Yes, she's engaged to him all right. Been engaged close on a coupla months now."

"I say! That's frightfully interesting! Fearfully interesting, really!"

"It's funny about that guy," said the cigar-stand girl. "He's a nut! The fellow who said there's plenty of room at the top must have been thinking of Gus Biddle's head! He's crazy about m' girl friend, y' know, and, whenever they have a fuss, it seems like he sort of flies right off the handle."

"Goes in off the deep end, eh?"

"Yes, SIR! Loses what little sense he's got. Why, the last time him and m' girl friend got to scrapping was when he was going on to Pittsburg to play, about a month ago. He'd been out with her the day he left for there, and he had a grouch or something, and he started making low, sneaky cracks about her Uncle Sigsbee. Well, m' girl friend's got a nice disposition, but she c'n get mad, and she just left him flat and told him all was over. And he went off to Pittsburg, and, when he started in to pitch the opening game, he just couldn't keep his mind on his job, and look what them assassins done to him! Five runs in the first innings! Yessir, he's a nut all right!"

Archie was deeply concerned. So this was the explanation of that mysterious disaster, that weird tragedy which had puzzled the sporting press from coast to coast.

"Good God! Is he often taken like that?"

"Oh, he's all right when he hasn't had a fuss with m' girl friend," said the cigar-stand girl, indifferently. Her interest in baseball was tepid. Women are too often like this—mere butterflies, with no concern for the deeper side of life.

"Yes, but I say! What I mean to say, you know! Are they pretty pally now? The good old Dove of Peace flapping its little wings fairly briskly and all that?"

"Oh, I guess everything's nice and smooth just now. I seen m' girl friend yesterday, and Gus was taking her to the movies last night, so I guess everything's nice and smooth."

Archie breathed a sigh of relief.

"Took her to the movies, did he? Stout fellow!"

"I was at the funniest picture last week," said the cigar-stand girl. "Honest, it was a scream! It was like this—"

Archie listened politely; then went in to get a bite of lunch. His equanimity, shaken by the discovery of the rift in the peerless one's armour, was restored. Good old Biddle had taken the girl to the movies last night. Probably he had squeezed her hand a goodish bit in the dark. With what result? Why, the fellow would be feeling like one of those chappies who used to joust for the smiles of females in the Middle Ages. What he meant to say, presumably the girl would be at the game this afternoon, whooping him on, and good old Biddle would be so full of beans and buck that there would be no holding him.

Encouraged by these thoughts, Archie lunched with an untroubled mind. Luncheon concluded, he proceeded to the lobby to buy back his hat and stick from the boy brigand with whom he had left them. It was while he was conducting this financial operation that he observed that at the cigar-stand, which adjoined the coat-and-hat alcove, his friend behind the counter had become engaged in conversation with another girl.

This was a determined looking young woman in a blue dress and a large hat of a bold and flowery species, Archie happening to attract her attention, she gave him a glance out of a pair of fine brown eyes, then, as if she did not think much of him, turned to her companion and resumed their conversation—which, being of an essentially private and intimate nature, she conducted, after the manner of her kind, in a ringing soprano which penetrated into every corner of the lobby. Archie, waiting while the brigand reluctantly made change for a dollar bill, was privileged to hear every word.

"Right from the start I seen he was in a ugly mood. YOU know how he gets, dearie! Chewing his upper lip and looking at you as if you were so much dirt beneath his feet! How was I to know he'd lost fifteen dollars fifty-five playing poker, and anyway, I don't see where he gets a licence to work off his grouches on me. And I told him so. I said to him, 'Gus,' I said, 'if you can't be bright and smiling and cheerful when you take me out, why do you come round at all? Was I wrong or right, dearie?"

The girl behind the counter heartily endorsed her conduct. "Once you let a man think he could use you as a door-mat, where were you?"

"What happened then, honey?"

"Well, after that we went to the movies."

Archie started convulsively. The change from his dollar-bill leaped in his hand. Some of it sprang overboard and tinkled across the floor, with the brigand in pursuit. A monstrous suspicion had begun, to take root in his mind.

"Well, we got good seats, but—well, you know how it is, once things start going wrong. You know that hat of mine, the one with the daisies and cherries and the feather—I'd taken it off and given it him to hold when we went in, and what do you think that fell'r'd done? Put it on the floor and crammed it under the seat, just to save himself the trouble of holding it on his lap! And, when I showed him I was upset, all he said was that he was a pitcher and not a hatstand!"

Archie was paralysed. He paid no attention to the hat-check boy, who was trying to induce him to accept treasure-trove to the amount of forty-five cents. His whole being was concentrated on this frightful tragedy which had burst upon him like a tidal wave. No possible room for doubt remained. "Gus" was the only Gus in New York that mattered, and this resolute and injured female before him was the Girl Friend, in whose slim hands rested the happiness of New York's baseball followers, the destiny of the unconscious Giants, and the fate of his thousand dollars. A strangled croak proceeded from his parched lips.

"Well, I didn't say anything at the moment. It just shows how them movies can work on a girl's feelings. It was a Bryant Washburn film, and somehow, whenever I see him on the screen, nothing else seems to matter. I just get that goo-ey feeling, and couldn't start a fight if you asked me to. So we go off to have a soda, and I said to him, 'That sure was a lovely film, Gus!' and would you believe me, he says straight out that he didn't think it was such a much, and he thought Bryant Washburn was a pill! A pill!" The Girl Friend's penetrating voice shook with emotion.

"He never!" exclaimed the shocked cigar-stand girl.

"He did, if I die the next moment! I wasn't more than half-way through my vanilla and maple, but I got up without a word and left him. And I ain't seen a sight of him since. So there you are, dearie! Was I right or wrong?"

The cigar-stand girl gave unqualified approval. What men like Gus Biddle needed for the salvation of their souls was an occasional good jolt right where it would do most good.

"I'm glad you think I acted right, dearie," said the Girl Friend. "I guess I've been too weak with Gus, and he's took advantage of it. I

93

s'pose I'll have to forgive him one of these old days, but, believe me, it won't be for a week."

The cigar-stand girl was in favour of a fortnight.

"No," said the Girl Friend, regretfully. "I don't believe I could hold out that long. But, if I speak to him inside a week, well—! Well, I gotta be going. Goodbye, honey."

The cigar-stand girl turned to attend to an impatient customer, and the Girl Friend, walking with the firm and decisive steps which indicate character, made for the swing-door leading to the street. And as she went, the paralysis which had pipped Archie released its hold. Still ignoring the forty-five cents which the boy continued to proffer, he leaped in her wake like a panther and came upon her just as she was stepping into a car. The car was full, but not too full for Archie. He dropped his five cents into the box and reached for a vacant strap. He looked down upon the flowered hat. There she was. And there he was. Archie rested his left ear against the forearm of a long, strongly-built young man in a grey suit who had followed him into the car and was sharing his strap, and pondered.

CHAPTER XV

SUMMER STORMS

Of course, in a way, the thing was simple. The wheeze was, in a sense, straightforward and uncomplicated. What he wanted to do was to point out to the injured girl all that hung on her. He wished to touch her heart, to plead with her, to desire her to restate her war-aims, and to persuade her—before three o'clock when that stricken gentleman would be stepping into the pitcher's box to loose off the first ball against the Pittsburg Pirates—to let bygones be bygones and forgive Augustus Biddle. But the blighted problem was, how the deuce to find the opportunity to start. He couldn't yell at the girl in a crowded street-car; and, if he let go of his strap and bent over her, somebody would step on his neck.

The Girl Friend, who for the first five minutes had remained entirely concealed beneath her hat, now sought diversion by looking up and examining the faces of the upper strata of passengers. Her eye caught Archie's in a glance of recognition, and he smiled feebly, endeavouring to register bonhomie and good-will. He was surprised to see a startled expression come into her brown eyes. Her face turned pink. At least, it was pink already, but it turned pinker. The next moment, the car having stopped to pick up more passengers, she jumped off and started to hurry across the street.

Archie was momentarily taken aback. When embarking on this business he had never intended it to become a blend of otter-hunting and a moving-picture chase. He followed her off the car with a sense that his grip on the affair was slipping. Preoccupied with these thoughts, he did not perceive that the long young man who had shared his strap had alighted too. His eyes were fixed on the vanishing figure of the Girl Friend, who, having buzzed at a smart pace into Sixth Avenue, was now legging it in the direction of the staircase leading to one of the stations of the Elevated Railroad. Dashing up the stairs after her, he shortly afterwards found himself suspended as before from a strap, gazing upon the now familiar flowers on top of her hat. From another strap farther down the carriage swayed the long young man in the grey suit.

The train rattled on. Once or twice, when it stopped, the girl seemed undecided whether to leave or remain. She half rose, then sank back again. Finally she walked resolutely out of the car, and Archie, following, found himself in a part of New York strange to him. The inhabitants of this district appeared to eke out a precarious existence, not by taking in one another's washing, but by selling one another second-hand clothes.

Archie glanced at his watch. He had lunched early, but so crowded with emotions had been the period following lunch that he was surprised to find that the hour was only just two. The discovery was a pleasant one. With a full hour before the scheduled start of the game, much might be achieved. He hurried after the girl, and came up with her just as she turned the corner into one of those forlorn New York side-streets which are populated chiefly by children, cats, desultory loafers, and empty meat-tins.

The girl stopped and turned. Archie smiled a winning smile.

"I say, my dear sweet creature!" he said. "I say, my dear old thing, one moment!"

"Is that so?" said the Girl Friend.

"I beg your pardon?"

"Is that so?"

Archie began to feel certain tremors. Her eyes were gleaming, and her determined mouth had become a perfectly straight line of scarlet. It was going to be difficult to be chatty to this girl. She was going to be a hard audience. Would mere words be able to touch her heart? The thought suggested itself that, properly speaking, one would need to use a pick-axe.

"If you could spare me a couples of minutes of your valuable time—"

"Say!" The lady drew herself up menacingly. "You tie a can to yourself and disappear! Fade away, or I'll call a cop!"

Archie was horrified at this misinterpretation of his motives. One or two children, playing close at hand, and a loafer who was trying to keep the wall from falling down, seemed pleased. Theirs was a colourless existence and to the rare purple moments which had enlivened it in the past the calling of a cop had been the unfailing preliminary. The loafer nudged a fellow-loafer, sunning himself against the same wall. The children, abandoning the meat-tin round which their game had centred, drew closer.

"My dear old soul!" said Archie. "You don't understand!"

"Don't I! I know your sort, you trailing arbutus!"

"No, no! My dear old thing, believe me! I wouldn't dream!"

"Are you going or aren't you?"

Eleven more children joined the ring of spectators. The loafers stared silently, like awakened crocodiles.

"But, I say, listen! I only wanted—"

At this point another voice spoke.

"Say!"

The word "Say!" more almost than any word in the American language, is capable of a variety of shades of expression. It can be genial, it can be jovial, it can be appealing. It can also be truculent The "Say!" which at this juncture smote upon Archie's ear-drum with a suddenness which made him leap in the air was truculent; and the two loafers and twenty-seven children who now formed the audience were well satisfied with the dramatic development of the performance. To their experienced ears the word had the right ring.

Archie spun round. At his elbow stood a long, strongly-built young man in a grey suit.

"Well!" said the young man, nastily. And he extended a large, freckled face toward Archie's. It seemed to the latter, as he backed against the wall, that the young man's neck must be composed of india-rubber. It appeared to be growing longer every moment. His face, besides being freckled, was a dull brick-red in colour; his lips curled back in an unpleasant snarl, showing a gold tooth; and beside him, swaying in an ominous sort of way, hung two clenched red hands about the size of two young legs of mutton. Archie eyed him with a growing apprehension. There are moments in life when, passing idly on our way, we see a strange face, look into strange eyes, and with a sudden glow of human warmth say to ourselves, "We have found a friend!" This was not one of those moments. The only person Archie had ever seen in his life who looked less friendly was the sergeant-major who had trained him in the early days of the war, before he had got his commission.

"I've had my eye on you!" said the young man.

He still had his eye on him. It was a hot, gimlet-like eye, and it pierced the recesses of Archie's soul. He backed a little farther against the wall.

Archie was frankly disturbed. He was no poltroon, and had proved the fact on many occasions during the days when the entire German army seemed to be picking on him personally, but he hated and shrank from anything in the nature of a bally public scene.

"What," enquired the young man, still bearing the burden of the conversation, and shifting his left hand a little farther behind his back, "do you mean by following this young lady?"

Archie was glad he had asked him. This was precisely what he wanted to explain.

"My dear old lad—" he began.

In spite of the fact that he had asked a question and presumably desired a reply, the sound of Archie's voice seemed to be more than the young man could endure. It deprived him of the

97

last vestige of restraint. With a rasping snarl he brought his left fist round in a sweeping semicircle in the direction of Archie's head.

Archie was no novice in the art of self-defence. Since his early days at school he had learned much from leather-faced professors of the science. He had been watching this unpleasant young man's eyes with close attention, and the latter could not have indicated his scheme of action more clearly if he had sent him a formal note. Archie saw the swing all the way. He stepped nimbly aside, and the fist crashed against the wall. The young man fell back with a yelp of anguish.

"Gus!" screamed the Girl Friend, bounding forward.

She flung her arms round the injured man, who was ruefully examining a hand which, always of an out-size, was now swelling to still further dimensions.

"Gus, darling!"

A sudden chill gripped Archie. So engrossed had he been with his mission that it had never occurred to him that the love-lorn pitcher might have taken it into his head to follow the girl as well in the hope of putting in a word for himself. Yet such apparently had been the case. Well, this had definitely torn it. Two loving hearts were united again in complete reconciliation, but a fat lot of good that was. It would be days before the misguided Looney Biddle would be able to pitch with a hand like that. It looked like a ham already, and was still swelling. Probably the wrist was sprained. For at least a week the greatest left-handed pitcher of his time would be about as much use to the Giants in any professional capacity as a cold in the head. And on that crippled hand depended the fate of all the money Archie had in the world. He wished now that he had not thwarted the fellow's simple enthusiasm. To have had his head knocked forcibly through a brick wall would not have been pleasant, but the ultimate outcome would not have been as unpleasant as this. With a heavy heart Archie prepared to withdraw, to be alone with his sorrow.

At this moment, however, the Girl Friend, releasing her wounded lover, made a sudden dash for him, with the plainest intention of blotting him from the earth.

"No, I say! Really!" said Archie, bounding backwards. "I mean to say!"

In a series of events, all of which had been a bit thick, this, in his opinion, achieved the maximum of thickness. It was the extreme ragged, outside edge of the limit. To brawl with a fellow-man in a public street had been bad, but to be brawled with by a girl—the shot was not on the board. Absolutely not on the board. There was only one thing to be done. It was dashed undignified, no doubt, for a fellow to pick up the old waukeesis and leg it in the face of the enemy, but there was no other course. Archie started to run; and, as he did so, one of the loafers made the mistake of gripping him by the collar of his coat.

"I got him!" observed the loafer.-There is a time for all things. This was essentially not the time for anyone of the male sex to grip the collar of Archie's coat. If a syndicate of Dempsey, Carpentier, and one of the Zoo gorillas had endeavoured to stay his progress at that moment, they would have had reason to consider it a rash move. Archie wanted to be elsewhere, and the blood of generations of Moffams, many of whom had swung a wicked axe in the free-for-all mix-ups of the Middle Ages, boiled within him at any attempt to revise his plans. There was a good deal of the loafer, but it was all soft. Releasing his hold when Archie's heel took him shrewdly on the shin, he received a nasty punch in what would have been the middle of his waistcoat if he had worn one, uttered a gurgling bleat like a wounded sheep, and collapsed against the wall. Archie, with a torn coat, rounded the corner, and sprinted down Ninth Avenue.

The suddenness of the move gave him an initial advantage. He was halfway down the first block before the vanguard of the pursuit poured out of the side street. Continuing to travel well, he skimmed past a large dray which had pulled up across the road, and moved on. The noise of those who pursued was loud and clamorous in the rear, but the dray hid him momentarily from their sight, and it was this fact which led Archie, the old campaigner, to take his next step.

It was perfectly obvious—he was aware of this even in the novel excitement of the chase—that a chappie couldn't hoof it at twenty-five miles an hour indefinitely along a main thoroughfare of a great city without exciting remark. He must take cover. Cover! That was the wheeze. He looked about him for cover.

"You want a nice suit?"

It takes a great deal to startle your commercial New Yorker. The small tailor, standing in his doorway, seemed in no way surprised at the spectacle of Archie, whom he had seen pass at a conventional walk some five minutes before, returning like this at top speed. He assumed that Archie had suddenly remembered that he wanted to buy something.

This was exactly what Archie had done. More than anything else in the world, what he wanted to do now was to get into that shop and have a long talk about gents' clothing. Pulling himself up abruptly, he shot past the small tailor into the dim interior. A confused aroma of cheap clothing greeted him. Except for a small

99

oasis behind a grubby counter, practically all the available space was occupied by suits. Stiff suits, looking like the body when discovered by the police, hung from hooks. Limp suits, with the appearance of having swooned from exhaustion, lay about on chairs and boxes. The place was a cloth morgue, a Sargasso Sea of serge.

Archie would not have had it otherwise. In these quiet groves of clothing a regiment could have lain hid.

"Something nifty in tweeds?" enquired the business-like proprietor of this haven, following him amiably into the shop, "Or, maybe, yes, a nice serge? Say, mister, I got a sweet thing in blue serge that'll fit you like the paper on the wall!"

Archie wanted to talk about clothes, but not yet.

"I say, laddie," he said, hurriedly. "Lend me, your ear for half a jiffy!" Outside the baying of the pack had become imminent. "Stow me away for a moment in the undergrowth, and I'll buy anything you want."

He withdrew into the jungle. The noise outside grew in volume. The pursuit had been delayed for a priceless few instants by the arrival of another dray, moving northwards, which had drawn level with the first dray and dexterously bottled up the fairway. This obstacle had now been overcome, and the original searchers, their ranks swelled by a few dozen more of the leisured classes, were hot on the trail again.

"You done a murder?" enquired the voice of the proprietor, mildly interested, filtering through a wall of cloth. "Well, boys will be boys!" he said, philosophically. "See anything there that you like? There some sweet things there!"

"I'm inspecting them narrowly," replied Archie. "If you don't let those chappies find me, I shouldn't be surprised if I bought one."

"One?" said the proprietor, with a touch of austerity.

"Two," said Archie, quickly. "Or possibly three or six."

The proprietor's cordiality returned.

"You can't have too many nice suits," he said, approvingly, "not a young feller like you that wants to look nice. All the nice girls like a young feller that dresses nice. When you go out of here in a suit I got hanging up there at the back, the girls 'll be all over you like flies round a honey-pot."

"Would you mind," said Archie, "would you mind, as a personal favour to me, old companion, not mentioning that word 'girls'?"

He broke off. A heavy foot had crossed the threshold of the shop.

"Say, uncle," said a deep voice, one of those beastly voices that

100

only the most poisonous blighters have, "you seen a young feller run past here?"

"Young feller?" The proprietor appeared to reflect. "Do you mean a young feller in blue, with a Homburg hat?"

"That's the duck! We lost him. Where did he go?"

"Him! Why, he come running past, quick as he could go. I wondered what he was running for, a hot day like this. He went round the corner at the bottom of the block."

There was a silence.

"Well, I guess he's got away," said the voice, regretfully.

"The way he was travelling," agreed the proprietor, "I wouldn't be surprised if he was in Europe by this. You want a nice suit?"

The other, curtly expressing a wish that the proprietor would go to eternal perdition and take his entire stock with him, stumped out.

"This," said the proprietor, tranquilly, burrowing his way to where Archie stood and exhibiting a saffron-coloured outrage, which appeared to be a poor relation of the flannel family, "would put you back fifty dollars. And cheap!"

"Fifty dollars!"

"Sixty, I said. I don't speak always distinct."

Archie regarded the distressing garment with a shuddering horror. A young man with an educated taste in clothes, it got right in among his nerve centres.

"But, honestly, old soul, I don't want to hurt your feelings, but that isn't a suit, it's just a regrettable incident!"

The proprietor turned to the door in a listening attitude.

"I believe I hear that feller coming back," he said.

Archie gulped.

"How about trying it on?" he said. "I'm not sure, after all, it isn't fairly ripe."

"That's the way to talk," said the proprietor, cordially. "You try it on. You can't judge a suit, not a real nice suit like this, by looking at it. You want to put it on. There!" He led the way to a dusty mirror at the back of the shop. "Isn't that a bargain at seventy dollars?...Why, say, your mother would be proud if she could see her boy now!"

A quarter of an hour later, the proprietor, lovingly kneading a little sheaf of currency bills, eyed with a fond look the heap of clothes which lay on the counter.

"As nice a little lot as I've ever had in my shop!" Archie did not deny this. It was, he thought, probably only too true.

"I only wish I could see you walking up Fifth Avenue in them!" rhapsodised the proprietor. "You'll give 'em a treat! What you going to do with 'em? Carry 'em under your arm?" Archie shuddered strongly. "Well, then, I can send 'em for you anywhere you like. It's all the same to me. Where'll I send 'em?"

Archie meditated. The future was black enough as it was. He shrank from the prospect of being confronted next day, at the height of his misery, with these appalling reach-me-downs.

An idea struck him.

"Yes, send 'em," he said.

"What's the name and address?"

"Daniel Brewster," said Archie, "Hotel Cosmopolis."

It was a long time since he had given his father-in-law a present.

Archie went out into the street, and began to walk pensively down a now peaceful Ninth Avenue. Out of the depths that covered him, black as the pit from pole to pole, no single ray of hope came to cheer him. He could not, like the poet, thank whatever gods there be for his unconquerable soul, for his soul was licked to a splinter. He felt alone and friendless in a rotten world. With the best intentions, he had succeeded only in landing himself squarely amongst the ribstons. Why had he not been content with his wealth, instead of risking it on that blighted bet with Reggie? Why had he trailed the Girl Friend, dash her! He might have known that he would only make an ass of himself, And, because he had done so, Looney Biddle's left hand, that priceless left hand before which opposing batters quailed and wilted, was out of action, resting in a sling, careened like a damaged battleship; and any chance the Giants might have had of beating the Pirates was gone—gone—as surely as that thousand dollars which should have bought a birthday present for Lucille.

A birthday present for Lucille! He groaned in bitterness of spirit. She would be coming back to-night, dear girl, all smiles and happiness, wondering what he was going to give her tomorrow. And when to-morrow dawned, all he would be able to give her would be a kind smile. A nice state of things! A jolly situation! A thoroughly good egg, he did NOT think!

It seemed to Archie that Nature, contrary to her usual custom of indifference to human suffering, was mourning with him. The sky was overcast, and the sun had ceased to shine. There was a sort of sombreness in the afternoon, which fitted in with his mood. And then something splashed on his face.

It says much for Archie's pre-occupation that his first thought, as, after a few scattered drops, as though the clouds were submitting samples for approval, the whole sky suddenly began to stream like a shower-bath, was that this was simply an additional infliction which he was called upon to bear, On top of all his other troubles he would get soaked to the skin or have to hang about in some doorway. He cursed richly, and sped for shelter.

The rain was setting about its work in earnest. The world was full of that rending, swishing sound which accompanies the more violent summer storms. Thunder crashed, and lightning flicked out of the grey heavens. Out in the street the raindrops bounded up off the stones like fairy fountains. Archie surveyed them morosely from his refuge in the entrance of a shop.

And then, suddenly, like one of those flashes which were lighting up the gloomy sky, a thought lit up his mind.

"By Jove! If this keeps up, there won't be a ball-game to-day!"

With trembling fingers he pulled out his watch. The hands pointed to five minutes to three. A blessed vision came to him of a moist and disappointed crowd receiving rain-checks up at the Polo Grounds.

"Switch it on, you blighters!" he cried, addressing the leaden clouds. "Switch it on more and more!"

It was shortly before five o'clock that a young man bounded into a jeweller's shop near the Hotel Cosmopolis—a young man who, in spite of the fact that his coat was torn near the collar and that he oozed water from every inch of his drenched clothes, appeared in the highest spirits.. It was only when he spoke that the jeweller recognised in the human sponge the immaculate youth who had looked in that morning to order a bracelet.

"I say, old lad," said this young man, "you remember that jolly little what-not you showed me before lunch?"

"The bracelet, sir?"

"As you observe with a manly candour which does you credit, my dear old jeweller, the bracelet. Well, produce, exhibit, and bring it forth, would you mind? Trot it out! Slip it across on a lordly dish!"

"You wished me, surely, to put it aside and send it to the Cosmopolis to-morrow?"

The young man tapped the jeweller earnestly on his substantial chest.

"What I wished and what I wish now are two bally separate and dashed distinct things, friend of my college days! Never put off till to-morrow what you can do to-day, and all that! I'm not taking any more chances. Not for me! For others, yes, but not for

103

Archibald! Here are the doubloons, produce the jolly bracelet Thanks!"

The jeweller counted the notes with the same unction which Archie had observed earlier in the day in the proprietor of the second-hand clothes-shop. The process made him genial.

"A nasty, wet day, sir, it's been," he observed, chattily.

Archie shook his head.

"Old friend," he said, "you're all wrong. Far otherwise, and not a bit like it, my dear old trafficker in gems! You've put your finger on the one aspect of this blighted p.m. that really deserves credit and respect. Rarely in the experience of a lifetime have I encountered a day so absolutely bally in nearly every shape and form, but there was one thing that saved it, and that was its merry old wetness! Toodle-oo, laddie!"

"Good evening, sir," said the jeweller.

CHAPTER XVI

ARCHIE ACCEPTS A SITUATION

Lucille moved her wrist slowly round, the better to examine the new bracelet.

"You really are an angel, angel!" she murmured.

"Like it?" said Archie complacently.

"LIKE it! Why, it's gorgeous! It must have cost a fortune."

"Oh, nothing to speak of. Just a few hard-earned pieces of eight. Just a few doubloons from the old oak chest."

"But I didn't know there were any doubloons in the old oak chest."

"Well, as a matter of fact," admitted Archie, "at one point in the proceedings there weren't. But an aunt of mine in England—peace be on her head!—happened to send me a chunk of the necessary at what you might call the psychological moment."

"And you spent it all on a birthday present for me! Archie!" Lucille gazed at her husband adoringly. "Archie, do you know what I think?"

"What?"

"You're the perfect man!"

"No, really! What ho!"

"Yes," said Lucille firmly. "I've long suspected it, and now I know. I don't think there's anybody like you in the world."

Archie patted her hand.

"It's a rummy thing," he observed, "but your father said almost exactly that to me only yesterday. Only I don't fancy he meant the same as you. To be absolutely frank, his exact expression was that he thanked God there was only one of me."

A troubled look came into Lucille's grey eyes.

"It's a shame about father. I do wish he appreciated you. But you mustn't be too hard on him."

"Me?" said Archie. "Hard on your father? Well, dash it all, I don't think I treat him with what you might call actual brutality, what! I mean to say, my whole idea is rather to keep out of the old lad's way and curl up in a ball if I can't dodge him. I'd just as soon be hard on a stampeding elephant! I wouldn't for the world say anything derogatory, as it were, to your jolly old pater, but there is no getting away from the fact that he's by way of being one of our leading man-eating fishes. It would be idle to deny that he considers

105

that you let down the proud old name of Brewster a bit when you brought me in and laid me on the mat."

"Anyone would be lucky to get you for a son-in-law, precious."

"I fear me, light of my life, the dad doesn't see eye to eye with you on that point. No, every time I get hold of a daisy, I give him another chance, but it always works out at 'He loves me not!'"

"You must make allowances for him, darling."

"Right-o! But I hope devoutly that he doesn't catch me at it. I've a sort of idea that if the old dad discovered that I was making allowances for him, he would have from ten to fifteen fits."

"He's worried just now, you know."

"I didn't know. He doesn't confide in me much."

"He's worried about that waiter."

"What waiter, queen of my soul?"

"A man called Salvatore. Father dismissed him some time ago."

"Salvatore!"

"Probably you don't remember him. He used to wait on this table."

"Why—"

"And father dismissed him, apparently, and now there's all sorts of trouble. You see, father wants to build this new hotel of his, and he thought he'd got the site and everything and could start building right away: and now he finds that this man Salvatore's mother owns a little newspaper and tobacco shop right in the middle of the site, and there's no way of getting him out without buying the shop, and he won't sell. At least, he's made his mother promise that she won't sell."

"A boy's best friend is his mother," said Archie approvingly. "I had a sort of idea all along—"

"So father's in despair."

Archie drew at his cigarette meditatively.

"I remember a chappie—a policeman he was, as a matter of fact, and incidentally a fairly pronounced blighter—remarking to me some time ago that you could trample on the poor man's face but you mustn't be surprised if he bit you in the leg while you were doing it. Apparently this is what has happened to the old dad. I had a sort of idea all along that old friend Salvatore would come out strong in the end if you only gave him time. Brainy sort of feller! Great pal of mine."—Lucille's small face lightened. She gazed at Archie with proud affection. She felt that she ought to have known that he was the one to solve this difficulty.

"You're wonderful, darling! Is he really a friend of yours?"

"Absolutely. Many's the time he and I have chatted in this very grill-room."

"Then it's all right. If you went to him and argued with him, he would agree to sell the shop, and father would be happy. Think how grateful father would be to you! It would make all the difference."

Archie turned this over in his mind.

"Something in that," he agreed.

"It would make him see what a pet lambkin you really are!"

"Well," said Archie, "I'm bound to say that any scheme which what you might call culminates in your father regarding me as a pet lambkin ought to receive one's best attention. How much did he offer Salvatore for his shop?"

"I don't know. There is father.—Call him over and ask him."

Archie glanced over to where Mr. Brewster had sunk moodily into a chair at a neighbouring table. It was plain even at that distance that Daniel Brewster had his troubles and was bearing them with an ill grace. He was scowling absently at the table-cloth.

"YOU call him," said Archie, having inspected his formidable relative. "You know him better."

"Let's go over to him."

They crossed the room. Lucille sat down opposite her father.- Archie draped himself over a chair in the background.

"Father, dear," said Lucille. "Archie has got an idea."

"Archie?" said Mr. Brewster incredulously.

"This is me," said Archie, indicating himself with a spoon. "The tall, distinguished-looking bird."

"What new fool-thing is he up to now?"

"It's a splendid idea, father. He wants to help you over your new hotel."

"Wants to run it for me, I suppose?"

"By Jove!" said Archie, reflectively. "That's not a bad scheme! I never thought of running an hotel. I shouldn't mind taking a stab at it."

"He has thought of a way of getting rid of Salvatore and his shop."

For the first time Mr. Brewster's interest in the conversation seemed to stir. He looked sharply at his son-in-law.

"He has, has he?" he said.

Archie balanced a roll on a fork and inserted a plate underneath. The roll bounded away into a corner.

"Sorry!" said Archie. "My fault, absolutely! I owe you a roll. I'll sign a bill for it. Oh, about this sportsman Salvatore, Well, it's like this, you know. He and I are great pals. I've known him for years and years. At least, it seems like years and years. Lu was suggesting that I seek him out in his lair and ensnare him with my diplomatic manner and superior brain power and what not."

"It was your idea, precious," said Lucille.

Mr. Brewster was silent.—Much as it went against the grain to have to admit it, there seemed to be something in this.

"What do you propose to do?"

"Become a jolly old ambassador. How much did you offer the chappie?"

"Three thousand dollars. Twice as much as the place is worth. He's holding out on me for revenge."

"Ah, but how did you offer it to him, what? I mean to say, I bet you got your lawyer to write him a letter full of whereases, peradventures, and parties of the first part, and so forth. No good, old companion!"

"Don't call me old companion!"

"All wrong, laddie! Nothing like it, dear heart! No good at all, friend of my youth! Take it from your Uncle Archibald! I'm a student of human nature, and I know a thing or two."

"That's not much," growled Mr. Brewster, who was finding his son-in-law's superior manner a little trying.

"Now, don't interrupt, father," said Lucille, severely. "Can't you see that Archie is going to be tremendously clever in a minute?"

"He's got to show me!"

"What you ought to do," said Archie, "is to let me go and see him, taking the stuff in crackling bills. I'll roll them about on the table in front of him. That'll fetch him!" He prodded Mr. Brewster encouragingly with a roll. "I'll tell you what to do. Give me three thousand of the best and crispest, and I'll undertake to buy that shop. It can't fail, laddie!"

"Don't call me laddie!" Mr. Brewster pondered. "Very well," he said at last. "I didn't know you had so much sense," he added grudgingly.

"Oh, positively!" said Archie. "Beneath a rugged exterior I hide a brain like a buzz-saw. Sense? I exude it, laddie; I drip with it."

There were moments during the ensuing days when Mr. Brewster permitted himself to hope; but more frequent were the moments when he told himself that a pronounced chump like his son-in-law could not fail somehow to make a mess of the negotiations. His relief, therefore, when Archie curveted into his private room and announced that he had succeeded was great.

"You really managed to make that wop sell out?"

Archie brushed some papers off the desk with a careless gesture, and seated himself on the vacant spot.

"Absolutely! I spoke to him as one old friend to another,

sprayed the bills all over the place; and he sang a few bars from 'Rigoletto,' and signed on the dotted line."

"You're not such a fool as you look," owned Mr. Brewster.

Archie scratched a match on the desk and lit a cigarette.

"It's a jolly little shop," he said. "I took quite a fancy to it. Full of newspapers, don't you know, and cheap novels, and some weird-looking sort of chocolates, and cigars with the most fearfully attractive labels. I think I'll make a success of it. It's bang in the middle of a dashed good neighbourhood. One of these days somebody will be building a big hotel round about there, and that'll help trade a lot. I look forward to ending my days on the other side of the counter with a full set of white whiskers and a skull-cap, beloved by everybody. Everybody'll say, 'Oh, you MUST patronise that quaint, delightful old blighter! He's quite a character.'"

Mr. Brewster's air of grim satisfaction had given way to a look of discomfort, almost of alarm. He presumed his son-in-law was merely indulging in badinage; but even so, his words were not soothing.

"Well, I'm much obliged," he said. "That infernal shop was holding up everything. Now I can start building right away."

Archie raised his eyebrows.

"But, my dear old top, I'm sorry to spoil your daydreams and stop you chasing rainbows, and all that, but aren't you forgetting that the shop belongs to me? I don't at all know that I want to sell, either!"

"I gave you the money to buy that shop!"

"And dashed generous of you it was, too!" admitted Archie, unreservedly. "It was the first money you ever gave me, and I shall always, tell interviewers that it was you who founded my fortunes. Some day, when I'm the Newspaper-and-Tobacco-Shop King, I'll tell the world all about it in my autobiography."

Mr. Brewster rose dangerously from his seat.

"Do you think you can hold me up, you—you worm?"

"Well," said Archie, "the way I look at it is this. Ever since we met, you've been after me to become one of the world's workers, and earn a living for myself, and what not; and now I see a way to repay you for your confidence and encouragement. You'll look me up sometimes at the good old shop, won't you?" He slid off the table and moved towards the door. "There won't be any formalities where you are concerned. You can sign bills for any reasonable amount any time you want a cigar or a stick of chocolate. Well, toodle-oo!"

"Stop!"

"Now what?"

"How much do you want for that damned shop?"

"I don't want money.-I want a job.-If you are going to take my life-work away from me, you ought to give me something else to do."

"What job?"

"You suggested it yourself the other day. I want to manage your new hotel."

"Don't be a fool! What do you know about managing an hotel?"

"Nothing. It will be your pleasing task to teach me the business while the shanty is being run up."

There was a pause, while Mr. Brewster chewed three inches off a pen-holder.

"Very well," he said at last.

"Topping!" said Archie. "I knew you'd, see it. I'll study your methods, what! Adding some of my own, of course. You know, I've thought of one improvement on the Cosmopolis already."

"Improvement on the Cosmopolis!" cried Mr. Brewster, gashed in his finest feelings.

"Yes. There's one point where the old Cosmop slips up badly, and I'm going to see that it's corrected at my little shack. Customers will be entreated to leave their boots outside their doors at night, and they'll find them cleaned in the morning. Well, pip, pip! I must be popping. Time is money, you know, with us business men."

110

CHAPTER XVII

BROTHER BILL'S ROMANCE

"Her eyes," said Bill Brewster, "are like—like—what's the word I want?"

He looked across at Lucille and Archie. Lucille was leaning forward with an eager and interested face; Archie was leaning back with his finger-tips together and his eyes closed. This was not the first time since their meeting in Beale's Auction Rooms that his brother-in-law had touched on the subject of the girl he had become engaged to marry during his trip to England. Indeed, Brother Bill had touched on very little else: and Archie, though of a sympathetic nature and fond of his young relative, was beginning to feel that he had heard all he wished to hear about Mabel Winchester. Lucille, on the other hand, was absorbed. Her brother's recital had thrilled her.

"Like—" said Bill. "Like—"

"Stars?" suggested Lucille.

"Stars," said Bill gratefully. "Exactly the word. Twin stars shining in a clear sky on a summer night. Her teeth are like—what shall I say?"

"Pearls?"

"Pearls. And her hair is a lovely brown, like leaves in autumn. In fact," concluded Bill, slipping down from the heights with something of a jerk, "she's a corker. Isn't she, Archie?"

Archie opened his eyes.

"Quite right, old top!" he said. "It was the only thing to do."

"What the devil are you talking about?" demanded Bill coldly. He had been suspicious all along of Archie's statement that he could listen better with his eyes shut.

"Eh? Oh, sorry! Thinking of something else."

"You were asleep."

"No, no, positively and distinctly not. Frightfully interested and rapt and all that, only I didn't quite get what you said."

"I said that Mabel was a corker."

"Oh, absolutely in every respect."

"There!" Bill turned to Lucille triumphantly. "You hear that? And Archie has only seen her photograph. Wait till he sees her in the flesh."

"My dear old chap!" said Archie, shocked. "Ladies present! I mean to say, what!"

111

"I'm afraid that father will be the one you'll find it hard to convince."

"Yes," admitted her brother gloomily.

"Your Mabel sounds perfectly charming, but—well, you know what father is. It IS a pity she sings in the chorus."

"She-hasn't much of a voice,"—argued Bill—in extenuation.

"All the same—"

Archie, the conversation having reached a topic on which he considered himself one of the greatest living authorities—to wit, the unlovable disposition of his father-in-law—addressed the meeting as one who has a right to be heard.

"Lucille's absolutely right, old thing.—Absolutely correct-o! Your esteemed progenitor is a pretty tough nut, and it's no good trying to get away from it.-And I'm sorry to have to say it, old bird, but, if you come bounding in with part of the personnel of the ensemble on your arm and try to dig a father's blessing out of him, he's extremely apt to stab you in the gizzard."

"I wish," said Bill, annoyed, "you wouldn't talk as though Mabel were the ordinary kind of chorus-girl. She's only on the stage because her mother's hard-up and she wants to educate her little brother."

"I say," said Archie, concerned. "Take my tip, old top. In chatting the matter over with the pater, don't dwell too much on that aspect of the affair.—I've been watching him closely, and it's about all he can stick, having to support ME. If you ring in a mother and a little brother on him, he'll crack under the strain."

"Well, I've got to do something about it. Mabel will be over here in a week."

"Great Scot! You never told us that."

"Yes. She's going to be in the new Billington show. And, naturally, she will expect to meet my family. I've told her all about you."

"Did you explain father to her?" asked Lucille.

"Well, I just said she mustn't mind him, as his bark was worse than his bite."

"Well," said Archie, thoughtfully, "he hasn't bitten me yet, so you may be right. But you've got to admit that he's a bit of a barker."

Lucille considered.

"Really, Bill, I think your best plan would be to go straight to father and tell him the whole thing.—You don't want him to hear about it in a roundabout way."

"The trouble is that, whenever I'm with father, I can't think of anything to say."

Archie found himself envying his father-in-law this merciful

112

dispensation of Providence; for, where he himself was concerned, there had been no lack of eloquence on Bill's part. In the brief period in which he had known him, Bill had talked all the time and always on the one topic. As unpromising a subject as the tariff laws was easily diverted by him into a discussion of the absent Mabel.

"When I'm with father," said Bill, "I sort of lose my nerve, and yammer."

"Dashed awkward," said Archie, politely. He sat up suddenly. "I say! By Jove! I know what you want, old friend! Just thought of it!"

"That busy brain is never still," explained Lucille.

"Saw it in the paper this morning. An advertisement of a book, don't you know."

"I've no time for reading."

"You've time for reading this one, laddie, for you can't afford to miss it. It's a what-d'you-call-it book. What I mean to say is, if you read it and take its tips to heart, it guarantees to make you a convincing talker. The advertisement says so. The advertisement's all about a chappie whose name I forget, whom everybody loved because he talked so well. And, mark you, before he got hold of this book—The Personality That Wins was the name of it, if I remember rightly—he was known to all the lads in the office as Silent Samuel or something. Or it may have been Tongue-Tied Thomas. Well, one day he happened by good luck to blow in the necessary for the good old P. that W.'s, and now, whenever they want someone to go and talk Rockefeller or someone into lending them a million or so, they send for Samuel. Only now they call him Sammy the Spell-Binder and fawn upon him pretty copiously and all that. How about it, old son? How do we go?"

"What perfect nonsense," said Lucille.

"I don't know," said Bill, plainly impressed. "There might be something in it."

"Absolutely!" said Archie. "I remember it said, 'Talk convincingly, and no man will ever treat you with cold, unresponsive indifference.' Well, cold, unresponsive indifference is just what you don't want the pater to treat you with, isn't it, or is it, or isn't it, what? I mean, what?"

"It sounds all right," said Bill.

"It IS all right," said Archie. "It's a scheme! I'll go farther. It's an egg!"

"The idea I had," said Bill, "was to see if I couldn't get Mabel a job in some straight comedy. That would take the curse off the thing a bit. Then I wouldn't have to dwell on the chorus end of the business, you see."

"Much more sensible," said Lucille.

"But what a-deuce of a sweat"—argued Archie. "I mean to say, having to pop round and nose about and all that."

"Aren't you willing to take a little trouble for your stricken brother-in-law, worm?" said Lucille severely.

"Oh, absolutely! My idea was to get this book and coach the dear old chap. Rehearse him, don't you know. He could bone up the early chapters a bit and then drift round and try his convincing talk on me."

"It might be a good idea," said Bill reflectively.

"Well, I'll tell you what I'm going to do," said Lucille. "I'm going to get Bill to introduce me to his Mabel, and, if she's as nice as he says she is, I'll go to father and talk convincingly to him."

"You're an ace!" said Bill.

"Absolutely!" agreed Archie cordially. "MY partner, what! All the same, we ought to keep the book as a second string, you know. I mean to say, you are a young and delicately nurtured girl—full of sensibility and shrinking what's-its-name and all that—and you know what the jolly old pater is. He might bark at you and put you out of action in the first round. Well, then, if anything like that happened, don't you see, we could unleash old Bill, the trained silver-tongued expert, and let him have a shot. Personally, I'm all for the P. that W.'s."—"Me, too," said Bill.

Lucille looked at her watch.

"Good gracious! It's nearly one o'clock!"

"No!" Archie heaved himself up from his chair. "Well, it's a shame to break up this feast of reason and flow of soul and all that, but, if we don't leg it with some speed, we shall be late."

"We're lunching at the Nicholson's!" explained Lucille to her brother. "I wish you were coming too."

"Lunch!" Bill shook his head with a kind of tolerant scorn. "Lunch means nothing to me these days. I've other things to think of besides food." He looked as spiritual as his rugged features would permit. "I haven't written to Her yet to-day."

"But, dash it, old scream, if she's going to be over here in a week, what's the good of writing? The letter would cross her."

"I'm not mailing my letters to England." said Bill. "I'm keeping them for her to read when she arrives."

"My sainted aunt!" said Archie.

Devotion like this was something beyond his outlook.

CHAPTER XVIII

THE SAUSAGE CHAPPIE

The personality that wins cost Archie two dollars in cash and a lot of embarrassment when he asked for it at the store. To buy a treatise of that name would automatically seem to argue that you haven't a winning personality already, and Archie was at some pains to explain to the girl behind the counter that he wanted it for a friend. The girl seemed more interested in his English accent than in his explanation, and Archie was uncomfortably aware, as he receded, that she was practising it in an undertone for the benefit of her colleagues and fellow-workers. However, what is a little discomfort, if endured in friendship's name?

He was proceeding up Broadway after leaving the store when he encountered Reggie van Tuyl, who was drifting along in somnambulistic fashion near Thirty-Ninth Street.

"Hullo, Reggie old thing!" said Archie.

"Hullo!" said Reggie, a man of few words.

"I've just been buying a book for Bill Brewster," went on Archie. "It appears that old Bill—What's the matter?"

He broke off his recital abruptly. A sort of spasm had passed across his companion's features. The hand holding Archie's arm had tightened convulsively. One would have said that Reginald had received a shock.

"It's nothing," said Reggie. "I'm all right now. I caught sight of that fellow's clothes rather suddenly. They shook me a bit. I'm all right now," he said, bravely.

Archie, following his friend's gaze, understood. Reggie van Tuyl was never at his strongest in the morning, and he had a sensitive eye for clothes. He had been known to resign from clubs because members exceeded the bounds in the matter of soft shirts with dinner-jackets. And the short, thick-set man who was standing just in front of them in attitude of restful immobility was certainly no dandy. His best friend could not have called him dapper. Take him for all in all and on the hoof, he might have been posing as a model for a sketch of What the Well-Dressed Man Should Not Wear.

In costume, as in most other things, it is best to take a definite line and stick to it. This man had obviously vacillated. His neck was swathed in a green scarf; he wore an evening-dress coat; and his lower limbs were draped in a pair of tweed trousers built for a larger

115

man. To the north he was bounded by a straw hat, to the south by brown shoes.

Archie surveyed the man's back carefully.

"Bit thick!" he said, sympathetically. "But of course Broadway isn't Fifth Avenue. What I mean to say is, Bohemian licence and what not. Broadway's crammed with deuced brainy devils who don't care how they look. Probably this bird is a master-mind of some species."

"All the same, man's no right to wear evening-dress coat with tweed trousers."

"Absolutely not! I see what you mean."

At this point the sartorial offender turned. Seen from the front, he was even more unnerving. He appeared to possess no shirt, though this defect was offset by the fact that the tweed trousers fitted snugly under the arms. He was not a handsome man. At his best he could never have been that, and in the recent past he had managed to acquire a scar that ran from the corner of his mouth half-way across his cheek. Even when his face was in repose he had an odd expression; and when, as he chanced to do now, he smiled, odd became a mild adjective, quite inadequate for purposes of description. It was not an unpleasant face, however. Unquestionably genial, indeed. There was something in it that had a quality of humorous appeal.

Archie started. He stared at the man, Memory stirred.

"Great Scot!" he cried. "It's the Sausage Chappie!"

Reginald van Tuyl gave a little moan. He was not used to this sort of thing. A sensitive young man as regarded scenes, Archie's behaviour unmanned him. For Archie, releasing his arm, had bounded forward and was shaking the other's hand warmly.

"Well, well, well! My dear old chap! You must remember me, what? No? Yes?"

The man with the scar seemed puzzled. He shuffled the brown shoes, patted the straw hat, and eyed Archie questioningly.

"I don't seem to place you," he said.

Archie slapped the back of the evening-dress coat. He linked his arm affectionately with that of the dress-reformer.

"We met outside St Mihiel in the war. You gave me a bit of sausage. One of the most sporting events in history. Nobody but a real sportsman would have parted with a bit of sausage at that moment to a stranger. Never forgotten it, by Jove. Saved my life, absolutely. Hadn't chewed a morsel for eight hours. Well, have you got anything on? I mean to say, you aren't booked for lunch or any rot of that species, are you? Fine! Then I move we all toddle off and get a bite somewhere." He squeezed the other's arm fondly. "Fancy meeting you again like this! I've often wondered what became of you. But, by Jove, I was forgetting. Dashed rude of me. My friend, Mr. van Tuyl."

Reggie gulped. The longer he looked at it, the harder this man's costume was to bear. His eye passed shudderingly from the brown shoes to the tweed trousers, to the green scarf, from the green scarf to the straw hat.

"Sorry," he mumbled. "Just remembered. Important date. Late already. Er—see you some time—"

He melted away, a broken man. Archie was not sorry to see him go. Reggie was a good chap, but he would undoubtedly have been de trop at this reunion.

"I vote we go to the Cosmopolis," he said, steering his newly-found friend through the crowd. "The browsing and sluicing isn't bad there, and I can sign the bill which is no small consideration nowadays."

The Sausage Chappie chuckled amusedly.

"I can't go to a place like the Cosmopolis looking like this."

Archie, was a little embarrassed.

"Oh, I don't know, you know, don't you know!" he said. "Still, since you have brought the topic up, you DID get the good old wardrobe a bit mixed this morning what? I mean to say, you seem absent-mindedly, as it were, to have got hold of samples from a good number of your various suitings."

"Suitings? How do you mean, suitings? I haven't any suitings! Who do you think I am? Vincent Astor? All I have is what I stand up in."

Archie was shocked. This tragedy touched him. He himself had never had any money in his life, but somehow he had always seemed to manage to have plenty of clothes. How this was he could not say. He had always had a vague sort of idea that tailors were kindly birds who never failed to have a pair of trousers or something up their sleeve to present to the deserving. There was the drawback, of course, that once they had given you things they were apt to write you rather a lot of letters about it; but you soon managed to recognise their handwriting, and then it was a simple task to extract their communications from your morning mail and drop them in the waste-paper basket. This was the first case he had encountered of a man who was really short of clothes.

"My dear old lad," he said, briskly, "this must be remedied! Oh, positively! This must be remedied at once! I suppose my things wouldn't fit you? No. Well, I tell you what. We'll wangle something from my father-in-law. Old Brewster, you know, the fellow who runs the Cosmopolis. His'll fit you like the paper on the wall, because he's

117

a tubby little blighter, too. What I mean to say is, he's also one of those sturdy, square, fine-looking chappies of about the middle height. By the way, where are you stopping these days?"

"Nowhere just at present. I thought of taking one of those self-contained Park benches."

"Are you broke?"

"Am I!"

Archie was concerned.

"You ought to get a job."

"I ought. But somehow I don't seem able to."

"What did you do before the war?"

"I've forgotten."

"Forgotten!"

"Forgotten."

"How do you mean—forgotten? You can't mean—FORGOTTEN?"

"Yes. It's quite gone."

"But I mean to say. You can't have forgotten a thing like that."

"Can't I! I've forgotten all sorts of things. Where I was born. How old I am. Whether I'm married or single. What my name is—"

"Well, I'm dashed!" said Archie, staggered. "But you remembered about giving me a bit of sausage outside St. Mihiel?"

"No, I didn't. I'm taking your word for it. For all I know you may be luring me into some den to rob me of my straw hat. I don't know you from Adam. But I like your conversation—especially the part about eating—and I'm taking a chance."

Archie was concerned.

"Listen, old bean. Make an effort. You must remember that sausage episode? It was just outside St. Mihiel, about five in the evening. Your little lot were lying next to my little lot, and we happened to meet, and I said 'What ho!' and you said 'Halloa!' and I said 'What ho! What ho!' and you said 'Have a bit of sausage?' and I said 'What ho! What ho! What HO!'"

"The dialogue seems to have been darned sparkling but I don't remember it. It must have been after that that I stopped one. I don't seem quite to have caught up with myself since I got hit."

"Oh! That's how you got that scar?"

"No. I got that jumping through a plate-glass window in London on Armistice night."

"What on earth did you do that for?"

"Oh, I don't know. It seemed a good idea at the time."

"But if you can remember a thing like that, why can't you remember your name?"

118

"I remember everything that happened after I came out of hospital. It's the part before that's gone."

Archie patted him on the shoulder.

"I know just what you want. You need a bit of quiet and repose, to think things over and so forth. You mustn't go sleeping on Park benches. Won't do at all. Not a bit like it. You must shift to the Cosmopolis. It isn't half a bad spot, the old Cosmop. I didn't like it much the first night I was there, because there was a dashed tap that went drip-drip-drip all night and kept me awake, but the place has its points."

"Is the Cosmopolis giving free board and lodging these days?"

"Rather! That'll be all right. Well, this is the spot. We'll start by trickling up to the old boy's suite and looking over his reach-me-downs. I know the waiter on his floor. A very sound chappie. He'll let us in with his pass-key."

And so it came about that Mr. Daniel Brewster, returning to his suite in the middle of lunch in order to find a paper dealing with the subject he was discussing with his guest, the architect of his new hotel, was aware of a murmur of voices behind the closed door of his bedroom. Recognising the accents of his son-in-law, he breathed an oath and charged in. He objected to Archie wandering at large about his suite.

The sight that met his eyes when he opened the door did nothing to soothe him. The floor was a sea of clothes. There were coats on the chairs, trousers on the bed, shirts on the bookshelf. And in the middle of his welter stood Archie, with a man who, to Mr. Brewster's heated eye, looked like a tramp comedian out of a burlesque show.

"Great Godfrey!" ejaculated Mr. Brewster.

Archie looked up with a friendly smile.

"Oh, halloa-halloa!" he said, affably, "We were just glancing through your spare scenery to see if we couldn't find something for my pal here. This is Mr. Brewster, my father-in-law, old man."

Archie scanned his relative's twisted features. Something in his expression seemed not altogether encouraging. He decided that the negotiations had better be conducted in private. "One moment, old lad," he said to his new friend. "I just want to have a little talk with my father-in-law in the other room. Just a little friendly business chat. You stay here."

In the other room Mr. Brewster turned on Archie like a wounded lion of the desert.

"What the—!"

Archie secured one of his coat-buttons and began to massage it affectionately.

119

"Ought to have explained!" said Archie, "only didn't want to interrupt your lunch. The sportsman on the horizon is a dear old pal of mine—"

Mr. Brewster wrenched himself free.

"What the devil do you mean, you worm, by bringing tramps into my bedroom and messing about with my clothes?"

"That's just what I'm trying to explain, if you'll only listen. This bird is a bird I met in France during the war. He gave me a bit of sausage outside St. Mihiel—"

"Damn you and him and the sausage!"

"Absolutely. But listen. He can't remember who he is or where he was born or what his name is, and he's broke; so, dash it, I must look after him. You see, he gave me a bit of sausage."

Mr. Brewster's frenzy gave way to an ominous calm.

"I'll give him two seconds to clear out of here. If he isn't gone by then I'll have him thrown out."

Archie was shocked.

"You don't mean that?"

"I do mean that."

"But where is he to go?"

"Outside."

"But you don't understand. This chappie has lost his memory because he was wounded in the war. Keep that fact firmly fixed in the old bean. He fought for you. Fought and bled for you. Bled profusely, by Jove. AND he saved my life!"

"If I'd got nothing else against him, that would be enough."

"But you can't sling a chappie out into the cold hard world who bled in gallons to make the world safe for the Hotel Cosmopolis."

Mr. Brewster looked ostentatiously at his watch.

"Two seconds!" he said.

There was a silence. Archie appeared to be thinking. "Right-o!" he said at last. "No need to get the wind up. I know where he can go. It's just occurred to me I'll put him up at my little shop."

The purple ebbed from Mr. Brewster's face. Such was his emotion that he had forgotten that infernal shop. He sat down. There was more silence.

"Oh, gosh!" said Mr. Brewster.

"I knew you would be reasonable about it," said Archie, approvingly. "Now, honestly, as man to man, how do we go?"

"What do you want me to do?" growled Mr. Brewster.

"I thought you might put the chappie up for a while, and give him a chance to look round and nose about a bit."

"I absolutely refuse to give any more loafers free board and lodging."

"Any MORE?"

"Well, he would be the second, wouldn't he?"

Archie looked pained.

"It's true," he said, "that when I first came here I was temporarily resting, so to speak; but didn't I go right out and grab the managership of your new hotel? Positively!"

"I will NOT adopt this tramp."

"Well, find him a job, then."

"What sort of a job?"

"Oh, any old sort"

"He can be a waiter if he likes."

"All right; I'll put the matter before him."

He returned to the bedroom. The Sausage Chappie was gazing fondly into the mirror with a spotted tie draped round his neck.

"I say, old top," said Archie, apologetically, "the Emperor of the Blighters out yonder says you can have a job here as waiter, and he won't do another dashed thing for you. How about it?"

"Do waiters eat?"

"I suppose so. Though, by Jove, come to think of it, I've never seen one at it."

"That's good enough for me!" said the Sausage Chappie. "When do I begin?"

CHAPTER XIX

REGGIE COMES TO LIFE

The advantage of having plenty of time on one's hands is that one has leisure to attend to the affairs of all one's circle of friends; and Archie, assiduously as he watched over the destinies of the Sausage Chappie, did not neglect the romantic needs of his brother-in-law Bill. A few days later, Lucille, returning one morning to their mutual suite, found her husband seated in an upright chair at the table, an unusually stern expression on his amiable face. A large cigar was in the corner of his mouth. The fingers of one hand rested in the armhole of his waistcoat: with the other hand he tapped menacingly on the table.

As she gazed upon him, wondering what could be the matter with him, Lucille was suddenly aware of Bill's presence. He had emerged sharply from the bedroom and was walking briskly across the floor. He came to a halt in front of the table.

"Father!" said Bill.

Archie looked up sharply, frowning heavily over his cigar.

"Well, my boy," he said in a strange, rasping voice. "What is it? Speak up, my boy, speak up! Why the devil can't you speak up? This is my busy day!"

"What on earth are you doing?" asked Lucille.

Archie waved her away with the large gesture of a man of blood and iron interrupted while concentrating.

"Leave us, woman! We would be alone! Retire into the jolly old background and amuse yourself for a bit. Read a book. Do acrostics. Charge ahead, laddie."

"Father!" said Bill, again.

"Yes, my boy, yes? What is it?"

"Father!"

Archie picked up the red-covered volume that lay on the table.

"Half a mo', old son. Sorry to stop you, but I knew there was something. I've just remembered. Your walk. All wrong!"

"All wrong?"

"All wrong! Where's the chapter on the Art. of Walking? Here we are. Listen, dear old soul. Drink this in. 'In walking, one should strive to acquire that swinging, easy movement from the hips. The correctly-poised walker seems to float along, as it were.' Now, old bean, you didn't float a dam' bit. You just galloped in like a chappie charging into a railway restaurant for a bowl of soup when his train

122

leaves in two minutes. Dashed important, this walking business, you know. Get started wrong, and where are you? Try it again.... Much better." He turned to Lucille. "Notice him float along that time? Absolutely skimmed, what?"

Lucille had taken a seat,-and was waiting for enlightenment.

"Are you and Bill going into vaudeville?" she asked.

Archie, scrutinising-his-brother-in-law closely, had further criticism to make.

"'The man of self-respect and self-confidence,'" he read, "'stands erect in an easy, natural, graceful attitude. Heels not too far apart, head erect, eyes to the front with a level gaze'—get your gaze level, old thing!—'shoulders thrown back, arms hanging naturally at the sides when not otherwise employed'—that means that, if he tries to hit you, it's all right to guard—'chest expanded naturally, and abdomen'—this is no place for you, Lucille. Leg it out of earshot— 'ab—what I said before—drawn in somewhat and above all not protruded.' Now, have you got all that? Yes, you look all right. Carry on, laddie, carry on. Let's have two-penn'orth of the Dynamic Voice and the Tone of Authority—some of the full, rich, round stuff we hear so much about!"

Bill fastened a gimlet eye upon his brother-in-law and drew a deep breath.

"Father!" he said. "Father!"

"You'll have to brighten up Bill's dialogue a lot," said Lucille, critically, "or you will never get bookings."

"Father!"

"I mean, it's all right as far as it goes, but it's sort of monotonous. Besides, one of you ought to be asking questions and the other answering. Bill ought to be saying, 'Who was that lady I saw you coming down the street with?' so that you would be able to say, 'That wasn't a lady. That was my wife.' I KNOW! I've been to lots of vaudeville shows."

Bill relaxed his attitude. He deflated his chest, spread his heels, and ceased to draw in his abdomen.

"We'd better try this another time, when we're alone," he said, frigidly. "I can't do myself justice."

"Why do you want to do yourself justice?" asked Lucille.

"Right-o!" said Archie, affably, casting off his forbidding expression like a garment. "Rehearsal postponed. I was just putting old Bill through it," he explained, "with a view to getting him into mid-season form for the jolly old pater."

"Oh!" Lucille's voice was the voice of one who sees light in darkness. "When Bill walked in like a cat on hot bricks and stood there looking stuffed, that was just the Personality That Wins!"

"That was it."

"Well, you couldn't blame me for not recognising it, could you?"

Archie patted her head paternally.

"A little less of the caustic critic stuff," he said. "Bill will be all right on the night. If you hadn't come in then and put him off his stroke, he'd have shot out some amazing stuff, full of authority and dynamic accents and what not. I tell you, light of my soul, old Bill is all right! He's got the winning personality up a tree, ready whenever he wants to go and get it. Speaking as his backer and trainer, I think he'll twist your father round his little finger. Absolutely! It wouldn't surprise me if at the end of five minutes the good old dad started pumping through hoops and sitting up for lumps of sugar."

"It would surprise ME."

"Ah, that's because you haven't seen old Bill in action. You crabbed his act before he had begun to spread himself."

"It isn't that at all. The reason why I think that Bill, however winning his personality may be, won't persuade father to let him marry a girl in the chorus is something that happened last night."

"Last night?"

"Well, at three o'clock this morning. It's on the front page of the early editions of the evening papers. I brought one in for you to see, only you were so busy. Look! There it is!"

Archie seized the paper.

"Oh, Great Scot!"

"What is it?" asked Bill, irritably. "Don't stand goggling there! What the devil is it?"

"Listen to this, old thing!"

REVELRY BY NIGHT.
SPIRITED BATTLE ROYAL AT HOTEL COSMOPOLIS.
THE HOTEL DETECTIVE HAD A GOOD HEART BUT PAULINE PACKED THE PUNCH.

The logical contender for Jack Dempsey's championship honours has been discovered; and, in an age where women are stealing men's jobs all the time, it will not come as a surprise to our readers to learn that she belongs to the sex that is more deadly than the male. Her name is Miss Pauline Preston, and her wallop is vouched for under oath—under many oaths—by Mr. Timothy O'Neill, known to his intimates as Pie-Face, who holds down the arduous job of detective at the Hotel Cosmopolis.

At three o'clock this morning, Mr. O'Neill was advised by the

124

night-clerk that the occupants of every room within earshot of number 618 had 'phoned the desk to complain of a disturbance, a noise, a vocal uproar proceeding from the room mentioned. Thither, therefore, marched Mr. O'Neill, his face full of cheese-sandwich, (for he had been indulging in an early breakfast or a late supper) and his heart of devotion to duty. He found there the Misses Pauline Preston and "Bobbie" St. Clair, of the personnel of the chorus of the Frivolities, entertaining a few friends of either sex. A pleasant time was being had by all, and at the moment of Mr. O'Neill's entry the entire strength of the company was rendering with considerable emphasis that touching ballad, "There's a Place For Me In Heaven, For My Baby-Boy Is There."

The able and efficient officer at once suggested that there was a place for them in the street and the patrol-wagon was there; and, being a man of action as well as words, proceeded to gather up an armful of assorted guests as a preliminary to a personally-conducted tour onto the cold night. It was at this point that Miss Preston stepped into the limelight. Mr. O'Neill contends that she hit him with a brick, an iron casing, and the Singer Building. Be that as it may, her efforts were sufficiently able to induce him to retire for reinforcements, which, arriving, arrested the supper-party regardless of age or sex.

At the police-court this morning Miss Preston maintained that she and her friends were merely having a quiet home-evening and that Mr. O'Neill was no gentleman. The male guests gave their names respectively as Woodrow Wilson, David Lloyd-George, and William J. Bryan. These, however, are believed to be incorrect. But the moral is, if you want excitement rather than sleep, stay at the Hotel Cosmopolis.

Bill may have quaked inwardly as he listened to this epic but outwardly he was unmoved.

"Well," he said, "what about it?"

"What about it!" said Lucille.

"What about it!" said Archie. "Why, my dear old friend, it simply means that all the time we've been putting in making your personality winning has been chucked away. Absolutely a dead loss! We might just as well have read a manual on how to knit sweaters."

"I don't see it," maintained Bill, stoutly.

Lucille turned apologetically to her husband.

"You mustn't judge me by him, Archie, darling. This sort of thing doesn't run in the family.-We are supposed to be rather bright on the whole. But poor Bill was dropped by his nurse when he was a baby, and fell on his head."

"I suppose what you're driving at," said the goaded Bill, "is

125

that what has happened will make father pretty sore against girls who happen to be in the chorus?"

"That's absolutely it, old thing, I'm sorry to say. The next person who mentions the word chorus-girl in the jolly old governor's presence is going to take his life in his hands. I tell you, as one man to another, that I'd much rather be back in France hopping over the top than do it myself."

"What darned nonsense! Mabel may be in the chorus, but she isn't like those girls."

"Poor old Bill!" said Lucille. "I'm awfully sorry, but it's no use not facing facts. You know perfectly well that the reputation of the hotel is the thing father cares more about than anything else in the world, and that this is going to make him furious with all the chorus-girls in creation. It's no good trying to explain to him that your Mabel is in the chorus but not of the chorus, so to speak."

"Deuced well put!" said Archie, approvingly. "You're absolutely right. A chorus-girl by the river's brim, so to speak, a simple chorus-girl is to him, as it were, and she is nothing more, if you know what I mean."

"So now," said Lucille, "having shown you that the imbecile scheme which you concocted with my poor well-meaning husband is no good at all, I will bring you words of cheer. Your own original plan—of getting your Mabel a part in a comedy—was always the best one. And you can do it. I wouldn't have broken the bad news so abruptly if I hadn't had some consolation to give you afterwards. I met Reggie van Tuyl just now, wandering about as if the cares of the world were on his shoulders, and he told me that he was putting up most of the money for a new play that's going into rehearsal right away. Reggie's an old friend of yours. All you have to do is to go to him and ask him to use his influence to get your Mabel a small part. There's sure to be a maid or something with only a line or two that won't matter."

"A ripe scheme!" said Archie. "Very sound and fruity!"

The cloud did not lift from Bill's corrugated brow.

"That's all very well," he said. "But you know what a talker Reggie is. He's an obliging sort of chump, but his tongue's fastened on at the middle and waggles at both ends. I don't want the whole of New York to know about my engagement, and have somebody spilling the news to father, before I'm ready."

"That's all right," said Lucille. "Archie can speak to him. There's no need for him to mention your name at all. He can just say there's a girl he wants to get a part for. You would do it, wouldn't you, angel-face?"

"Like a bird, queen of my soul."

"Then that's splendid. You'd better give Archie that photograph of Mabel to give to Reggie, Bill."

"Photograph?" said Bill. "Which photograph? I have twenty-four!"

Archie found Reggie van Tuyl brooding in a window of his club that looked over Fifth Avenue. Reggie was a rather melancholy young man who suffered from elephantiasis of the bank-roll and the other evils that arise from that complaint. Gentle and sentimental by nature, his sensibilities had been much wounded by contact with a sordid world; and the thing that had first endeared Archie to him was the fact that the latter, though chronically hard-up, had never made any attempt to borrow money from him. Reggie would have parted with it on demand, but it had delighted him to find that Archie seemed to take a pleasure in his society without having any ulterior motives. He was fond of Archie, and also of Lucille; and their happy marriage was a constant source of gratification to him.

For Reggie was a sentimentalist. He would have liked to live in a world of ideally united couples, himself ideally united to some charming and affectionate girl. But, as a matter of cold fact, he was a bachelor, and most of the couples he knew were veterans of several divorces. In Reggie's circle, therefore, the home-life of Archie and Lucille shone like a good deed in a naughty world. It inspired him. In moments of depression it restored his waning faith in human nature.

Consequently, when Archie, having greeted him and slipped into a chair at his side, suddenly produced from his inside pocket the photograph of an extremely pretty girl and asked him to get her a small part in the play which he was financing, he was shocked and disappointed. He was in a more than usually sentimental mood that afternoon, and had, indeed, at the moment of Archie's arrival, been dreaming wistfully of soft arms clasped snugly about his collar and the patter of little feet and all that sort of thing.-He gazed reproachfully at Archie.

"Archie!" his voice quivered with emotion. "Is it worth it?, is it worth it, old man?-Think of the poor little woman at home!"

Archie was puzzled.

"Eh, old top? Which poor little woman?"

"Think of her trust in you, her faith—".

"I don't absolutely get you, old bean."

"What would Lucille say if she knew about this?"

"Oh, she does. She knows all about it."

"Good heavens!" cried Reggie.-He was shocked to the core of his being.-One of the articles of his faith was, that the union of Lucille and Archie was different from those loose partnerships which were the custom in his world.-He had not been conscious of such a poignant feeling that the foundations of the universe were cracked and tottering and that there was no light and sweetness in life since the morning, eighteen months back, when a negligent valet had sent him out into Fifth Avenue with only one spat on.

"It was Lucille's idea," explained Archie. He was about to mention his brother-in-law's connection with the matter, but checked himself in time, remembering Bill's specific objection to having his secret revealed to Reggie. "It's like this, old thing, I've never met this female, but she's a pal of Lucille's"—he comforted his conscience by the reflection that, if she wasn't now, she would be in a few days-"and Lucille wants to do her a bit of good. She's been on the stage in England, you know, supporting a jolly old widowed mother and educating a little brother and all that kind and species of rot, you understand, and now she's coming over to America, and Lucille wants you to rally round and shove her into your show and generally keep the home fires burning and so forth. How do we go?"

Reggie beamed with relief. He felt just as he had felt on that other occasion at the moment when a taxi-cab had rolled up and enabled him to hide his spatless leg from the public gaze.

"Oh, I see!" he said. "Why, delighted, old man, quite delighted!"

"Any small part would do. Isn't there a maid or something in your bob's-worth of refined entertainment who drifts about saying, 'Yes, madam,' and all that sort of thing? Well, then that's just the thing. Topping! I knew I could rely on you, old bird. I'll get Lucille to ship her round to your address when she arrives. I fancy she's due to totter in somewhere in the next few days. Well, I must be popping. Toodle-oo!"

"Pip-pip!" said Reggie.

It was about a week later that Lucille came into the suite at the Hotel Cosmopolis that was her home, and found Archie lying on the couch,
smoking a refreshing pipe after the labours of the day. It seemed to Archie that his wife was not in her usual cheerful frame of mind. He kissed her, and, having relieved her of her parasol, endeavoured without success to balance it on his chin. Having picked it up from the floor and placed it on the table, he became aware that Lucille was looking at him in a despondent sort of way. Her grey eyes were clouded.

"Halloa, old thing," said Archie. "What's up?"

Lucille sighed wearily.

"Archie, darling, do you know any really good swear-words?"

"Well," said Archie, reflectively, "let me see. I did pick up a few tolerably ripe and breezy expressions out in France. All through my military career there was something about me—some subtle magnetism, don't you know, and that sort of thing—that seemed to make colonels and blighters of that order rather inventive. I sort of inspired them, don't you know. I remember one brass-hat addressing me for quite ten minutes, saying something new all the time. And even then he seemed to think he had only touched the fringe of the subject. As a matter of fact, he said straight out in the most frank and confiding way that mere words couldn't do justice to me. But why?"

"Because I want to relieve my feelings."

"Anything wrong?"

"Everything's wrong. I've just been having tea with Bill and his Mabel."

"Oh, ah!" said Archie, interested. "And what's the verdict?"

"Guilty!" said Lucille. "And the sentence, if I had anything to do with it, would be transportation for life." She peeled off her gloves irritably. "What fools men are! Not you, precious! You're the only man in the world that isn't, it seems to me. You did marry a nice girl, didn't you? YOU didn't go running round after females with crimson hair, goggling at them with your eyes popping out of your head like a bulldog waiting for a bone."

"Oh, I say! Does old Bill look like that?"

"Worse!"

Archie rose to a point of order.

"But one moment, old lady. You speak of crimson hair. Surely old Bill—in the extremely jolly monologues he used to deliver whenever I didn't see him coming and he got me alone—used to allude to her hair as brown."

"It isn't brown now. It's bright scarlet. Good gracious, I ought to know. I've been looking at it all the afternoon. It dazzled me. If I've got to meet her again, I mean to go to the oculist's and get a pair of those smoked glasses you wear at Palm Beach." Lucille brooded silently for a while over the tragedy. "I don't want to say anything against her, of course."

"No, no, of course not."

"But of all the awful, second-rate girls I ever met, she's the worst! She has vermilion hair and an imitation Oxford manner. She's so horribly refined that it's dreadful to listen to her. She's a sly, creepy, slinky, made-up, insincere vampire! She's common! She's awful! She's a cat!"

"You're quite right not to say anything against her," said Archie, approvingly. "It begins to look," he went on, "as if the good old pater was about due for another shock. He has a hard life!"

"If Bill DARES to introduce that girl to Father, he's taking his life in his hands."

"But surely that was the idea—the scheme—the wheeze, wasn't it? Or do you think there's any chance of his weakening?"

"Weakening! You should have seen him looking at her! It was like a small boy flattening his nose against the window of a candy-store."

"Bit thick!"

Lucille kicked the leg of the table.

"And to think," she said, "that, when I was a little girl, I used to look up to Bill as a monument of wisdom. I used to hug his knees and gaze into his face and wonder how anyone could be so magnificent." She gave the unoffending table another kick. "If I could have looked into the future," she said, with feeling, "I'd have bitten him in the ankle!"

In the days which followed, Archie found himself a little out of touch with Bill and his romance. Lucille referred to the matter only when he brought the subject up, and made it plain that the topic of her future sister-in-law was not one which she enjoyed discussing. Mr. Brewster, senior, when Archie, by way of delicately preparing his mind for what was to befall, asked him if he liked red hair, called him a fool, and told him to go away and bother someone else when they were busy. The only person who could have kept him thoroughly abreast of the trend of affairs was Bill himself; and experience had made Archie wary in the matter of meeting Bill. The position of confidant to a young man in the early stages of love is no sinecure, and it made Archie sleepy even to think of having to talk to his brother-in-law. He sedulously avoided his love-lorn relative, and it was with a sinking feeling one day that, looking over his shoulder as he sat in the Cosmopolis grill-room preparatory to ordering lunch, he perceived Bill bearing down upon him, obviously resolved upon joining his meal.

To his surprise, however, Bill did not instantly embark upon his usual monologue. Indeed, he hardly spoke at all. He champed a chop, and seemed to Archie to avoid his eye. It was not till lunch was over and they were smoking that he unburdened himself.

"Archie!" he said.

"Hallo, old thing!" said Archie. "Still there? I thought you'd died or something. Talk about our old pals, Tongue-tied Thomas and Silent Sammy! You could beat 'em both on the same evening."

"It's enough to make me silent."

"What is?"

Bill had relapsed into a sort of waking dream. He sat frowning sombrely, lost to the world. Archie, having waited what seemed to him a sufficient length of time for an answer to his question, bent forward and touched his brother-in-law's hand gently with the lighted end of his cigar. Bill came to himself with a howl.

"What is?" said Archie.

"What is what?" said Bill.

"Now listen, old thing," protested Archie. "Life is short and time is flying. Suppose we cut out the cross-talk. You hinted there was something on your mind—something worrying the old bean—and I'm waiting to hear what it is."

Bill fiddled a moment with his coffee-spoon.

"I'm in an awful hole," he said at last.

"What's the trouble?"

"It's about that darned girl!"

Archie blinked.

"What!"

"That darned girl!"

Archie could scarcely credit his senses. He had been prepared—indeed, he had steeled himself—to hear Bill allude to his affinity in a number of ways. But "that darned girl" was not one of them.

"Companion of my riper years," he said, "let's get this thing straight. When you say 'that darned girl,' do you by any possibility allude to—?"

"Of course I do!"

"But, William, old bird—"

"Oh, I know, I know, I know!" said Bill, irritably. "You're surprised to hear me talk like that about her?"

"A trifle, yes. Possibly a trifle. When last heard from, laddie, you must recollect, you were speaking of the lady as your soul-mate, and at least once—if I remember rightly—you alluded to her as your little dusky-haired lamb."

A sharp howl escaped Bill.

"Don't!" A strong shudder convulsed his frame. "Don't remind me of it!"

"There's been a species of slump, then, in dusky-haired lambs?"

"How," demanded Bill, savagely, "can a girl be a dusky-haired lamb when her hair's bright scarlet?"

"Dashed difficult!" admitted Archie.

"I suppose Lucille told you about that?"

"She did touch on it. Lightly, as it were. With a sort of gossamer touch, so to speak."

Bill threw off the last fragments of reserve.

"Archie, I'm in the devil of a fix. I don't know why it was, but directly I saw her—things seemed so different over in England—I

131

mean." He swallowed ice-water in gulps. "I suppose it was seeing her with Lucille. Old Lu is such a thoroughbred. Seemed to kind of show her up. Like seeing imitation pearls by the side of real pearls. And that crimson hair! It sort of put the lid on it." Bill brooded morosely. "It ought to be a criminal offence for women to dye their hair. Especially red. What the devil do women do that sort of thing for?"

"Don't blame me, old thing. It's not my fault."

Bill looked furtive and harassed.

"It makes me feel such a cad. Here am I, feeling that I would give all I've got in the world to get out of the darned thing, and all the time the poor girl seems to be getting fonder of me than ever."

"How do you know?" Archie surveyed his brother-in-law critically. "Perhaps her feelings have changed too. Very possibly she may not like the colour of YOUR hair. I don't myself. Now if you were to dye yourself crimson—"

"Oh, shut up! Of course a man knows when a girl's fond of him."

"By no means, laddie. When you're my age—"

"I AM your age."

"So you are! I forgot that. Well, now, approaching the matter from another angle, let us suppose, old son, that Miss What's-Her-Name—the party of the second part—"

"Stop it!" said Bill suddenly. "Here comes Reggie!"

"Eh?"

"Here comes Reggie van Tuyl. I don't want him to hear us talking about the darned thing."

Archie looked over his shoulder and perceived that it was indeed so. Reggie was threading his way among the tables.

"Well, HE looks pleased with things, anyway," said Bill, enviously. "Glad somebody's happy."

He was right. Reggie van Tuyl's usual mode of progress through a restaurant was a somnolent slouch. Now he was positively bounding along. Furthermore, the usual expression on Reggie's face was a sleepy sadness. Now he smiled brightly and with animation. He curveted towards their table, beaming and erect, his head up, his gaze level, and his chest expanded, for all the world as if he had been reading the hints in "The Personality That Wins."

Archie was puzzled. Something had plainly happened to Reggie. But what? It was idle to suppose that somebody had left him money, for he had been left practically all the money there was a matter of ten years before.

"Hallo, old bean," he said, as the new-comer, radiating good will and bonhomie, arrived at the table and hung over it like a noon-

132

day sun. "We've finished. But rally round and we'll watch you eat. Dashed interesting, watching old Reggie eat. Why go to the Zoo?"

Reggie shook his head.

"Sorry, old man. Can't. Just on my way to the Ritz. Stepped in because I thought you might be here. I wanted you to be the first to hear the news."

"News?"

"I'm the happiest man alive!"

"You look it, darn you!" growled Bill, on whose mood of grey gloom this human sunbeam was jarring heavily.

"I'm engaged to be married!"

"Congratulations, old egg!" Archie shook his hand cordially. "Dash it, don't you know, as an old married man I like to see you young fellows settling down."

"I don't know how to thank you enough, Archie, old man," said Reggie, fervently.

"Thank me?"

"It was through you that I met her. Don't you remember the girl you sent to me? You wanted me to get her a small part—"

He stopped, puzzled. Archie had uttered a sound that was half gasp and half gurgle, but it was swallowed up in the extraordinary noise from the other side of the table. Bill Brewster was leaning forward with bulging eyes and soaring eyebrows.

"Are you engaged to Mabel Winchester?"

"Why, by George!" said Reggie. "Do you know her?"

Archie recovered himself.

"Slightly," he said. "Slightly. Old Bill knows her slightly, as it were. Not very well, don't you know, but—how shall I put it?"

"Slightly," suggested Bill.

"Just the word. Slightly."

"Splendid!" said Reggie van Tuyl. "Why don't you come along to the Ritz and meet her now?"

Bill stammered. Archie came to the rescue again.

"Bill can't come now. He's got a date."

"A date?" said Bill.

"A date," said Archie. "An appointment, don't you know. A—a—in fact, a date."

"But—er—wish her happiness from me," said Bill, cordially.

"Thanks very much, old man," said Reggie.

"And say I'm delighted, will you?"

"Certainly."

"You won't forget the word, will you? Delighted."

"Delighted."

"That's right. Delighted."

133

Reggie looked at his watch.

"Halloa! I must rush!"

Bill and Archie watched him as he bounded out of the restaurant.

"Poor old Reggie!" said Bill, with a fleeting compunction.

"Not necessarily," said Archie. "What I mean to say is, tastes differ, don't you know. One man's peach is another man's poison, and vice versa."

"There's something in that."

"Absolutely! Well," said Archie, judicially, "this would appear to be, as it were, the maddest, merriest day in all the glad New Year, yes, no?"

Bill drew a deep breath.

"You bet your sorrowful existence it is!" he said. "I'd like to do something to celebrate it."

"The right spirit!" said Archie. "Absolutely the right spirit! Begin by paying for my lunch!"

CHAPTER XX

THE-SAUSAGE-CHAPPIE-CLICKS

Rendered restless by relief, Bill Brewster did not linger long at the luncheon-table. Shortly after Reggie van Tuyl had retired, he got up and announced his intention of going for a bit of a walk to calm his excited mind. Archie dismissed him with a courteous wave of the hand; and, beckoning to the Sausage Chappie, who in his role of waiter was hovering near, requested him to bring the best cigar the hotel could supply. The padded seat in which he sat was comfortable; he had no engagements; and it seemed to him that a pleasant half-hour could be passed in smoking dreamily and watching his fellow-men eat.

The grill-room had filled up. The Sausage Chappie, having brought Archie his cigar, was attending to a table close by, at which a woman with a small boy in a sailor suit had seated themselves. The woman was engrossed with the bill of fare, but the child's attention seemed riveted upon the Sausage Chappie. He was drinking him in with wide eyes. He seemed to be brooding on him.

Archie, too, was brooding on the Sausage Chappie, The latter made an excellent waiter: he was brisk and attentive, and did the work as if he liked it; but Archie was not satisfied. Something seemed to tell him that the man was fitted for higher things. Archie was a grateful soul. That sausage, coming at the end of a five-hour hike, had made a deep impression on his plastic nature. Reason told him that only an exceptional man could have parted with half a sausage at such a moment; and he could not feel that a job as waiter at a New York hotel was an adequate job for an exceptional man. Of course, the root of the trouble lay in the fact that the fellow could not remember what his real life-work had been before the war. It was exasperating to reflect, as the other moved away to take his order to the kitchen, that there, for all one knew, went the dickens of a lawyer or doctor or architect or what not.

His meditations were broken by the voice of the child.

"Mummie," asked the child interestedly, following the Sausage Chappie with his eyes as the latter disappeared towards the kitchen, "why has that man got such a funny face?"

"Hush, darling."

"Yes, but why HAS he?"

"I don't know, darling."

The child's faith in the maternal omniscience seemed to have received a shock. He had the air of a seeker after truth who has been baffled. His eyes roamed the room discontentedly.

"He's got a funnier face than that man there," he said, pointing to Archie.

"Hush, darling!"

"But he has. Much funnier."

In a way it was a sort of compliment, but Archie felt embarrassed. He withdrew coyly into the cushioned recess. Presently the Sausage Chappie returned, attended to the needs of the woman and the child, and came over to Archie. His homely face was beaming.

"Say, I had a big night last night," he said, leaning on the table.

"Yes?" said Archie. "Party or something?"

"No, I mean I suddenly began to remember things. Something seems to have happened to the works."

Archie sat up excitedly. This was great news.

"No, really? My dear old lad, this is absolutely topping. This is priceless."

"Yessir! First thing I remembered was that I was born at Springfield, Ohio. It was like a mist starting to lift. Springfield, Ohio. That was it. It suddenly came back to me."

"Splendid! Anything else?"

"Yessir! Just before I went to sleep I remembered my name as well."

Archie was stirred to his depths.

"Why, the thing's a walk-over!" he exclaimed. "Now you've once got started, nothing can stop you. What is your name?"

"Why, it's—That's funny! It's gone again. I have an idea it began with an S. What was it? Skeffington? Skillington?"

"Sanderson?"

"No; I'll get it in a moment. Cunningham? Carrington? Wilberforce? Debenham?"

"Dennison?" suggested Archie, helpfully.—"No, no, no. It's on the tip of my tongue. Barrington? Montgomery? Hepplethwaite? I've got it! Smith!"

"By Jove! Really?"

"Certain of it."

"What's the first name?"

An anxious expression came into the man's eyes. He hesitated. He lowered his voice.

"I have a horrible feeling that it's Lancelot!"

"Good God!" said Archie.

"It couldn't really be that, could it?"

Archie looked grave. He hated to give pain, but he felt he must be honest.

"It might," he said. "People give their children all sorts of rummy names. My second name's Tracy. And I have a pal in England who was christened Cuthbert de la Hay Horace. Fortunately everyone calls him Stinker."

The head-waiter began to drift up like a bank of fog, and the Sausage Chappie returned to his professional duties. When he came back, he was beaming again.

"Something else I remembered," he said, removing the cover. "I'm married!"

"Good Lord!"

"At least I was before the war. She had blue eyes and brown hair and a Pekingese dog."

"What was her name?"

"I don't know."

"Well, you're coming on," said Archie. "I'll admit that. You've still got a bit of a way to go before you become like one of those blighters who take the Memory Training Courses in the magazine advertisements—I mean to say, you know, the lads who meet a fellow once for five minutes, and then come across him again ten years later and grasp him by the hand and say, 'Surely this is Mr. Watkins of Seattle?' Still, you're doing fine. You only need patience. Everything comes to him who waits." Archie sat up, electrified. "I say, by Jove, that's rather good, what! Everything comes to him who waits, and you're a waiter, what, what. I mean to say, what!"

"Mummie," said the child at the other table, still speculative, "do you think something trod on his face?"

"Hush, darling."

"Perhaps it was bitten by something?"

"Eat your nice fish, darling," said the mother, who seemed to be one of those dull-witted persons whom it is impossible to interest in a discussion on first causes.

Archie felt stimulated. Not even the advent of his father-in-law, who came in a few moments later and sat down at the other end of the room, could depress his spirits.

The Sausage Chappie came to his table again.

"It's a funny thing," he said. "Like waking up after you've been asleep. Everything seems to be getting clearer. The dog's name was Marie. My wife's dog, you know. And she had a mole on her chin."

"The dog?"

"No. My wife. Little beast! She bit me in the leg once."

"Your wife?"

"No. The dog. Good Lord!" said the Sausage Chappie.

Archie looked up and followed his gaze.

A couple of tables away, next to a sideboard on which the management exposed for view the cold meats and puddings and pies mentioned in volume two of the bill of fare ("Buffet Froid"), a man and a girl had just seated themselves. The man was stout and middle-aged. He bulged in practically every place in which a man can bulge, and his head was almost entirely free from hair. The girl was young and pretty. Her eyes were blue. Her hair was brown. She had a rather attractive little mole on the left side of her chin.

"Good Lord!" said the Sausage Chappie.

"Now what?" said Archie.

"Who's that? Over at the table there?"

Archie, through long attendance at the Cosmopolis Grill, knew most of the habitues by sight.

"That's a man named Gossett. James J. Gossett. He's a motion-picture man. You must have seen his name around."

"I don't mean him. Who's the girl?"

"I've never seen her before."

"It's my wife!" said the Sausage Chappie.

"Your wife!"

"Yes!"

"Are you sure?"

"Of course I'm sure!"

"Well, well, well!" said Archie. "Many happy returns of the day!"

At the other table, the girl, unconscious of the drama which was about to enter her life, was engrossed in conversation with the stout man. And at this moment the stout man leaned forward and patted her on the cheek.

It was a paternal pat, the pat which a genial uncle might bestow on a favourite niece, but it did not strike the Sausage Chappie in that light. He had been advancing on the table at a fairly rapid pace, and now, stirred to his depths, he bounded forward with a hoarse cry.

Archie was at some pains to explain to his father-in-law later that, if the management left cold pies and things about all over the place, this sort of thing was bound to happen sooner or later. He urged that it was putting temptation in people's way, and that Mr. Brewster had only himself to blame. Whatever the rights of the case, the Buffet Froid undoubtedly came in remarkably handy at this crisis in the Sausage Chappie's life. He had almost reached the sideboard when the stout man patted the girl's cheek, and to seize a huckleberry pie was with him the work of a moment. The next instant the pie had whizzed past the other's head and burst like a shell against the wall.

There are, no doubt, restaurants where this sort of thing would have excited little comment, but the Cosmopolis was not one of them. Everybody had something to say, but the only one among those present who had anything sensible to say was the child in the sailor suit.

"Do it again!" said the child, cordially.

The Sausage Chappie did it again. He took up a fruit salad, poised it for a moment, then decanted it over Mr. Gossett's bald head. The child's happy laughter rang over the restaurant. Whatever anybody else might think of the affair, this child liked it and was prepared to go on record to that effect.

Epic events have a stunning quality. They paralyse the faculties. For a moment there was a pause. The world stood still. Mr. Brewster bubbled inarticulately. Mr. Gossett dried himself sketchily with a napkin. The Sausage Chappie snorted.

The girl had risen to her feet and was staring wildly.

"John!" she cried.

Even at this moment of crisis the Sausage Chappie was able to look relieved.

"So it is!" he said. "And I thought it was Lancelot!"

"I thought you were dead!"

"I'm not!" said the Sausage Chappie.

Mr. Gossett, speaking thickly through the fruit-salad, was understood to say that he regretted this. And then confusion broke loose again. Everybody began to talk at once.

"I say!" said Archie. "I say! One moment!"

Of the first stages of this interesting episode Archie had been a paralysed spectator. The thing had numbed him. And then—

Sudden a thought came, like a full-blown rose.
Flushing his brow.

When he reached the gesticulating group, he was calm and business-like. He had a constructive policy to suggest.

"I say," he said. "I've got an idea!"

"Go away!" said Mr. Brewster. "This is bad enough without you butting in."

Archie quelled him with a gesture.

"Leave us," he said. "We would be alone. I want to have a little business-talk with Mr. Gossett." He turned to the movie-magnate, who was gradually emerging from the fruit-salad rather after the

139

manner of a stout Venus rising from the sea. "Can you spare me a moment of your valuable time?"

"I'll have him arrested!"

"Don't you do it, laddie. Listen!"

"The man's mad. Throwing pies!"

Archie attached himself to his coat-button.

"Be calm, laddie. Calm and reasonable!"

For the first time Mr. Gossett seemed to become aware that what he had been looking on as a vague annoyance was really an individual.

"Who the devil are you?"

Archie drew himself up with dignity.

"I am this gentleman's representative," he replied, indicating the Sausage Chappie with a motion of the hand. "His jolly old personal representative. I act for him. And on his behalf I have a pretty ripe proposition to lay before you. Reflect, dear old bean," he proceeded earnestly. "Are you going to let this chance slip? The opportunity of a lifetime which will not occur again. By Jove, you ought to rise up and embrace this bird. You ought to clasp the chappie to your bosom! He has thrown pies at you, hasn't he? Very well. You are a movie-magnate. Your whole fortune is founded on chappies who throw pies. You probably scour the world for chappies who throw pies. Yet, when one comes right to you without any fuss or trouble and demonstrates before your very eyes the fact that he is without a peer as a pie-propeller, you get the wind up and talk about having him arrested. Consider! (There's a bit of cherry just behind your left ear.) Be sensible. Why let your personal feeling stand in the way of doing yourself a bit of good? Give this chappie a job and give it him quick, or we go elsewhere. Did you ever see Fatty Arbuckle handle pastry with a surer touch? Has Charlie Chaplin got this fellow's speed and control. Absolutely not. I tell you, old friend, you're in danger of throwing away a good thing!"

He paused. The Sausage Chappie beamed.

"I've aways wanted to go into the movies," he said. "I was an actor before the war. Just remembered."

Mr. Brewster attempted to speak. Archie waved him down.

"How many times have I got to tell you not to butt in?" he said, severely.

Mr. Gossett's militant demeanour had become a trifle modified during Archie's harangue. First and foremost a man of business, Mr. Gossett was not insensible to the arguments which had been put forward. He brushed a slice of orange from the back of his neck, and mused awhile.

"How do I know this fellow would screen well?" he said, at length.

"Screen well!" cried Archie. "Of course he'll screen well. Look at his face. I ask you! The map! I call your attention to it." He turned apologetically to the Sausage Chappie. "Awfully sorry, old lad, for dwelling on this, but it's business, you know." He turned to Mr. Gossett. "Did you ever see a face like that? Of course not. Why should I, as this gentleman's personal representative, let a face like that go to waste? There's a fortune in it. By Jove, I'll give you two minutes to think the thing over, and, if you don't talk business then, I'll jolly well take my man straight round to Mack Sennett or someone. We don't have to ask for jobs. We consider offers."

There was a silence. And then the clear voice of the child in the sailor suit made itself heard again.

"Mummie!"

"Yes, darling?"

"Is the man with the funny face going to throw any more pies?"

"No, darling."

The child uttered a scream of disappointed fury.

"I want the funny man to throw some more pies! I want the funny man to throw some more pies!"

A look almost of awe came into Mr. Gossett's face. He had heard the voice of the Public. He had felt the beating of the Public's pulse.

"Out of the mouths of babes and sucklings," he said, picking a piece of banana off his right eyebrow, "Out of the mouths of babes and sucklings. Come round to my office!"

141

CHAPTER XXI

THE GROWING BOY

The lobby of the Cosmopolis Hotel was a favourite stamping-ground of Mr. Daniel Brewster, its proprietor. He liked to wander about there, keeping a paternal eye on things, rather in the manner of the Jolly Innkeeper (hereinafter to be referred to as Mine Host) of the old-fashioned novel. Customers who, hurrying in to dinner, tripped over Mr. Brewster, were apt to mistake him for the hotel detective—for his eye was keen and his aspect a trifle austere—but, nevertheless, he was being as jolly an innkeeper as he knew how. His presence in the lobby supplied a personal touch to the Cosmopolis which other New York hotels lacked, and it undeniably made the girl at the book-stall extraordinarily civil to her clients, which was all to the good.

Most of the time Mr. Brewster stood in one spot and just looked thoughtful; but now and again he would wander to the marble slab behind which he kept the desk-clerk and run his eye over the register, to see who had booked rooms—like a child examining the stocking on Christmas morning to ascertain what Santa Claus had brought him.

As a rule, Mr. Brewster concluded this performance by shoving the book back across the marble slab and resuming his meditations. But one night a week or two after the Sausage Chappie's sudden restoration to the normal, he varied this procedure by starting rather violently, turning purple, and uttering an exclamation which was manifestly an exclamation of chagrin. He turned abruptly and cannoned into Archie, who, in company with Lucille, happened to be crossing the lobby at the moment on his way to dine in their suite.

Mr. Brewster apologised gruffly; then, recognising his victim, seemed to regret having done so.

"Oh, it's you! Why can't you look where you're going?" he demanded. He had suffered much from his son-in-law.

"Frightfully sorry," said Archie, amiably. "Never thought you were going to fox-trot backwards all over the fairway."

"You mustn't bully Archie," said Lucille, severely, attaching herself to her father's back hair and giving it a punitive tug, "because he's an angel, and I love him, and you must learn to love him, too."

"Give you lessons at a reasonable rate," murmured Archie.

Mr. Brewster regarded his young relative with a lowering eye.

"What's the matter, father darling?" asked Lucille. "You seem upset"

"I am upset!" Mr. Brewster snorted. "Some people have got a nerve!" He glowered forbiddingly at an inoffensive young man in a light overcoat who had just entered, and the young man, though his conscience was quite clear and Mr. Brewster an entire stranger to him, stopped dead, blushed, and went out again—to dine elsewhere. "Some people have got the nerve of an army mule!"

"Why, what's happened?"

"Those darned McCalls have registered here!"

"No!"

"Bit beyond me, this," said Archie, insinuating himself into the conversation. "Deep waters and what not! Who are the McCalls?"

"Some people father dislikes," said Lucille. "And they've chosen his hotel to stop at. But, father dear, you mustn't mind. It's really a compliment. They've come because they know it's the best hotel in New York."

"Absolutely!" said Archie. "Good accommodation for man and beast! All the comforts of home! Look on the bright side, old bean. No good getting the wind up. Cherrio, old companion!"

"Don't call me old companion!"

"Eh, what? Oh, right-o!"

Lucille steered her husband out of the danger zone, and they entered the lift.

"Poor father!" she said, as they went to their suite, "it's a shame. They must have done it to annoy him. This man McCall has a place next to some property father bought in Westchester, and he's bringing a law-suit against father about a bit of land which he claims belongs to him. He might have had the tact to go to another hotel. But, after all, I don't suppose it was the poor little fellow's fault. He does whatever his wife tells him to."

"We all do that," said Archie the married man.

Lucille eyed him fondly.

"Isn't it a shame, precious, that all husbands haven't nice wives like me?"

"When I think of you, by Jove," said Archie, fervently, "I want to babble, absolutely babble!"

"Oh, I was telling you about the McCalls. Mr. McCall is one of those little, meek men, and his wife's one of those big, bullying women. It was she who started all the trouble with father. Father and Mr. McCall were very fond of each other till she made him begin the suit. I feel sure she made him come to this hotel just to

143

annoy father. Still, they've probably taken the most expensive suite in the place, which is something."

Archie was at the telephone. His mood was now one of quiet peace. Of all the happenings which went to make up existence in New York, he liked best the cosy tete-a-tete dinners with Lucille in their suite, which, owing to their engagements—for Lucille was a popular girl, with many friends—occurred all too seldom.

"Touching now the question of browsing and sluicing," he said. "I'll be getting them to send along a waiter."

"Oh, good gracious!"

"What's the matter?"

"I've just remembered. I promised faithfully I would go and see Jane Murchison to-day. And I clean forgot. I must rush."

"But light of my soul, we are about to eat. Pop around and see her after dinner."

"I can't. She's going to a theatre to-night."

"Give her the jolly old miss-in-baulk, then, for the nonce, and spring round to-morrow."

"She's sailing for England to-morrow morning, early. No, I must go and see her now. What a shame! She's sure to make me stop to dinner, I tell you what. Order something for me, and, if I'm not back in half an hour, start."

"Jane Murchison," said Archie, "is a bally nuisance."

"Yes. But I've known her since she was eight."

"If her parents had had any proper feeling," said Archie, "they would have drowned her long before that."

He unhooked the receiver, and asked despondently to be connected with Room Service. He thought bitterly of the exigent Jane, whom he recollected dimly as a tall female with teeth. He half thought of going down to the grill-room on the chance of finding a friend there, but the waiter was on his way to the room. He decided that he might as well stay where he was.

The waiter arrived, booked the order, and departed. Archie had just completed his toilet after a shower-bath when a musical clinking without announced the advent of the meal. He opened the door. The waiter was there with a table congested with things under covers, from which escaped a savoury and appetising odour. In spite of his depression, Archie's soul perked up a trifle.

Suddenly he became aware that he was not the only person present who was deriving enjoyment from the scent of the meal. Standing beside the waiter and gazing wistfully at the foodstuffs was a long, thin boy of about sixteen. He was one of those boys who seem all legs and knuckles. He had pale red hair, sandy eyelashes, and a long neck; and his eyes, as he removed them from the table and raised them to Archie's, had a hungry look. He reminded Archie of a half-grown, half-starved hound.

"That smells good!" said the long boy. He inhaled deeply. "Yes, sir," he continued, as one whose mind is definitely made up, "that smells good!"

Before Archie could reply, the telephone bell rang. It was Lucille, confirming her prophecy that the pest Jane would insist on her staying to dine.

"Jane," said Archie, into the telephone, "is a pot of poison. The waiter is here now, setting out a rich banquet, and I shall have to eat two of everything by myself."

He hung up the receiver, and, turning, met the pale eye of the long boy, who had propped himself up in the doorway.

"Were you expecting somebody to dinner?" asked the boy.

"Why, yes, old friend, I was."

"I wish—"

"Yes?"

"Oh, nothing."

The waiter left. The long boy hitched his back more firmly against the doorpost, and returned to his original theme.

"That surely does smell good!" He basked a moment in the aroma. "Yes, sir! I'll tell the world it does!"

Archie was not an abnormally rapid thinker, but he began at this point to get a clearly defined impression that this lad, if invited, would waive the formalities and consent to join his meal. Indeed, the idea Archie got was that, if he were not invited pretty soon, he would invite himself.

"Yes," he agreed. "It doesn't smell bad, what!"

"It smells GOOD!" said the boy. "Oh, doesn't it! Wake me up in the night and ask me if it doesn't!"

"Poulet en casserole," said Archie.

"Golly!" said the boy, reverently.

There was a pause. The situation began to seem to Archie a trifle difficult. He wanted to start his meal, but it began to appear that he must either do so under the penetrating gaze of his new friend or else eject the latter forcibly. The boy showed no signs of ever wanting to leave the doorway.

"You've dined, I suppose, what?" said Archie.

"I never dine."

"What!"

"Not really dine, I mean. I only get vegetables and nuts and things."

"Dieting?"

"Mother is."

145

"I don't absolutely catch the drift, old bean," said Archie. The boy sniffed with half-closed eyes as a wave of perfume from the poulet en casserole floated past him. He seemed to be anxious to intercept as much of it as possible before it got through the door.

"Mother's a food-reformer," he vouchsafed. "She lectures on it. She makes Pop and me live on vegetables and nuts and things."

Archie was shocked. It was like listening to a tale from the abyss.

"My dear old chap, you must suffer agonies—absolute shooting pains!" He had no hesitation now. Common humanity pointed out his course. "Would you care to join me in a bite now?"

"Would I!" The boy smiled a wan smile. "Would I! Just stop me on the street and ask me!"

"Come on in, then," said Archie, rightly taking this peculiar phrase for a formal acceptance. "And close the door. The fatted calf is getting cold."

Archie was not a man with a wide visiting-list among people with families, and it was so long since he had seen a growing boy in action at the table that he had forgotten what sixteen is capable of doing with a knife and fork, when it really squares its elbows, takes a deep breath, and gets going. The spectacle which he witnessed was consequently at first a little unnerving. The long boy's idea of trifling with a meal appeared to be to swallow it whole and reach out for more. He ate like a starving Eskimo. Archie, in the time he had spent in the trenches making the world safe for the working-man to strike in, had occasionally been quite peckish, but he sat dazed before this majestic hunger. This was real eating.

There was little conversation. The growing boy evidently did not believe in table-talk when he could use his mouth for more practical purposes. It was not until the final roll had been devoured to its last crumb that the guest found leisure to address his host. Then he leaned back with a contented sigh.

"Mother," said the human python, "says you ought to chew every mouthful thirty-three times...."

"Yes, sir! Thirty-three times!" He sighed again, "I haven't ever had meal like that."

"All right, was it, what?"

"Was it! Was it! Call me up on the 'phone and ask me!-Yes, sir!-Mother's tipped off these darned waiters not to serve-me anything but vegetables and nuts and things, darn it!"

"The mater seems to have drastic ideas about the good old feed-bag, what!"

"I'll say she has! Pop hates it as much as me, but he's scared to kick. Mother says vegetables contain all the proteins you want.

Mother says, if you eat meat, your blood-pressure goes all blooey. Do you think it does?"

"Mine seems pretty well in the pink."

"She's great on talking," conceded the boy. "She's out to-night somewhere, giving a lecture on Rational Eating to some ginks. I'll have to be slipping up to our suite before she gets back." He rose, sluggishly. "That isn't a bit of roll under that napkin, is it?" he asked, anxiously.

Archie raised the napkin.

"No. Nothing of that species."

"Oh, well!" said the boy, resignedly. "Then I believe I'll be going. Thanks very much for the dinner."

"Not a bit, old top. Come again if you're ever trickling round in this direction."

The long boy removed himself slowly, loath to leave. At the door he cast an affectionate glance back at the table.

"Some meal!" he said, devoutly. "Considerable meal!"

Archie lit a cigarette. He felt like a Boy Scout who has done his day's Act of Kindness.

On the following morning it chanced that Archie needed a fresh supply of tobacco. It was his custom, when this happened, to repair to a small shop on Sixth Avenue which he had discovered accidentally in the course of his rambles about the great city. His relations with Jno. Blake, the proprietor, were friendly and intimate. The discovery that Mr. Blake was English and had, indeed, until a few years back maintained an establishment only a dozen doors or so from Archie's London club, had served as a bond.

To-day he found Mr. Blake in a depressed mood. The tobacconist was a hearty, red-faced man, who looked like an English sporting publican—the kind of man who wears a fawn-coloured top-coat and drives to the Derby in a dog-cart; and usually there seemed to be nothing on his mind except the vagaries of the weather, concerning which he was a great conversationalist. But now moodiness had claimed him for its own. After a short and melancholy "Good morning," he turned to the task of measuring out the tobacco in silence.

Archie's sympathetic nature was perturbed.—"What's the matter, laddie?" he enquired. "You would seem to be feeling a bit of an onion this bright morning, what, yes, no? I can see it with the naked eye."

Mr. Blake grunted sorrowfully.

"I've had a knock, Mr. Moffam."

"Tell me all, friend of my youth."

147

Mr. Blake, with a jerk of his thumb, indicated a poster which hung on the wall behind the counter. Archie had noticed it as he came in, for it was designed to attract the eye. It was printed in black letters on a yellow ground, and ran as follows:

CLOVER-LEAF SOCIAL AND OUTING CLUB
GRAND CONTEST
PIE-EATING CHAMPIONSHIP OF THE WEST SIDE
SPIKE O'DOWD
(Champion)
v.
BLAKE'S UNKNOWN
FOR A PURSE OF $50 AND SIDE-BET

Archie examined this document gravely. It conveyed nothing to him except—what he had long suspected—that his sporting-looking friend had sporting blood as well as that kind of exterior. He expressed a kindly hope that the other's Unknown would bring home the bacon.

Mr. Blake laughed one of those hollow, mirthless laughs.

"There ain't any blooming Unknown," he said, bitterly. This man had plainly suffered. "Yesterday, yes, but not now."

Archie sighed.

"In the midst of life—Dead?" he enquired, delicately.

"As good as," replied the stricken tobacconist. He cast aside his artificial restraint and became voluble. Archie was one of those sympathetic souls in whom even strangers readily confided their most intimate troubles. He was to those in travail of spirit very much what catnip is to a cat. "It's 'ard, sir, it's blooming 'ard! I'd got the event all sewed up in a parcel, and now this young feller-me-lad 'as to give me the knock. This lad of mine—sort of cousin 'e is; comes from London, like you and me—'as always 'ad, ever since he landed in this country, a most amazing knack of stowing away grub. 'E'd been a bit underfed these last two or three years over in the old country, what with food restrictions and all, and 'e took to the food over 'ere amazing. I'd 'ave backed 'im against a ruddy orstridge! Orstridge! I'd 'ave backed 'im against 'arff a dozen orstridges—take 'em on one after the other in the same ring on the same evening— and given 'em a handicap, too! 'E was a jewel, that boy. I've seen him polish off four pounds of steak and mealy potatoes and then look round kind of wolfish, as much as to ask when dinner was going to begin! That's the kind of a lad 'e was till this very morning. 'E would have out-swallowed this 'ere O'Dowd without turning a
148

hair, as a relish before 'is tea! I'd got a couple of 'undred dollars on 'im, and thought myself lucky to get the odds. And now—"

Mr. Blake relapsed into a tortured silence.

"But what's the matter with the blighter? Why can't he go over the top? Has he got indigestion?"

"Indigestion?" Mr. Blaife laughed another of his hollow laughs. "You couldn't give that boy indigestion if you fed 'im in on safety-razor blades. Religion's more like what 'e's got."

"Religion?"

"Well, you can call it that. Seems last night, instead of goin' and resting 'is mind at a picture-palace like I told him to, 'e sneaked off to some sort of a lecture down on Eighth Avenue. 'E said 'e'd seen a piece about it in the papers, and it was about Rational Eating, and that kind of attracted 'im. 'E sort of thought 'e might pick up a few hints, like. 'E didn't know what rational eating was, but it sounded to 'im as if it must be something to do with food, and 'e didn't want to miss it. 'E came in here just now," said Mr. Blake, dully, "and 'e was a changed lad! Scared to death 'e was! Said the way 'e'd been goin' on in the past, it was a wonder 'e'd got any stummick left! It was a lady that give the lecture, and this boy said it was amazing what she told 'em about blood-pressure and things 'e didn't even know 'e 'ad. She showed 'em pictures, coloured pictures, of what 'appens inside the injudicious eater's stummick who doesn't chew his food, and it was like a battlefield! 'E said 'e would no more think of eatin' a lot of pie than 'e would of shootin' 'imself, and anyhow eating pie would be a quicker death. I reasoned with 'im, Mr. Moffam, with tears in my eyes. I asked 'im was he goin' to chuck away fame and wealth just because a woman who didn't know what she was talking about had shown him a lot of faked pictures. But there wasn't any doin' anything with him. 'E give me the knock and 'opped it down the street to buy nuts." Mr. Blake moaned. "Two 'undred dollars and more gone pop, not to talk of the fifty dollars 'e would have won and me to get twenty-five of!"

Archie took his tobacco and walked pensively back to the hotel. He was fond of Jno. Blake, and grieved for the trouble that had come upon him. It was odd, he felt, how things seemed to link themselves up together. The woman who had delivered the fateful lecture to injudicious eaters could not be other than the mother of his young guest of last night. An uncomfortable woman! Not content with starving her own family—Archie stopped in his tracks. A pedestrian, walking behind him, charged into his back, but Archie paid no attention. He had had one of those sudden, luminous ideas, which help a man who does not do much thinking as a rule to restore his average. He stood there for a moment, almost dizzy at

149

the brilliance of his thoughts; then hurried on. Napoleon, he mused as he walked, must have felt rather like this after thinking up a hot one to spring on the enemy.

As if Destiny were suiting her plans to his, one of the first persons he saw as he entered the lobby of the Cosmopolis was the long boy. He was standing at the bookstall, reading as much of a morning paper as could be read free under the vigilant eyes of the presiding girl. Both he and she were observing the unwritten rules which govern these affairs—to wit, that you may read without interference as much as can be read without touching the paper. If you touch the paper, you lose, and have to buy.

"Well, well, well!" said Archie. "Here we are again, what!" He prodded the boy amiably in the lower ribs. "You're just the chap I was looking for. Got anything on for the time being?"

The boy said he had no engagements.

"Then I want you to stagger round with me to a chappie I know on Sixth Avenue. It's only a couple of blocks away. I think I can do you a bit of good. Put you on to something tolerably ripe, if you know what I mean. Trickle along, laddie. You don't need a hat."

They found Mr. Blake brooding over his troubles in an empty shop.

"Cheer up, old thing!" said Archie. "The relief expedition has arrived." He directed his companion's gaze to the poster. "Cast your eye over that. How does that strike you?"

The long boy scanned the poster. A gleam appeared in his rather dull eye.

"Well?"

"Some people have all the luck!" said the long boy, feelingly.

"Would you like to compete, what?"

The boy smiled a sad smile.

"Would I! Would I! Say!..."

"I know," interrupted Archie. "Wake you up in the night and ask you! I knew I could rely on you, old thing." He turned to Mr. Blake. "Here's the fellow you've been wanting to meet. The finest left-and-right-hand eater east of the Rockies! He'll fight the good fight for you."

Mr. Blake's English training had not been wholly overcome by residence in New York. He still retained a nice eye for the distinctions of class.

"But this is young gentleman's a young gentleman," he urged, doubtfully, yet with hope shining in his eye. "He wouldn't do it."

"Of course, he would. Don't be ridic, old thing."

"Wouldn't do what?" asked the boy.

"Why save the old homestead by taking on the champion.

Dashed sad case, between ourselves! This poor egg's nominee has given him the raspberry at the eleventh hour, and only you can save him. And you owe it to him to do something you know, because it was your jolly old mater's lecture last night that made the nominee quit. You must charge in and take his place. Sort of poetic justice, don't you know, and what not!" He turned to Mr. Blake. "When is the conflict supposed to start? Two-thirty? You haven't any important engagement for two-thirty, have you?"

"No. Mother's lunching at some ladies' club, and giving a lecture afterwards. I can slip away."

Archie patted his head.

"Then leg it where glory waits you, old bean!"

The long boy was gazing earnestly at the poster. It seemed to fascinate him.

"Pie!" he said in a hushed voice.

The word was like a battle-cry.

CHAPTER XXII

WASHY STEPS INTO THE HALL OF FAME

At about nine o'clock next morning, in a suite at the Hotel Cosmopolis, Mrs. Cora Bates McCall, the eminent lecturer on Rational Eating, was seated at breakfast with her family. Before her sat Mr. McCall, a little hunted-looking man, the natural peculiarities of whose face were accentuated by a pair of glasses of semicircular shape, like half-moons with the horns turned up. Behind these, Mr. McCall's eyes played a perpetual game of peekaboo, now peering over them, anon ducking down and hiding behind them. He was sipping a cup of anti-caffeine. On his right, toying listlessly with a plateful of cereal, sat his son, Washington. Mrs. McCall herself was eating a slice of Health Bread and nut butter. For she practised as well as preached the doctrines which she had striven for so many years to inculcate in an unthinking populace. Her day always began with a light but nutritious breakfast, at which a peculiarly uninviting cereal, which looked and tasted like an old straw hat that had been run through a meat chopper, competed for first place in the dislike of her husband and son with a more than usually offensive brand of imitation coffee. Mr. McCall was inclined to think that he loathed the imitation coffee rather more than the cereal, but Washington held strong views on the latter's superior ghastliness. Both Washington and his father, however, would have been fair-minded enough to admit that it was a close thing.

Mrs. McCall regarded her offspring with grave approval.

"I am glad to see, Lindsay," she said to her husband, whose eyes sprang dutifully over the glass fence as he heard his name, "that Washy has recovered his appetite. When he refused his dinner last night, I was afraid that he might be sickening for something. Especially as he had quite a flushed look. You noticed his flushed look?"

"He did look flushed."

"Very flushed. And his breathing was almost stertorous. And, when he said that he had no appetite, I am bound to say that I was anxious. But he is evidently perfectly well this morning. You do feel perfectly well this morning, Washy?"

The heir of the McCall's looked up from his cereal. He was a long, thin boy of about sixteen, with pale red hair, sandy eyelashes, and a long neck.

"Uh-huh," he said.

152

Mrs. McCall nodded.

"Surely now you will agree, Lindsay, that a careful and rational diet is what a boy needs? Washy's constitution is superb. He has a remarkable stamina, and I attribute it entirely to my careful supervision of his food. I shudder when I think of the growing boys who are permitted by irresponsible people to devour meat, candy, pie—" She broke off. "What is the matter, Washy?"

It seemed that the habit of shuddering at the thought of pie ran in the McCall family, for at the mention of the word a kind of internal shimmy had convulsed Washington's lean frame, and over his face there had come an expression that was almost one of pain. He had been reaching out his hand for a slice of Health Bread, but now he withdrew it rather hurriedly and sat back breathing hard.

"I'm all right," he said, huskily.

"Pie," proceeded Mrs. McCall, in her platform voice. She stopped again abruptly. "Whatever is the matter, Washington? You are making me feel nervous."

"I'm all right."

Mrs. McCall had lost the thread of her remarks. Moreover, having now finished her breakfast, she was inclined for a little light reading. One of the subjects allied to the matter of dietary on which she felt deeply was the question of reading at meals. She was of the opinion that the strain on the eye, coinciding with the strain on the digestion, could not fail to give the latter the short end of the contest; and it was a rule at her table that the morning paper should not even be glanced at till the conclusion of the meal. She said that it was upsetting to begin the day by reading the paper, and events were to prove that she was occasionally right.

All through breakfast the New York Chronicle had been lying neatly folded beside her plate. She now opened it, and, with a remark about looking for the report of her yesterday's lecture at the Butterfly Club, directed her gaze at the front page, on which she hoped that an editor with the best interests of the public at heart had decided to place her.

Mr. McCall, jumping up and down behind his glasses, scrutinised her face closely as she began to read. He always did this on these occasions, for none knew better than he that his comfort for the day depended largely on some unknown reporter whom he had never met. If this unseen individual had done his work properly and as befitted the importance of his subject, Mrs. McCall's mood for the next twelve hours would be as uniformly sunny as it was possible for it to be. But sometimes the fellows scamped their job disgracefully; and once, on a day which lived in Mr. McCall's memory, they had failed to make a report at all.

To-day, he noted with relief, all seemed to be well. The report actually was on the front page, an honour rarely accorded to his wife's utterances. Moreover, judging from the time it took her to read the thing, she had evidently been reported at length.

"Good, my dear?" he ventured. "Satisfactory?"

"Eh?" Mrs. McCall smiled meditatively. "Oh, yes, excellent. They have used my photograph, too. Not at all badly reproduced."

"Splendid!" said Mr. McCall.

Mrs. McCall gave a sharp shriek, and the paper fluttered from her hand.

"My dear!" said Mr. McCall, with concern.

His wife had recovered the paper, and was reading with burning eyes. A bright wave of colour had flowed over her masterful features. She was breathing as stertorously as ever her son Washington had done on the previous night.

"Washington!"

A basilisk glare shot across the table and turned the long boy to stone—all except his mouth, which opened feebly.

"Washington! Is this true?"

Washy closed his mouth, then let it slowly open again.

"My dear!" Mr. McCall's voice was alarmed. "What is it?" His eyes had climbed up over his glasses and remained there. "What is the matter? Is anything wrong?"

"Wrong! Read for yourself!"

Mr. McCall was completely mystified. He could not even formulate a guess at the cause of the trouble. That it appeared to concern his son Washington seemed to be the one solid fact at his disposal, and that only made the matter still more puzzling. Where, Mr. McCall asked himself, did Washington come in?

He looked at the paper, and received immediate enlightenment. Headlines met his eyes:

GOOD STUFF IN THIS BOY.
ABOUT A TON OF IT.
SON OF CORA BATES McCALL
FAMOUS FOOD-REFORM LECTURER
WINS PIE-EATING CHAMPIONSHIP OF
WEST SIDE.

There followed a lyrical outburst. So uplifted had the reporter evidently felt by the importance of his news that he had been unable to confine himself to prose:—

154

My children, if you fail to shine or triumph in your
special line; if, let us say, your hopes are bent on
some day being President, and folks ignore your proper
worth, and say you've not a chance on earth—Cheer up!
for in these stirring days Fame may be won in many ways.
Consider, when your spirits fall, the case of Washington
McCall.

Yes, cast your eye on Washy, please! He looks just like
a piece of cheese: he's not a brilliant sort of chap: he
has a dull and vacant map: his eyes are blank, his face
is red, his ears stick out beside his head. In fact, to
end these compliments, he would be dear at thirty cents.
Yet Fame has welcomed to her Hall this self-same
Washington McCall.

His mother (nee Miss Cora Bates) is one who frequently
orates upon the proper kind of food which every menu
should include. With eloquence the world she weans from
chops and steaks and pork and beans. Such horrid things
she'd like to crush, and make us live on milk and mush.
But oh! the thing that makes her sigh is when she sees
us eating pie. (We heard her lecture last July upon "The
Nation's Menace—Pie.") Alas, the hit it made was small
with Master Washington McCall.

For yesterday we took a trip to see the great Pie
Championship, where men with bulging cheeks and eyes
consume vast quantities of pies. A fashionable West Side
crowd beheld the champion, Spike O'Dowd, endeavour to
defend his throne against an upstart, Blake's Unknown.
He wasn't an Unknown at all. He was young Washington
McCall.

We freely own we'd give a leg if we could borrow, steal,
or beg the skill old Homer used to show. (He wrote the
Iliad, you know.) Old Homer swung a wicked pen, but we
are ordinary men, and cannot even start to dream of
doing justice to our theme. The subject of that great
repast is too magnificent and vast. We can't describe
(or even try) the way those rivals wolfed their pie.
Enough to say that, when for hours each had extended all
his pow'rs, toward the quiet evenfall O'Dowd succumbed
to young McCall.

155

*The champion was a willing lad. He gave the public all
he had. His was a genuine fighting soul. He'd lots of
speed and much control. No yellow streak did he evince.
He tackled apple-pie and mince. This was the motto on
his shield—"O'Dowds may burst. They never yield." His
eyes began to start and roll. He eased his belt another
hole. Poor fellow! With a single glance one saw that he
had not a chance. A python would have had to crawl and
own defeat from young McCall.*

*At last, long last, the finish came. His features
overcast with shame, O'Dowd, who'd faltered once or
twice, declined to eat another slice. He tottered off,
and kindly men rallied around with oxygen. But Washy,
Cora Bates's son, seemed disappointed it was done. He
somehow made those present feel he'd barely started on
his meal. We ask him, "Aren't you feeling bad?" "Me!"
said the lion-hearted lad. "Lead me"—he started for the
street—"where I can get a bite to eat!" Oh, what a
lesson does it teach to all of us, that splendid speech!
How better can the curtain fall on Master Washington
McCall!*

Mr. McCall read this epic through, then he looked at his son. He first looked at him over his glasses, then through his glasses, then over his glasses again, then through his glasses once more. A curious expression was in his eyes. If such a thing had not been so impossible, one would have said that his gaze had in it something of respect, of admiration, even of reverence.

"But how did they find out your name?" he asked, at length.

Mrs. McCall exclaimed impatiently.

"Is THAT all you have to say?"

"No, no, my dear, of course not, quite so. But the point struck me as curious."

"Wretched boy," cried Mrs. McCall, "were you insane enough to reveal your name?"

Washington wriggled uneasily. Unable to endure the piercing stare of his mother, he had withdrawn to the window, and was looking out with his back turned. But even there he could feel her eyes on the back of his neck.

"I didn't think it 'ud matter," he mumbled. "A fellow with tortoiseshell-rimmed specs asked me, so I told him. How was I to know—"

His stumbling defence was cut short by the opening of the door.

"Hallo-allo-allo! What ho! What ho!"

Archie was standing in the doorway, beaming ingratiatingly on the family.

The apparition of an entire stranger served to divert the lightning of Mrs. McCall's gaze from the unfortunate Washy. Archie, catching it between the eyes, blinked and held on to the wall. He had begun to regret that he had yielded so weakly to Lucille's entreaty that he should look in on the McCalls and use the magnetism of his personality upon them in the hope of inducing them to settle the lawsuit. He wished, too, if the visit had to be paid that he had postponed it till after lunch, for he was never at his strongest in the morning. But Lucille had urged him to go now and get it over, and here he was.

"I think," said Mrs. McCall, icily, "that you must have mistaken your room."

Archie rallied his shaken forces.

"Oh, no. Rather not. Better introduce myself, what? My name's Moffam, you know. I'm old Brewster's son-in-law, and all that sort of rot, if you know what I mean." He gulped and continued. "I've come about this jolly old lawsuit, don't you know."

Mr. McCall seemed about to speak, but his wife anticipated him.

"Mr. Brewster's attorneys are in communication with ours. We do not wish to discuss the matter."

Archie took an uninvited seat, eyed the Health Bread on the breakfast table for a moment with frank curiosity, and resumed his discourse.

"No, but I say, you know! I'll tell you what happened. I hate to totter in where I'm not wanted and all that, but my wife made such a point of it. Rightly or wrongly she regards me as a bit of a hound in the diplomacy line, and she begged me to look you up and see whether we couldn't do something about settling the jolly old thing. I mean to say, you know, the old bird—old Brewster, you know—is considerably perturbed about the affair—hates the thought of being in a posish where he has either got to bite his old pal McCall in the neck or be bitten by him—and—well, and so forth, don't you know! How about it?" He broke off. "Great Scot! I say, what!"

So engrossed had he been in his appeal that he had not observed the presence of the pie-eating champion, between whom and himself a large potted plant intervened. But now Washington, hearing the familiar voice, had moved from the window and was confronting him with an accusing stare.

157

"HE made me do it!" said Washy, with the stern joy a sixteen-year-old boy feels when he sees somebody on to whose shoulders he can shift trouble from his own. "That's the fellow who took me to the place!"

"What are you talking about, Washington?"

"I'm telling you! He got me into the thing."

"Do you mean this—this—" Mrs. McCall shuddered. "Are you referring to this pie-eating contest?"

"You bet I am!"

"Is this true?" Mrs. McCall glared stonily at Archie, "Was it you who lured my poor boy into that—that—"

"Oh, absolutely. The fact is, don't you know, a dear old pal of mine who runs a tobacco shop on Sixth Avenue was rather in the soup. He had backed a chappie against the champion, and the chappie was converted by one of your lectures and swore off pie at the eleventh hour. Dashed hard luck on the poor chap, don't you know! And then I got the idea that our little friend here was the one to step in and save the situash, so I broached the matter to him. And I'll tell you one thing," said Archie, handsomely, "I don't know what sort of a capacity the original chappie had, but I'll bet he wasn't in your son's class. Your son has to be seen to be believed! Absolutely! You ought to be proud of him!" He turned in friendly fashion to Washy. "Rummy we should meet again like this! Never dreamed I should find you here. And, by Jove, it's absolutely marvellous how fit you look after yesterday. I had a sort of idea you would be groaning on a bed of sickness and all that."

There was a strange gurgling sound in the background. It resembled something getting up steam. And this, curiously enough, is precisely what it was. The thing that was getting up steam was Mr. Lindsay McCall.

The first effect of the Washy revelations on Mr. McCall had been merely to stun him. It was not until the arrival of Archie that he had had leisure to think; but since Archie's entrance he had been thinking rapidly and deeply.

For many years Mr. McCall had been in a state of suppressed revolution. He had smouldered, but had not dared to blaze. But this startling upheaval of his fellow-sufferer, Washy, had acted upon him like a high explosive. There was a strange gleam in his eye, a gleam of determination. He was breathing hard.

"Washy!"

His voice had lost its deprecating mildness. It rang strong and clear.

"Yes, pop?"

"How many pies did you eat yesterday?"

Washy considered.

"A good few."

"How many? Twenty?"

"More than that. I lost count. A good few."

"And you feel as well as ever?"

"I feel fine."

Mr. McCall dropped his glasses. He glowered for a moment at the breakfast table. His eye took in the Health Bread, the imitation coffee-pot, the cereal, the nut-butter. Then with a swift movement he seized the cloth, jerked it forcibly, and brought the entire contents rattling and crashing to the floor.

"Lindsay!"

Mr. McCall met his wife's eye with quiet determination. It was plain that something had happened in the hinterland of Mr. McCall's soul.

"Cora," he said, resolutely, "I have come to a decision. I've been letting you run things your own way a little too long in this family. I'm going to assert myself. For one thing, I've had all I want of this food-reform foolery. Look at Washy! Yesterday that boy seems to have consumed anything from a couple of hundredweight to a ton of pie, and he has thriven on it! Thriven! I don't want to hurt your feelings, Cora, but Washington and I have drunk our last cup of anti-caffeine! If you care to go on with the stuff, that's your look-out. But Washy and I are through."

He silenced his wife with a masterful gesture and turned to Archie. "And there's another thing. I never liked the idea of that lawsuit, but I let you talk me into it. Now I'm going to do things my way. Mr. Moffam, I'm glad you looked in this morning. I'll do just what you want. Take me to Dan Brewster now, and let's call the thing off, and shake hands on it."

"Are you mad, Lindsay?"

It was Cora Bates McCall's last shot. Mr. McCall paid no attention to it. He was shaking hands with Archie.

"I consider you, Mr. Moffam," he said, "the most sensible young man I have ever met!"

Archie blushed modestly.

"Awfully good of you, old bean," he said. "I wonder if you'd mind telling my jolly old father-in-law that? It'll be a bit of news for him!"

159

CHAPTER XXIII

MOTHER'S KNEE

Archie Moffam's connection with that devastatingly popular ballad, "Mother's Knee," was one to which he always looked back later with a certain pride. "Mother's Knee," it will be remembered, went through the world like a pestilence. Scots elders hummed it on their way to kirk; cannibals crooned it to their offspring in the jungles of Borneo; it was a best-seller among the Bolshevists. In the United States alone three million copies were disposed of. For a man who has not accomplished anything outstandingly great in his life, it is something to have been in a sense responsible for a song like that; and, though there were moments when Archie experienced some of the emotions of a man who has punched a hole in the dam of one of the larger reservoirs, he never really regretted his share in the launching of the thing.

It seems almost bizarre now to think that there was a time when even one person in the world had not heard "Mother's Knee"; but it came fresh to Archie one afternoon some weeks after the episode of Washy, in his suite at the Hotel Cosmopolis, where he was cementing with cigarettes and pleasant conversation his renewed friendship with Wilson Hymack, whom he had first met in the neighbourhood of Armentieres during the war.

"What are you doing these days?" enquired Wilson Hymack.

"Me?" said Archie. "Well, as a matter of fact, there is what you might call a sort of species of lull in my activities at the moment. But my jolly old father-in-law is bustling about, running up a new hotel a bit farther down-town, and the scheme is for me to be manager when it's finished. From what I have seen in this place, it's a simple sort of job, and I fancy I shall be somewhat hot stuff. How are you filling in the long hours?"

"I'm in my uncle's office, darn it!"

"Starting at the bottom and learning the business and all that? A noble pursuit, no doubt, but I'm bound to say it would give me the pip in no uncertain manner."

"It gives me," said Wilson Hymack, "a pain in the thorax. I want to be a composer."

"A composer, eh?"

Archie felt that he should have guessed this. The chappie had a distinctly artistic look. He wore a bow-tie and all that sort of thing. His trousers bagged at the knees, and his hair, which during the

160

martial epoch of his career had been pruned to the roots, fell about his ears in luxuriant disarray.

"Say! Do you want to hear the best thing I've ever done?"

"Indubitably," said Archie, politely. "Carry on, old bird!"

"I wrote the lyric as well as the melody," said Wilson Hymack, who had already seated himself at the piano. "It's got the greatest title you ever heard. It's a lallapaloosa! It's called 'It's a Long Way Back to Mother's Knee.' How's that? Poor, eh?"

Archie expelled a smoke-ring doubtfully.

"Isn't it a little stale?"

"Stale? What do you mean, stale? There's always room for another song boosting Mother."

"Oh, is it boosting Mother?" Archie's face cleared. "I thought it was a hit at the short skirts. Why, of course, that makes all the difference. In that case, I see no reason why it should not be ripe, fruity, and pretty well all to the mustard. Let's have it."

Wilson Hymack pushed as much of his hair out of his eyes as he could reach with one hand, cleared his throat, looked dreamily over the top of the piano at a photograph of Archie's father-in-law, Mr. Daniel Brewster, played a prelude, and began to sing in a weak, high, composer's voice. All composers sing exactly alike, and they have to be heard to be believed.

"One night a young man wandered through the glitter of Broadway: His money he had squandered. For a meal he couldn't pay."

"Tough luck!" murmured Archie, sympathetically.

> *"He thought about the village where his boyhood he had spent, And yearned for all the simple joys with which he'd been content."*

"The right spirit!" said Archie, with approval. "I'm beginning to like this chappie!"

"Don't interrupt!"

"Oh, right-o! Carried away and all that!"

> *"He looked upon the city, so frivolous and gay; And, as he heaved a weary sigh, these words he then did say: It's a long way back to Mother's knee, Mother's knee, Mother's knee: It's a long way back to Mother's knee, Where I used to stand and prattle With my teddy-bear and rattle:*

> *Oh, those childhood days in Tennessee,*
> *They sure look good to me!*
> *It's a long, long way, but I'm gonna start to-day!*
> *I'm going back,*
> *Believe me, oh!*
> *I'm going back*
> *(I want to go!)*
> *I'm going back—back—on the seven-three*
> *To the dear old shack where I used to be!*
> *I'm going back to Mother's knee!"*

Wilson Hymack's voice cracked on the final high note, which was of an altitude beyond his powers. He turned with a modest cough.

"That'll give you an idea of it!"

"It has, old thing, it has!"

"Is it or is it not a ball of fire?"

"It has many of the earmarks of a sound egg," admitted Archie. "Of course—"

"Of course, it wants singing."

"Just what I was going to suggest."

"It wants a woman to sing it. A woman who could reach out for that last high note and teach it to take a joke. The whole refrain is working up to that. You need Tetrazzini or someone who would just pick that note off the roof and hold it till the janitor came round to lock up the building for the night."

"I must buy a copy for my wife. Where can I get it?"

"You can't get it! It isn't published. Writing music's the darndest job!" Wilson Hymack snorted fiercely. It was plain that the man was pouring out the pent-up emotion of many days. "You write the biggest thing in years and you go round trying to get someone to sing it, and they say you're a genius and then shove the song away in a drawer and forget about it."

Archie lit another cigarette.

"I'm a jolly old child in these matters, old lad," he said, "but why don't you take it direct to a publisher? As a matter of fact, if it would be any use to you, I was foregathering with a music-publisher only the other day. A bird of the name of Blumenthal. He was lunching in here with a pal of mine, and we got tolerably matey. Why not let me tool you round to the office to-morrow and play it to him?"

"No, thanks. Much obliged, but I'm not going to play that melody in any publisher's office with his hired gang of Tin-Pan Alley composers listening at the keyhole and taking notes. I'll have to wait till I can find somebody to sing it. Well, I must be going along. Glad to have seen you again. Sooner or later I'll take you to hear that high note sung by someone in a way that'll make your spine tie itself in knots round the back of your neck."

"I'll count the days," said Archie, courteously. "Pip-pip!"

Hardly had the door closed behind the composer when it opened again to admit Lucille.

"Hallo, light of my soul!" said Archie, rising and embracing his wife. "Where have you been all the afternoon? I was expecting you this many an hour past. I wanted you to meet—"

"I've been having tea with a girl down in Greenwich Village. I couldn't get away before. Who was that who went out just as I came along the passage?"

"Chappie of the name of Hymack. I met him in France. A composer and what not."

"We seem to have been moving in artistic circles this afternoon. The girl I went to see is a singer. At least, she wants to sing, but gets no encouragement."

"Precisely the same with my bird. He wants to get his music sung but nobody'll sing it. But I didn't know you knew any Greenwich Village warblers, sunshine of my home. How did you meet this female?"

Lucille sat down and gazed forlornly at him with her big grey eyes. She was registering something, but Archie could not gather what it was.

"Archie, darling, when you married me you undertook to share my sorrows, didn't you?"

"Absolutely! It's all in the book of words. For better or for worse, in sickness and in health, all-down-set-'em-up-in-the-other-alley. Regular iron-clad contract!"

"Then share 'em!" said Lucille. "Bill's in love again!"

Archie blinked.

"Bill? When you say Bill, do you mean Bill? Your brother Bill? My brother-in-law Bill? Jolly old William, the son and heir of the Brewsters?"

"I do."

"You say he's in love? Cupid's dart?"

"Even so!"

"But, I say! Isn't this rather—What I mean to say is, the lad's an absolute scourge! The Great Lover, what! Also ran, Brigham Young, and all that sort of thing! Why, it's only a few weeks ago that he was moaning brokenly about that vermilion-haired female who subsequently hooked on to old Reggie van Tuyl!"

"She's a little better than that girl, thank goodness. All the same, I don't think Father will approve."

"Of what calibre is the latest exhibit?"

"Well, she comes from the Middle West, and seems to be trying to be twice as Bohemian as the rest of the girls down in Greenwich Village. She wears her hair bobbed and goes about in a kimono. She's probably read magazine stories about Greenwich Village, and has modelled herself on them. It's so silly, when you can see Hicks Corners sticking out of her all the time."

"That one got past me before I could grab it. What did you say she had sticking out of her?"

"I meant that anybody could see that she came from somewhere out in the wilds. As a matter of fact, Bill tells me that she was brought up in Snake Bite, Michigan."

"Snake Bite? What rummy names you have in America! Still, I'll admit there's a village in England called Nether Wallop, so who am I to cast the first stone? How is old Bill? Pretty feverish?"

"He says this time it is the real thing."

"That's what they all say! I wish I had a dollar for every time— Forgotten what I was going to say!" broke off Archie, prudently. "So you think," he went on, after a pause, "that William's latest is going to be one more shock for the old dad?"

"I can't imagine Father approving of her."

"I've studied your merry old progenitor pretty closely," said Archie, "and, between you and me, I can't imagine him approving of anybody!"

"I can't understand why it is that Bill goes out of his way to pick these horrors. I know at least twenty delightful girls, all pretty and with lots of money, who would be just the thing for him; but he sneaks away and goes falling in love with someone impossible. And the worst of it is that one always feels one's got to do one's best to see him through."

"Absolutely! One doesn't want to throw a spanner into the works of Love's young dream. It behoves us to rally round. Have you heard this girl sing?"

"Yes. She sang this afternoon."

"What sort of a voice has she got?"

"Well, it's—loud!"

"Could she pick a high note off the roof and hold it till the janitor came round to lock up the building for the night?"

"What on earth do you mean?"

"Answer me this, woman, frankly. How is her high note? Pretty lofty?"

"Why, yes."

"Then say no more," said Archie. "Leave this to me, my dear old better four-fifths! Hand the whole thing over to Archibald, the man who never lets you down. I have a scheme!"

As Archie approached his suite on the following afternoon he heard through the closed door the drone of a gruff male voice; and, going in, discovered Lucille in the company of his brother-in-law. Lucille, Archie thought, was looking a trifle fatigued. Bill, on the other hand, was in great shape. His eyes were shining, and his face looked so like that of a stuffed frog that Archie had no difficulty in gathering that he had been lecturing on the subject of his latest enslaver.

"Hallo, Bill, old crumpet!" he said.

"Hallo, Archie!"

"I'm so glad you've come," said Lucille. "Bill is telling me all about Spectatia."

"Who?"

"Spectatia. The girl, you know. Her name is Spectatia Huskisson."

"It can't be!" said Archie, incredulously.

"Why not?" growled Bill.

"Well, how could it?" said Archie, appealing to him as a reasonable man. "I mean to say! Spectatia Huskisson! I gravely doubt whether there is such a name."

"What's wrong with it?" demanded the incensed Bill. "It's a darned sight better name than Archibald Moffam."

"Don't fight, you two children!" intervened Lucille, firmly. "It's a good old Middle West name. Everybody knows the Huskissons of Snake Bite, Michigan. Besides, Bill calls her Tootles."

"Pootles," corrected Bill, austerely.

"Oh, yes, Pootles. He calls her Pootles."

"Young blood! Young blood!" sighed Archie.

"I wish you wouldn't talk as if you were my grandfather."

"I look on you as a son, laddie, a favourite son!"

"If I had a father like you—!"-"Ah, but you haven't, young-feller-me-lad, and that's the trouble. If you had, everything would be simple. But as your actual father, if you'll allow me to say so, is one of the finest specimens of the human vampire-bat in captivity, something has got to be done about it, and you're dashed lucky to have me in your corner, a guide, philosopher, and friend, full of the fruitiest ideas. Now, if you'll kindly listen to me for a moment—"

"I've been listening to you ever since you came in."

"You wouldn't speak in that harsh tone of voice if you knew all! William, I have a scheme!"

"Well?"

165

"The scheme to which I allude is what Maeterlinck would call a lallapaloosa!"

"What a little marvel he is!" said Lucille, regarding her husband affectionately. "He eats a lot of fish, Bill. That's what makes him so clever!"

"Shrimps!" diagnosed Bill, churlishly.

"Do you know the leader of the orchestra in the restaurant downstairs?" asked Archie, ignoring the slur.

"I know there IS a leader of the orchestra. What about him?"

"A sound fellow. Great pal of mine. I've forgotten his name—"

"Call him Pootles!" suggested Lucille.

"Desist!" said Archie, as a wordless growl proceeded from his stricken brother-in-law. "Temper your hilarity with a modicum of reserve. This girlish frivolity is unseemly. Well, I'm going to have a chat with this chappie and fix it all up."

"Fix what up?"

"The whole jolly business. I'm going to kill two birds with one stone. I've a composer chappie popping about in the background whose one ambish. is to have his pet song sung before a discriminating audience. You have a singer straining at the leash. I'm going to arrange with this egg who leads the orchestra that your female shall sing my chappie's song downstairs one night during dinner. How about it? Is it or is it not a ball of fire?"

"It's not a bad idea," admitted Bill, brightening visibly. "I wouldn't have thought you had it in you."

"Why not?"

"Well—"

"It's a capital idea," said Lucille. "Quite out of the question, of course."

"How do you mean?"

"Don't you know that the one thing Father hates more than anything else in the world is anything like a cabaret? People are always coming to him, suggesting that it would brighten up the dinner hour if he had singers and things, and he crushes them into little bits. He thinks there's nothing that lowers the tone of a place more. He'll bite you in three places when you suggest it to him!"

"Ah! But has it escaped your notice, lighting system of my soul, that the dear old dad is not at present in residence? He went off to fish at Lake What's-its-name this morning."

"You aren't dreaming of doing this without asking him?"

"That was the general idea."

"But he'll be furious when he finds out."

"But will he find out? I ask you, will he?"

"Of course he will."

166

"I don't see why he should," said Bill, on whose plastic mind the plan had made a deep impression.

"He won't," said Archie, confidently. "This wheeze is for one night only. By the time the jolly old guv'nor returns, bitten to the bone by mosquitoes, with one small stuffed trout in his suit-case, everything will be over and all quiet once more along the Potomac. The scheme is this. My chappie wants his song heard by a publisher. Your girl wants her voice heard by one of the blighters who get up concerts and all that sort of thing. No doubt you know such a bird, whom you could invite to the hotel for a bit of dinner?"

"I know Carl Steinburg. As a matter of fact, I was thinking of writing to him about Spectatia."

"You're absolutely sure that IS her name?" said Archie, his voice still tinged with incredulity. "Oh, well, I suppose she told you so herself, and no doubt she knows best. That will be topping. Rope in your pal and hold him down at the table till the finish. Lucille, the beautiful vision on the sky-line yonder, and I will be at another table entertaining Maxie Blumenthal"

"Who on earth is Maxie Blumenthal?" asked Lucille.

"One of my boyhood chums. A music-publisher. I'll get him to come along, and then we'll all be set. At the conclusion of the performance Miss—" Archie winced—"Miss Spectatia Huskisson will be signed up for a forty weeks' tour, and jovial old Blumenthal will be making all arrangements for publishing the song. Two birds, as I indicated before, with one stone! How about it?"

"It's a winner," said Bill.

"Of course," said Archie, "I'm not urging you. I merely make the suggestion. If you know a better 'ole go to it!"

"It's terrific!" said Bill.

"It's absurd!" said Lucille.

"My dear old partner of joys and sorrows," said Archie, wounded, "we court criticism, but this is mere abuse. What seems to be the difficulty?"

"The leader of the orchestra would be afraid to do it."

"Ten dollars—supplied by William here—push it over, Bill, old man—will remove his tremors."

"And Father's certain to find out."

"Am I afraid of Father?" cried Archie, manfully. "Well, yes, I am!" he added, after a moment's reflection. "But I don't see how he can possibly get to know."

"Of course he can't," said Bill, decidedly. "Fix it up as soon as you can, Archie. This is what the doctor ordered."

167

CHAPTER XXIV

THE MELTING OF MR. CONNOLLY

The main dining-room of the Hotel Cosmopolis is a decorous place. The lighting is artistically dim, and the genuine old tapestries on the walls seem, with their mediaeval calm, to discourage any essay in the riotous. Soft-footed waiters shimmer to and fro over thick, expensive carpets to the music of an orchestra which abstains wholly from the noisy modernity of jazz. To Archie, who during the past few days had been privileged to hear Miss Huskisson rehearsing, the place had a sort of brooding quiet, like the ocean just before the arrival of a cyclone. As Lucille had said, Miss Huskisson's voice was loud. It was a powerful organ, and there was no doubt that it would take the cloistered stillness of the Cosmopolis dining-room and stand it on one ear. Almost unconsciously, Archie found himself bracing his muscles and holding his breath as he had done in France at the approach of the zero hour, when awaiting the first roar of a barrage. He listened mechanically to the conversation of Mr. Blumenthal.

The music-publisher was talking with some vehemence on the subject of Labour. A recent printers' strike had bitten deeply into Mr. Blumenthal's soul. The working man, he considered, was rapidly landing God's Country in the soup, and he had twice upset his glass with the vehemence of his gesticulation. He was an energetic right-and-left-hand talker.

"The more you give 'em the more they want!" he complained. "There's no pleasing 'em! It isn't only in my business. There's your father, Mrs. Moffam!"

"Good God! Where?" said Archie, starting.

"I say, take your father's case. He's doing all he knows to get this new hotel of his finished, and what happens? A man gets fired for loafing on his job, and Connolly calls a strike. And the building operations are held up till the thing's settled! It isn't right!"

"It's a great shame," agreed Lucille. "I was reading about it in the paper this morning."

"That man Connolly's a tough guy. You'd think, being a personal friend of your father, he would—"

"I didn't know they were friends."

"Been friends for years. But a lot of difference that makes. Out come the men just the same. It isn't right! I was saying it wasn't

168

right!" repeated Mr. Blumenthal to Archie, for he was a man who liked the attention of every member of his audience.

Archie did not reply. He was staring glassily across the room at two men who had just come in. One was a large, stout, square-faced man of commanding personality. The other was Mr. Daniel Brewster.

Mr. Blumenthal followed his gaze.

"Why, there is Connolly coming in now!"

"Father!" gasped Lucille.

Her eyes met Archie's. Archie took a hasty drink of ice-water.

"This," he murmured, "has torn it!"

"Archie, you must do something!"

"I know! But what?"

"What's the trouble?" enquired Mr. Blumenthal, mystified.

"Go over to their table and talk to them," said Lucille.

"Me!" Archie quivered. "No, I say, old thing, really!"

"Get them away!"

"How do you mean?"

"I know!" cried Lucille, inspired, "Father promised that you should be manager of the new hotel when it was built. Well, then, this strike affects you just as much as anybody else. You have a perfect right to talk it over with them. Go and ask them to have dinner up in our suite where you can discuss it quietly. Say that up there they won't be disturbed by the—the music."

At this moment, while Archie wavered, hesitating like a diver on the edge of a spring-board who is trying to summon up the necessary nerve to project himself into the deep, a bell-boy approached the table where the Messrs. Brewster and Connolly had seated themselves. He murmured something in Mr. Brewster's ear, and the proprietor of the Cosmopolis rose and followed him out of the room.

"Quick! Now's your chance!" said Lucille, eagerly. "Father's been called to the telephone. Hurry!"

Archie took another drink of ice-water to steady his shaking nerve-centers, pulled down his waistcoat, straightened his tie, and then, with something of the air of a Roman gladiator entering the arena, tottered across the room. Lucille turned to entertain the perplexed music-publisher.

The nearer Archie got to Mr. Aloysius Connolly the less did he like the looks of him. Even at a distance the Labour leader had had a formidable aspect. Seen close to, he looked even more uninviting. His face had the appearance of having been carved out of granite, and the eye which collided with Archie's as the latter, with an attempt at an ingratiating smile, pulled up a chair and sat down at

169

the table was hard and frosty. Mr. Connolly gave the impression that he would be a good man to have on your side during a rough-and-tumble fight down on the water-front or in some lumber-camp, but he did not look chummy.

"Hallo-allo-allo!" said Archie.

"Who the devil," inquired Mr. Connolly, "are you?"

"My name's Archibald Moffam."

"That's not my fault."

"I'm jolly old Brewster's son-in-law."

"Glad to meet you."

"Glad to meet YOU," said Archie, handsomely.

"Well, good-bye!" said Mr. Connolly.

"Eh?"

"Run along and sell your papers. Your father-in-law and I have business to discuss."

"Yes, I know."

"Private," added Mr. Connolly.

"Oh, but I'm in on this binge, you know. I'm going to be the manager of the new hotel."

"You!"

"Absolutely!"

"Well, well!" said Mr. Connolly, noncommittally.

Archie, pleased with the smoothness with which matters had opened, bent forward winsomely.

"I say, you know! It won't do, you know! Absolutely no! Not a bit like it! No, no, far from it! Well, how about it? How do we go? What? Yes? No?"

"What on earth are you talking about?"

"Call it off, old thing!"

"Call what off?"

"This festive old strike."

"Not on your—hallo, Dan! Back again?"

Mr. Brewster, looming over the table like a thundercloud, regarded Archie with more than his customary hostility. Life was no pleasant thing for the proprietor of the Cosmopolis just now. Once a man starts building hotels, the thing becomes like dram-drinking. Any hitch, any sudden cutting-off of the daily dose, has the worst effects; and the strike which was holding up the construction of his latest effort had plunged Mr. Brewster into a restless gloom. In addition to having this strike on his hands, he had had to abandon his annual fishing-trip just when he had begun to enjoy it; and, as if all this were not enough, here was his son-in-law sitting at his table. Mr. Brewster had a feeling that this was more than man was meant to bear.

"What do you want?" he demanded.

"Hallo, old thing!" said Archie. "Come and join the party!"

"Don't call me old thing!"

"Right-o, old companion, just as you say. I say, I was just going to suggest to Mr. Connolly that we should all go up to my suite and talk this business over quietly."

"He says he's the manager of your new hotel," said Mr. Connolly. "Is that right?"

"I suppose so," said Mr. Brewster, gloomily.

"Then I'm doing you a kindness," said Mr. Connolly, "in not letting it be built."

Archie dabbed at his forehead with his handkerchief. The moments were flying, and it began to seem impossible to shift these two men. Mr. Connolly was as firmly settled in his chair as some primeval rock. As for Mr. Brewster, he, too, had seated himself, and was gazing at Archie with a weary repulsion. Mr. Brewster's glance always made Archie feel as though there were soup on his shirt-front.

And suddenly from the orchestra at the other end of the room there came a familiar sound, the prelude of "Mother's Knee."

"So you've started a cabaret, Dan?" said Mr. Connolly, in a satisfied voice. "I always told you you were behind the times here!"

Mr. Brewster jumped.

"Cabaret!"

He stared unbelievingly at the white-robed figure which had just mounted the orchestra dais, and then concentrated his gaze on Archie.

Archie would not have looked at his father-in-law at this juncture if he had had a free and untrammelled choice; but Mr. Brewster's eye drew his with something of the fascination which a snake's has for a rabbit. Mr. Brewster's eye was fiery and intimidating. A basilisk might have gone to him with advantage for a course of lessons. His gaze went right through Archie till the latter seemed to feel his back-hair curling crisply in the flames.

"Is this one of your fool-tricks?"

Even in this tense moment Archie found time almost unconsciously to admire his father-in-law's penetration and intuition. He seemed to have a sort of sixth sense. No doubt this was how great fortunes were made.

"Well, as a matter of fact—to be absolutely accurate—it was like this—"

"Say, cut it out!" said Mr. Connolly. "Can the chatter! I want to listen."

Archie was only too ready to oblige him. Conversation at the

171

moment was the last thing he himself desired. He managed with a strong effort to disengage himself from Mr. Brewster's eye, and turned to the orchestra dais, where Miss Spectatia Huskisson was now beginning the first verse of Wilson Hymack's masterpiece.

Miss Huskisson, like so many of the female denizens of the Middle West, was tall and blonde and constructed on substantial lines. She was a girl whose appearance suggested the old homestead and fried pancakes and pop coming home to dinner after the morning's ploughing. Even her bobbed hair did not altogether destroy this impression. She looked big and strong and healthy, and her lungs were obviously good. She attacked the verse of the song with something of the vigour and breadth of treatment with which in other days she had reasoned with refractory mules. Her diction was the diction of one trained to call the cattle home in the teeth of Western hurricanes. Whether you wanted to or not, you heard every word.

The subdued clatter of knives and forks had ceased. The diners, unused to this sort of thing at the Cosmopolis, were trying to adjust their faculties to cope with the outburst. Waiters stood transfixed, frozen, in attitudes of service. In the momentary lull between verse and refrain Archie could hear the deep breathing of Mr. Brewster. Involuntarily he turned to gaze at him once more, as refugees from Pompeii may have turned to gaze upon Vesuvius; and, as he did so, he caught sight of Mr. Connolly, and paused in astonishment.

Mr. Connolly was an altered man. His whole personality had undergone a subtle change. His face still looked as though hewn from the living rock, but into his eyes had crept an expression which in another man might almost have been called sentimental. Incredible as it seemed to Archie, Mr. Connolly's eyes were dreamy. There was even in them a suggestion of unshed tears. And when with a vast culmination of sound Miss Huskisson reached the high note at the end of the refrain and, after holding it as some storming-party, spent but victorious, holds the summit of a hard-won redoubt, broke off suddenly, in the stillness which followed there proceeded from Mr. Connolly a deep sigh.

Miss Huskisson began the second verse. And Mr. Brewster, seeming to recover from some kind of a trance, leaped to his feet.

"Great Godfrey!"

"Sit down!" said Mr. Connolly, in a broken voice. "Sit down, Dan!"

"He went back to his mother on the train that very day:
He knew there was no other who could make him bright and gay:

172

He kissed her on the forehead and he whispered, 'I've come home!'
He told her he was never going any more to roam.
And onward through the happy years, till he grew old and grey,
He never once regretted those brave words he once did say:
It's a long way back to mother's knee—"

The last high note screeched across the room like a shell, and the applause that followed was like a shell's bursting. One could hardly have recognised the refined interior of the Cosmopolis dining-room. Fair women were waving napkins; brave men were hammering on the tables with the butt-end of knives, for all the world as if they imagined themselves to be in one of those distressing midnight-revue places. Miss Huskisson bowed, retired, returned, bowed, and retired again, the tears streaming down her ample face. Over in a corner Archie could see his brother-in-law clapping strenuously. A waiter, with a display of manly emotion that did him credit, dropped an order of new peas.

"Thirty years ago last October," said Mr. Connolly, in a shaking voice, "I—"

Mr. Brewster interrupted him violently.

"I'll fire that orchestra-leader! He goes to-morrow! I'll fire—" He turned on Archie. "What the devil do you mean by it, you—you"

"Thirty years ago," said Mr. Connolly, wiping away a tear with his napkin, "I left me dear old home in the old country—"

"MY hotel a bear-garden!"

"Frightfully sorry and all that, old companion—"

"Thirty years ago last October! 'Twas a fine autumn evening the finest ye'd ever wish to see. Me old mother, she came to the station to see me off."

Mr. Brewster, who was not deeply interested in Mr. Connolly's old mother, continued to splutter inarticulately, like a firework trying to go off.

"'Ye'll always be a good boy, Aloysius?' she said to me," said Mr. Connolly, proceeding with his autobiography. "And I said: 'Yes, Mother, I will!'" Mr. Connolly sighed and applied the napkin again. "'Twas a liar I was!" he observed, remorsefully. "Many's the dirty I've played since then. 'It's a long way back to Mother's knee.' 'Tis a true word!" He turned impulsively to Mr. Brewster. "Dan, there's a deal of trouble in this world without me going out of me way to make more. The strike is over! I'll send the men back tomorrow! There's me hand on it!"

Mr. Brewster, who had just managed to co-ordinate his views

on the situation and was about to express them with the generous strength which was ever his custom when dealing with his son-in-law, checked himself abruptly. He stared at his old friend and business enemy, wondering if he could have heard aright. Hope began to creep back into Mr. Brewster's heart, like a shamefaced dog that has been away from home hunting for a day or two.

"You'll what!"

"I'll send the men back to-morrow! That song was sent to guide me, Dan! It was meant! Thirty years ago last October me dear old mother—"

Mr. Brewster bent forward attentively. His views on Mr. Connolly's dear old mother had changed. He wanted to hear all about her.

"'Twas that last note that girl sang brought it all back to me as if 'twas yesterday. As we waited on the platform, me old mother and I, out comes the train from the tunnel, and the engine lets off a screech the way ye'd hear it ten miles away. 'Twas thirty years ago"

Archie stole softly from the table. He felt that his presence, if it had ever been required, was required no longer. Looking back, he could see his father-in-law patting Mr. Connolly affectionately on the shoulder.

Archie and Lucille lingered over their coffee. Mr. Blumenthal was out in the telephone-box settling the business end with Wilson Hymack. The music-publisher had been unstinted in his praise of "Mother's Knee." It was sure-fire, he said. The words, stated Mr. Blumenthal, were gooey enough to hurt, and the tune reminded him of every other song-hit he had ever heard. There was, in Mr. Blumenthal's opinion, nothing to stop this thing selling a million copies.

Archie smoked contentedly.

"Not a bad evening's work, old thing," he said. "Talk about birds with one stone!" He looked at Lucille reproachfully. "You don't seem bubbling over with joy."

"Oh, I am, precious!" Lucille sighed. "I was only thinking about Bill."

"What about Bill?"

"Well, it's rather awful to think of him tied for life to that-that steam-siren."

"Oh, we mustn't look on the jolly old dark side. Perhaps—Hallo, Bill, old top! We were just talking about you."

"Were you?" said Bill Brewster, in a dispirited voice.

"I take it that you want congratulations, what?"

"I want sympathy!"

"Sympathy?"

174

"Sympathy! And lots of it! She's gone!"

"Gone! Who?"

"Spectatia!"

"How do you mean, gone?"

Bill glowered at the tablecloth.

"Gone home. I've just seen her off in a cab. She's gone back to Washington Square to pack. She's catching the ten o'clock train back to Snake Bite. It was that damned song!" muttered Bill, in a stricken voice. "She says she never realised before she sang it to-night how hollow New York was. She said it suddenly came over her. She says she's going to give up her career and go back to her mother. What the deuce are you twiddling your fingers for?" he broke off, irritably.

"Sorry, old man. I was just counting."

"Counting? Counting what?"

"Birds, old thing. Only birds!" said Archie.

CHAPTER XXV

THE WIGMORE VENUS

The morning was so brilliantly fine; the populace popped to and fro in so active and cheery a manner; and everybody appeared to be so absolutely in the pink, that a casual observer of the city of New York would have said that it was one of those happy days. Yet Archie Moffam, as he turned out of the sun-bathed street into the ramshackle building on the third floor of which was the studio belonging to his artist friend, James B. Wheeler, was faintly oppressed with a sort of a kind of feeling that something was wrong. He would not have gone so far as to say that he had the pip—it was more a vague sense of discomfort. And, searching for first causes as he made his way upstairs, he came to the conclusion that the person responsible for this nebulous depression was his wife, Lucille. It seemed to Archie that at breakfast that morning Lucille's manner had been subtly rummy. Nothing you could put your finger on, still—rummy.

Musing thus, he reached the studio, and found the door open and the room empty. It had the air of a room whose owner has dashed in to fetch his golf-clubs and biffed off, after the casual fashion of the artist temperament, without bothering to close up behind him. And such, indeed, was the case. The studio had seen the last of J. B. Wheeler for that day: but Archie, not realising this and feeling that a chat with Mr. Wheeler, who was a light-hearted bird, was what he needed this morning, sat down to wait. After a few moments, his gaze, straying over the room, encountered a handsomely framed picture, and he went across to take a look at it.

J. B. Wheeler was an artist who made a large annual income as an illustrator for the magazines, and it was a surprise to Archie to find that he also went in for this kind of thing. For the picture, dashingly painted in oils, represented a comfortably plump young woman who, from her rather weak-minded simper and the fact that she wore absolutely nothing except a small dove on her left shoulder, was plainly intended to be the goddess Venus. Archie was not much of a lad around the picture-galleries, but he knew enough about Art to recognise Venus when he saw her; though once or twice, it is true, artists had double-crossed him by ringing in some such title as "Day Dreams," or "When the Heart is Young."

He inspected this picture for awhile, then, returning to his seat, lit a cigarette and began to meditate on Lucille once more.

"Yes, the dear girl had been rummy at breakfast. She had not exactly said anything or done anything out of the ordinary; but—well, you know how it is. We husbands, we lads of the for-better-or-for-worse brigade, we learn to pierce the mask. There had been in Lucille's manner that curious, strained sweetness which comes to women whose husbands have failed to match the piece of silk or forgotten to post an important letter. If his conscience had not been as clear as crystal, Archie would have said that that was what must have been the matter. But, when Lucille wrote letters, she just stepped out of the suite and dropped them in the mail-chute attached to the elevator. It couldn't be that. And he couldn't have forgotten anything else, because—"

"Oh my sainted aunt!"

Archie's cigarette smouldered, neglected, between his fingers. His jaw had fallen and his eyes were staring glassily before him. He was appalled. His memory was weak, he knew; but never before had it let him down, so scurvily as this. This was a record. It stood in a class by itself, printed in red ink and marked with a star, as the bloomer of a lifetime. For a man may forget many things: he may forget his name, his umbrella, his nationality, his spats, and the friends of his youth: but there is one thing which your married man, your in-sickness-and-in-health lizard must not forget: and that is the anniversary of his wedding-day.

Remorse swept over Archie like a wave. His heart bled for Lucille. No wonder the poor girl had been rummy at breakfast. What girl wouldn't be rummy at breakfast, tied for life to a ghastly outsider like himself? He groaned hollowly, and sagged forlornly in his chair: and, as he did so, the Venus caught his eye. For it was an eye-catching picture. You might like it or dislike it, but you could not ignore it.

As a strong swimmer shoots to the surface after a high dive, Archie's soul rose suddenly from the depths to which it had descended. He did not often get inspirations, but he got one now. Hope dawned with a jerk. The one way out had presented itself to him. A rich present! That was the wheeze. If he returned to her bearing a rich present, he might, with the help of Heaven and a face of brass, succeed in making her believe that he had merely pretended to forget the vital date in order to enhance the surprise.

It was a scheme. Like some great general forming his plan of campaign on the eve of battle, Archie had the whole binge neatly worked out inside a minute. He scribbled a note to Mr. Wheeler, explaining the situation and promising reasonable payment on the instalment system; then, placing the note in a conspicuous position on the easel, he leaped to the telephone: and presently found himself connected with Lucille's room at the Cosmopolis.

"Hullo, darling," he cooed.

There was a slight pause at the other end of the wire.

"Oh, hullo, Archie!"

Lucille's voice was dull and listless, and Archie's experienced ear could detect that she had been crying. He raised his right foot, and kicked himself indignantly on the left ankle.

"Many happy returns of the day, old thing!"

A muffled sob floated over the wire.

"Have you only just remembered?" said Lucille in a small voice.

Archie, bracing himself up, cackled gleefully into the receiver.

"Did I take you in, light of my home? Do you mean to say you really thought I had forgotten? For Heaven's sake!"

"You didn't say a word at breakfast."

"Ah, but that was all part of the devilish cunning. I hadn't got a present for you then. At least, I didn't know whether it was ready."

"Oh, Archie, you darling!" Lucille's voice had lost its crushed melancholy. She trilled like a thrush, or a linnet, or any bird that goes in largely for trilling. "Have you really got me a present?"

"It's here now. The dickens of a fruity picture. One of J. B. Wheeler's things. You'll like it."

"Oh, I know I shall. I love his work. You are an angel. We'll hang it over the piano."

"I'll be round with it in something under three ticks, star of my soul. I'll take a taxi."

"Yes, do hurry! I want to hug you!"

"Right-o!" said Archie. "I'll take two taxis."

It is not far from Washington Square to the Hotel Cosmopolis, and Archie made the journey without mishap. There was a little unpleasantness with the cabman before starting—he, on the prudish plea that he was a married man with a local reputation to keep up, declining at first to be seen in company with the masterpiece. But, on Archie giving a promise to keep the front of the picture away from the public gaze, he consented to take the job on; and, some ten minutes later, having made his way blushfully through the hotel lobby and endured the frank curiosity of the boy who worked the elevator, Archie entered his suite, the picture under his arm.

He placed it carefully against the wall in order to leave himself more scope for embracing Lucille, and when the joyful reunion—or the sacred scene, if you prefer so to call it, was concluded, he stepped forward to turn it round and exhibit it.

"Why, it's enormous," said Lucille. "I didn't know Mr. Wheeler ever painted pictures that size. When you said it was one of his, I thought it must be the original of a magazine drawing or something like—Oh!"

Archie had moved back and given her an uninterrupted view of the work of art, and she had started as if some unkindly disposed person had driven a bradawl into her.

"Pretty ripe, what?" said Archie enthusiastically.

Lucille did not speak for a moment. It may have been sudden joy that kept her silent. Or, on the other hand, it may not. She stood looking at the picture with wide eyes and parted lips.

"A bird, eh?" said Archie.

"Y—yes," said Lucille.

"I knew you'd like it," proceeded Archie with animation, "You see? you're by way of being a picture-hound—know all about the things, and what not—inherit it from the dear old dad, I shouldn't wonder. Personally, I can't tell one picture from another as a rule, but I'm bound to say, the moment I set eyes on this, I said to myself 'What ho!' or words to that effect, I rather think this will add a touch of distinction to the home, yes, no? I'll hang it up, shall I? 'Phone down to the office, light of my soul, and tell them to send up a nail, a bit of string, and the hotel hammer."

"One moment, darling. I'm not quite sure."

"Eh?"

"Where it ought to hang, I mean. You see—"

"Over the piano, you said. The jolly old piano."

"Yes, but I hadn't seen it then."

A monstrous suspicion flitted for an instant into Archie's mind.

"I say, you do like it, don't you?" he said anxiously.

"Oh, Archie, darling! Of course I do!-And it was so sweet of you to give it to me. But, what I was trying to say was that this picture is so—so striking that I feel that we ought to wait a little while and decide where it would have the best effect. The light over the piano is rather strong."

"You think it ought to hang in a dimmish light, what?"

"Yes, yes. The dimmer the—I mean, yes, in a dim light. Suppose we leave it in the corner for the moment—over there— behind the sofa, and—and I'll think it over. It wants a lot of thought, you know."

"Right-o! Here?"

"Yes, that will do splendidly. Oh, and, Archie."

"Hullo?"

"I think perhaps... Just turn its face to the wall, will you?" Lucille gave a little gulp. "It will prevent it getting dusty."

It perplexed Archie a little during the next few days to notice in Lucille, whom he had always looked on as pre-eminently a girl who knew her own mind, a curious streak of vacillation. Quite half a dozen times he suggested various spots on the wall as suitable for the Venus, but Lucille seemed unable to decide. Archie wished that she would settle on something definite, for he wanted to invite J. B. Wheeler to the suite to see the thing. He had heard nothing from the artist since the day he had removed the picture, and one morning, encountering him on Broadway, he expressed his appreciation of the very decent manner in which the other had taken the whole affair.

"Oh, that!" said J. B. Wheeler. "My dear fellow, you're welcome." He paused for a moment. "More than welcome," he added. "You aren't much of an expert on pictures, are you?"

"Well," said Archie, "I don't know that you'd call me an absolute nib, don't you know, but of course I know enough to see that this particular exhibit is not a little fruity. Absolutely one of the best things you've ever done, laddie."

A slight purple tinge manifested itself in Mr. Wheeler's round and rosy face. His eyes bulged.

"What are you talking about, you Tishbite? You misguided son of Belial, are you under the impression that I painted that thing?"

"Didn't you?"

Mr. Wheeler swallowed a little convulsively.

"My fiancee painted it," he said shortly.

"Your fiancee? My dear old lad, I didn't know you were engaged. Who is she? Do I know her?"

"Her name is Alice Wigmore. You don't know her."

"And she painted that picture?" Archie was perturbed. "But, I say! Won't she be apt to wonder where the thing has got to?"

"I told her it had been stolen. She thought it a great compliment, and was tickled to death. So that's all right."

"And, of course, she'll paint you another."

"Not while I have my strength she won't," said J. B. Wheeler firmly. "She's given up painting since I taught her golf, thank goodness, and my best efforts shall be employed in seeing that she doesn't have a relapse."

"But, laddie," said Archie, puzzled, "you talk as though there were something wrong with the picture. I thought it dashed hot stuff."

"God bless you!" said J. B. Wheeler.

Archie proceeded on his way, still mystified. Then he reflected that artists as a class were all pretty weird and rummy and talked more or less consistently through their hats. You couldn't ever take an artist's opinion on a picture. Nine out of ten of them had views on Art which would have admitted them to any looney-bin, and no questions asked. He had met several of the species who absolutely raved over things which any reasonable chappie would decline to be found dead in a ditch with. His admiration for the Wigmore Venus, which had faltered for a moment during his conversation with J. B. Wheeler, returned in all its pristine vigour. Absolute rot, he meant to say, to try to make out that it wasn't one of the ones and just like mother used to make. Look how Lucille had liked it!

At breakfast next morning, Archie once more brought up the question of the hanging of the picture. It was absurd to let a thing like that go on wasting its sweetness behind a sofa with its face to the wall.

"Touching the jolly old masterpiece," he said, "how about it? I think it's time we hoisted it up somewhere."

Lucille fiddled pensively with her coffee-spoon.

"Archie, dear," she said, "I've been thinking."

"And a very good thing to do," said Archie. "I've often meant to do it myself when I got a bit of time."

"About that picture, I mean. Did you know it was father's birthday to-morrow?"

"Why no, old thing, I didn't, to be absolutely honest. Your revered parent doesn't confide in me much these days, as a matter of fact."

"Well, it is. And I think we ought to give him a present."

"Absolutely. But how? I'm all for spreading sweetness and light, and cheering up the jolly old pater's sorrowful existence, but I haven't a bean. And, what is more, things have come to such a pass that I scan the horizon without seeing a single soul I can touch. I suppose I could get into Reggie van Tuyl's ribs for a bit, but—I don't know—touching poor old Reggie always seems to me rather like potting a sitting bird."

"Of course, I don't want you to do anything like that. I was thinking—Archie, darling, would you be very hurt if I gave father the picture?"

"Oh, I say!"

"Well, I can't think of anything else."

"But wouldn't you miss it most frightfully?"

"Oh, of course I should. But you see—father's birthday—"

Archie had always thought Lucille the dearest and most unselfish angel in the world, but never had the fact come home to him so forcibly as now. He kissed her fondly.

"By Jove!" he exclaimed. "You really are, you know! This is the biggest thing since jolly old Sir Philip What's-his-name gave the

181

drink of water to the poor blighter whose need was greater than his, if you recall the incident. I had to sweat it up at school, I remember. Sir Philip, poor old bean, had a most ghastly thirst on, and he was just going to have one on the house, so to speak, when... but it's all in the history-books. This is the sort of thing Boy Scouts do! Well, of course, it's up to you, queen of my soul. If you feel like making the sacrifice, right-o! Shall I bring the pater up here and show him the picture?"

"No, I shouldn't do that. Do you think you could get into his suite to-morrow morning and hang it up somewhere? You see, if he had the chance of—what I mean is, if—yes, I think it would be best to hang it up and let him discover it there."

"It would give him a surprise, you mean, what?"

"Yes."

Lucille sighed inaudibly. She was a girl with a conscience, and that conscience was troubling her a little. She agreed with Archie that the discovery of the Wigmore Venus in his artistically furnished suite would give Mr. Brewster a surprise. Surprise, indeed, was perhaps an inadequate word. She was sorry for her father, but the instinct of self-preservation is stronger than any other emotion.

Archie whistled merrily on the following morning as, having driven a nail into his father-in-law's wallpaper, he adjusted the cord from which the Wigmore Venus was suspended. He was a kind-hearted young man, and, though Mr. Daniel Brewster had on many occasions treated him with a good deal of austerity, his simple soul was pleased at the thought of doing him a good turn, He had just completed his work and was stepping cautiously down, when a voice behind him nearly caused him to overbalance.

"What the devil?"

Archie turned beamingly.

"Hullo, old thing! Many happy returns of the day!"

Mr. Brewster was standing in a frozen attitude. His strong face was slightly flushed.

"What—what—?" he gurgled.

Mr. Brewster was not in one of his sunniest moods that morning. The proprietor of a large hotel has many things to disturb him, and to-day things had been going wrong. He had come up to his suite with the idea of restoring his shaken nerve system with a quiet cigar, and the sight of his son-in-law had, as so frequently happened, made him feel worse than ever. But, when Archie had descended from the chair and moved aside to allow him an uninterrupted view of the picture, Mr. Brewster realised that a worse thing had befallen him than a mere visit from one who always made him feel that the world was a bleak place.

182

He stared at the Venus dumbly. Unlike most hotel-proprietors, Daniel Brewster was a connoisseur of Art. Connoisseuring was, in fact, his hobby. Even the public rooms of the Cosmopolis were decorated with taste, and his own private suite was a shrine of all that was best and most artistic. His tastes were quiet and restrained, and it is not too much to say that the Wigmore Venus hit him behind the ear like a stuffed eel-skin.

So great was the shock that for some moments it kept him silent, and before he could recover speech Archie had explained.

"It's a birthday present from Lucille, don't you know."

Mr. Brewster crushed down the breezy speech he had intended to utter.

"Lucille gave me—that?" he muttered.

He swallowed pathetically. He was suffering, but the iron courage of the Brewsters stood him in good stead. This man was no weakling. Presently the rigidity of his face relaxed. He was himself again. Of all things in the world he loved his daughter most, and if, in whatever mood of temporary insanity, she had brought herself to suppose that this beastly daub was the sort of thing he would like for a birthday present, he must accept the situation like a man. He would on the whole have preferred death to a life lived in the society of the Wigmore Venus, but even that torment must be endured if the alternative was the hurting of Lucille's feelings.

"I think I've chosen a pretty likely spot to hang the thing, what?" said Archie cheerfully. "It looks well alongside those Japanese prints, don't you think? Sort of stands out."

Mr. Brewster licked his dry lips and grinned a ghastly grin.

"It does stand out!" he agreed.

CHAPTER XXVI

A TALE OF A GRANDFATHER

Archie was not a man who readily allowed himself to become worried, especially about people who were not in his own immediate circle of friends, but in the course of the next week he was bound to admit that he was not altogether easy in his mind about his father-in-law's mental condition. He had read all sorts of things in the Sunday papers and elsewhere about the constant strain to which captains of industry are subjected, a strain which sooner or later is only too apt to make the victim go all blooey, and it seemed to him that Mr. Brewster was beginning to find the going a trifle too tough for his stamina. Undeniably he was behaving in an odd manner, and Archie, though no physician, was aware that, when the American business-man, that restless, ever-active human machine, starts behaving in an odd manner, the next thing you know is that two strong men, one attached to each arm, are hurrying him into the cab bound for Bloomingdale.

He did not confide his misgivings to Lucille, not wishing to cause her anxiety. He hunted up Reggie van Tuyl at the club, and sought advice from him.

"I say, Reggie, old thing—present company excepted—have there been any loonies in your family?"

Reggie stirred in the slumber which always gripped him in the early afternoon.

"Loonies?" he mumbled, sleepily. "Rather! My uncle Edgar thought he was twins."

"Twins, eh?"

"Yes. Silly idea! I mean, you'd have thought one of my uncle Edgar would have been enough for any man."

"How did the thing start?" asked Archie.

"Start? Well, the first thing we noticed was when he began wanting two of everything. Had to set two places for him at dinner and so on. Always wanted two seats at the theatre. Ran into money, I can tell you."

"He didn't behave rummily up till then? I mean to say, wasn't sort of jumpy and all that?"

"Not that I remember. Why?"

Archie's tone became grave.

"Well, I'll tell you, old man, though I don't want it to go any farther, that I'm a bit worried about my jolly old father-in-law. I

184

believe he's about to go in off the deep-end. I think he's cracking under the strain. Dashed weird his behaviour has been the last few days."

"Such as?" murmured Mr. van Tuyl.

"Well, the other morning I happened to be in his suite—incidentally he wouldn't go above ten dollars, and I wanted twenty-five-and he suddenly picked up a whacking big paper-weight and bunged it for all he was worth."

"At you?"

"Not at me. That was the rummy part of it. At a mosquito on the wall, he said. Well, I mean to say, do chappies bung paper-weights at mosquitoes? I mean, is it done?"

"Smash anything?"

"Curiously enough, no. But he only just missed a rather decent picture which Lucille had given him for his birthday. Another foot to the left and it would have been a goner."

"Sounds queer."

"And, talking of that picture, I looked in on him about a couple of afternoons later, and he'd taken it down from the wall and laid it on the floor and was staring at it in a dashed marked sort of manner. That was peculiar, what?"

"On the floor?"

"On the jolly old carpet. When I came in, he was goggling at it in a sort of glassy way. Absolutely rapt, don't you know. My coming in gave him a start—seemed to rouse him from a kind of trance, you know—and he jumped like an antelope; and, if I hadn't happened to grab him, he would have trampled bang on the thing. It was deuced unpleasant, you know. His manner was rummy. He seemed to be brooding on something. What ought I to do about it, do you think? It's not my affair, of course, but it seems to me that, if he goes on like this, one of these days he'll be stabbing someone with a pickle-fork."

To Archie's relief, his father-in-law's symptoms showed no signs of development. In fact, his manner reverted to the normal once more, and a few days later, meeting Archie in the lobby of the hotel, he seemed quite cheerful. It was not often that he wasted his time talking to his son-in-law, but on this occasion he chatted with him for several minutes about the big picture-robbery which had formed the chief item of news on the front pages of the morning papers that day. It was Mr. Brewster's opinion that the outrage had been the work of a gang and that nobody was safe.

Daniel Brewster had spoken of this matter with strange earnestness, but his words had slipped from Archie's mind when he made his way that night to his father-in-law's suite. Archie was in an

185

exalted mood. In the course of dinner he had had a bit of good news which was occupying his thoughts to the exclusion of all other matters. It had left him in a comfortable, if rather dizzy, condition of benevolence to all created things. He had smiled at the room-clerk as he crossed the lobby, and if he had had a dollar, he would have given it to the boy who took him up in the elevator.

He found the door of the Brewster suite unlocked which at any other time would have struck him as unusual; but to-night he was in no frame of mind to notice these trivialities. He went in, and, finding the room dark and no one at home, sat down, too absorbed in his thoughts to switch on the lights, and gave himself up to dreamy meditation.

There are certain moods in which one loses count of time, and Archie could not have said how long he had been sitting in the deep arm-chair near the window when he first became aware that he was not alone in the room. He had closed his eyes, the better to meditate, so had not seen anyone enter. Nor had he heard the door open. The first intimation he had that somebody had come in was when some hard substance knocked against some other hard object, producing a sharp sound which brought him back to earth with a jerk.

He sat up silently. The fact that the room was still in darkness made it obvious that something nefarious was afoot. Plainly there was dirty work in preparation at the cross-roads. He stared into the blackness, and, as his eyes grew accustomed to it, was presently able to see an indistinct form bending over something on the floor. The sound of rather stertorous breathing came to him.

Archie had many defects which prevented him being the perfect man, but lack of courage was not one of them. His somewhat rudimentary intelligence had occasionally led his superior officers during the war to thank God that Great Britain had a Navy, but even these stern critics had found nothing to complain of in the manner in which he bounded over the top. Some of us are thinkers, others men of action. Archie was a man of action, and he was out of his chair and sailing in the direction of the back of the intruder's neck before a wiser man would have completed his plan of campaign. The miscreant collapsed under him with a squashy sound, like the wind going out of a pair of bellows, and Archie, taking a firm seat on his spine, rubbed the other's face in the carpet and awaited the progress of events.

At the end of half a minute it became apparent that there was going to be no counter-attack. The dashing swiftness of the assault had apparently had the effect of depriving the marauder of his entire stock of breath. He was gurgling to himself in a pained sort of way and making no effort to rise. Archie, feeling that it would be safe to get up and switch on the light, did so, and, turning after completing this manoeuvre, was greeted by the spectacle of his father-in-law, seated on the floor in a breathless and dishevelled condition, blinking at the sudden illumination. On the carpet beside Mr. Brewster lay a long knife, and beside the knife lay the handsomely framed masterpiece of J. B. Wheeler's fiancee, Miss Alice Wigmore. Archie stared at this collection dumbly.

"Oh, what-ho!" he observed at length, feebly.

A distinct chill manifested itself in the region of Archie's spine. This could mean only one thing. His fears had been realised. The strain of modern life, with all its hustle and excitement, had at last proved too much for Mr. Brewster. Crushed by the thousand and one anxieties and worries of a millionaire's existence, Daniel Brewster had gone off his onion.

Archie was nonplussed. This was his first experience of this kind of thing. What, he asked himself, was the proper procedure in a situation of this sort? What was the local rule? Where, in a word, did he go from here? He was still musing in an embarrassed and baffled way, having taken the precaution of kicking the knife under the sofa, when Mr. Brewster spoke. And there was in, both the words and the method of their delivery so much of his old familiar self that Archie felt quite relieved.

"So it's you, is it, you wretched blight, you miserable weed!" said Mr. Brewster, having recovered enough breath to be going on with. He glowered at his son-in-law despondently. "I might have, expected it! If I was at the North Pole, I could count on you butting in!"

"Shall I get you a drink of water?" said Archie.

"What the devil," demanded Mr. Brewster, "do you imagine I want with a drink of water?"

"Well—" Archie hesitated delicately. "I had a sort of idea that you had been feeling the strain a bit. I mean to say, rush of modern life and all that sort of thing—"

"What are you doing in my room?" said Mr. Brewster, changing the subject.

"Well, I came to tell you something, and I came in here and was waiting for you, and I saw some chappie biffing about in the dark, and I thought it was a burglar or something after some of your things, so, thinking it over, I got the idea that it would be a fairly juicy scheme to land on him with both feet. No idea it was you, old thing! Frightfully sorry and all that. Meant well!"

Mr. Brewster sighed deeply. He was a just man, and he could

not but realise that, in the circumstances, Archie had behaved not unnaturally.

"Oh, well!" he said. "I might have known something would go wrong."

"Awfully sorry!"

"It can't be helped. What was it you wanted to tell me?" He eyed his son-in-law piercingly. "Not a cent over twenty dollars!" he said coldly.

Archie hastened to dispel the pardonable error.

"Oh, it wasn't anything like that," he said. "As a matter of fact, I think it's a good egg. It has bucked me up to no inconsiderable degree. I was dining with Lucille just now, and, as we dallied with the food-stuffs, she told me something which—well, I'm bound to say, it made me feel considerably braced. She told me to trot along and ask you if you would mind—"

"I gave Lucille a hundred dollars only last Tuesday."

Archie was pained.

"Adjust this sordid outlook, old thing!" he urged. "You simply aren't anywhere near it. Right off the target, absolutely! What Lucille told me to ask you was if you would mind—at some tolerably near date—being a grandfather! Rotten thing to be, of course," proceeded Archie commiseratingly, "for a chappie of your age, but there it is!"

Mr. Brewster gulped.

"Do you mean to say—?"

"I mean, apt to make a fellow feel a bit of a patriarch. Snowy hair and what not. And, of course, for a chappie in the prime of life like you—"

"Do you mean to tell me—? Is this true?"

"Absolutely! Of course, speaking for myself, I'm all for it. I don't know when I've felt more bucked. I sang as I came up here—absolutely warbled in the elevator. But you—"

A curious change had come over Mr. Brewster. He was one of those men who have the appearance of having been hewn out of the solid rock, but now in some indescribable way he seemed to have melted. For a moment he gazed at Archie, then, moving quickly forward, he grasped his hand in an iron grip.

"This is the best news I've ever had!" he mumbled.

"Awfully good of you to take it like this," said Archie cordially. "I mean, being a grandfather—"

Mr. Brewster smiled. Of a man of his appearance one could hardly say that he smiled playfully; but there was something in his expression that remotely suggested playfulness.

"My dear old bean," he said.

Archie started.

"My dear old bean," repeated Mr. Brewster firmly, "I'm the happiest man in America!" His eye fell on the picture which lay on the floor. He gave a slight shudder, but recovered himself immediately. "After this," he said, "I can reconcile myself to living with that thing for the rest of my life. I feel it doesn't matter."

"I say," said Archie, "how about that? Wouldn't have brought the thing up if you hadn't introduced the topic, but, speaking as man to man, what the dickens WERE you up to when I landed on your spine just now?"

"I suppose you thought I had gone off my head?"

"Well, I'm bound to say—"

Mr. Brewster cast an unfriendly glance at the picture.

"Well, I had every excuse, after living with that infernal thing for a week!"

Archie looked at him, astonished.

"I say, old thing, I don't know if I have got your meaning exactly, but you somehow give me the impression that you don't like that jolly old work of Art."

"Like it!" cried Mr. Brewster. "It's nearly driven me mad! Every time it caught my eye, it gave me a pain in the neck. To-night I felt as if I couldn't stand it any longer. I didn't want to hurt Lucille's feelings, by telling her, so I made up my mind I would cut the damned thing out of its frame and tell her it had been stolen."

"What an extraordinary thing! Why, that's exactly what old Wheeler did."

"Who is old Wheeler?"

"Artist chappie. Pal of mine. His fiancee painted the thing, and, when I lifted it off him, he told her it had been stolen. HE didn't seem frightfully keen on it, either."

"Your friend Wheeler has evidently good taste."

Archie was thinking.

"Well, all this rather gets past me," he said. "Personally, I've always admired the thing. Dashed ripe bit of work, I've always considered. Still, of course, if you feel that way—"

"You may take it from me that I do!"

"Well, then, in that case—You know what a clumsy devil I am—You can tell Lucille it was all my fault—"

The Wigmore Venus smiled up at Archie—it seemed to Archie with a pathetic, pleading smile. For a moment he was conscious of a feeling of guilt; then, closing his eyes and hardening his heart, he sprang lightly in the air and descended with both feet on the picture. There was a sound of rending canvas, and the Venus ceased to smile.

"Golly!" said Archie, regarding the wreckage remorsefully.

Mr. Brewster did not share his remorse. For the second time that night he gripped him by the hand.

"My boy!" he quavered. He stared at Archie as if he were seeing him with new eyes. "My dear boy, you were through the war, were you not?"

"Eh? Oh yes! Right through the jolly old war."

"What was your rank?"

"Oh, second lieutenant."

"You ought to have been a general!" Mr. Brewster clasped his hand once more in a vigorous embrace. "I only hope," he added "that your son will be like you!"

There are certain compliments, or compliments coming from certain sources, before which modesty reels, stunned. Archie's did.

He swallowed convulsively. He had never thought to hear these words from Daniel Brewster.

"How would it be, old thing," he said almost brokenly, "if you and I trickled down to the bar and had a spot of sherbet?"

THE END

www.ingramcontent.com/pod-product-compliance
Lightning Source LLC
Chambersburg PA
CBHW011523240626
47154CB00009B/2941